ELECTRIC SUNSHINE

BROOKLYN BOYS #1

E. DAVIES

Electric Sunshine / E. Davies. – 2nd ed.
ISBN-13: 978-1-912245-30-7

For all of us who felt alone in the crowd.

PROLOGUE

KEV - TWO WEEKS EARLIER

I'd never imagined a date kissing me good night on his front step before he tucked a tip into my shirt pocket. As it turned out, New York City was full of those kinds of dates—guys who wanted the boyfriend experience, but didn't want to worry about washing the sheets tomorrow.

Rick was another one of them, and it was strangely disappointing. I'd been all revved up to go, wondering if he'd pay extra for another couple hours. I didn't even have another date lined up after this, just in case. But Rick had meant it when he'd asked me for time together with no strings at all.

I couldn't stop myself from smiling as he leaned in to press his lips against mine and murmured, "Thanks for today."

"You're welcome," I answered, and I meant it. I could pay the rent, and he could go to bed feeling like someone in this goddamn city heard him, and liked him, and wanted him to be happy. And I did, on all counts.

He was a good guy. If he could let go of his self-esteem issues and his need to appear young and hip, he could find a guy his own age, or even a younger one—no problem. I was sure of it. But maybe I was young and overly optimistic. A lot of guys gave me patronizing smiles when I told them those things, like I was trying to flatter them, or like I had no idea what dating was like in the real world.

Maybe both of those things were true. I was twenty-three and fresh out of Tennessee, my head still spinning at every neon sign and shop display, not fifty-three and considering early retirement and a house in the sticks to escape the city.

"Bye, Rick. Have a good night," I said and finally stepped back with a wave, trotting down the steps of the brownstone house to head for the B train.

I spent the trip back to Brooklyn planning what I'd replace next in my wardrobe. I could use a Costco run to see what gay-approved underwear brand they had in stock so I could take new profile photos. Plus, we were nearly out of garlic, and Costco had the huge tubs. Garlic made any food palatable, even Adam's cooking.

At least my roommate took his turns cooking and cleaning. We'd gotten those roommate negotiations out of the way pretty early on, back in Tennessee. And he dealt with my doing sex work, so I couldn't complain.

Well, I did complain now and then when I got home to an empty, dark apartment.

Adam must be working a late shift. He split his time between jobs cleaning pools, stocking shelves, and stuffing flyers to make ends meet, and I met men for companionship. We were an odd couple of roommates, but we were happy.

That was what I told myself as I dropped onto the couch with a cheap crystal wine glass full of water. A boy needed to rehydrate his skin, after all.

For the first few minutes, the apartment was blissfully still, dark, and quiet after the hustle and bustle of Manhattan. Brooklyn was just a hop and skip away from where most of my clients lived or worked, but affordable for two country kids to split, if you squinted and tilted your head.

Our apartment had started life as a one-bedroom, but the landlord had seen a chance to hike the rent and installed a shoddy wall across the living room entrance to make it a two-bedroom apartment. Instead, we had a tiny living room where the dining room had once been.

I took the horrible bedroom, since I didn't really give a shit, and I was a lot less clumsy. Adam would have tripped and fallen into it and knocked a hole in the drywall in the first week, guaranteed. It did mean we couldn't have more than three friends over at once, and that was if two were willing to share the window seat, but it was cozy.

And boring when nobody was home.

"On the other hand…" I set aside my glass of water and twirled to the bedroom to grab my tweezers. I didn't keep them in the bathroom, or God knew what Adam would have used them to do.

I had to keep my eyebrows in tiptop shape, and I wanted some new profile photos, even if I didn't have new Diesels to take them in. I'd stop by TJ Maxx later that week, if none of the work I had lined up fell through. There was always that risk, among others.

I hummed and tilted my head this way and that, nabbing all the fine hairs. My hair was down to my chin now, but despite the waviness, it was under control. That would do just fine. I headed back to the living room and draped the fuzzy blanket across the couch. It made the perfect backdrop.

Maybe after taking some teasing shots, I'd head to my room and take care of the edge that had built up all evening in expectation. I'd watched Rick's time ticking down and given him a heads-up when there was enough time to get back to his place and screw, but he'd just smiled and waved it off.

The sexual frustration was real.

I pulled my pants off and my shirt up, arranging my body artistically. I'd been taking lewd selfies for long enough that I knew how to do it for maximum sex appeal. When my legs were arranged just so, I ran a finger along the head of my cock until it twitched to life in my underwear to give an extra little thickness to the bulge.

"Okay, now…" I bit my lip with concentration as I turned my phone to timer mode, curled my toes around the edges, and lifted it in the air. If I propped it between my toes and my other foot, I could hold it steady enough for a photo with my hands behind my head.

Thankful for my time at the ranch before I'd moved, I crunched up effortlessly, pressed the shutter button, arranged the phone between my feet, flopped down, stretched my arms casually above my head, and then gave the camera a sultry look.

Just in time, too.

I repeated the process a few times with different poses, and then balanced the camera in the usual places—on top of the TV stand, on the top of the armchair in the corner. I needed another set of professional photos soon, but this would have to do for now.

While I had the run of the place, it was time to reward myself for my hard modeling work. If I missed having someone to talk to about *my* day and *my* dreams, nobody had to know. Busting a good nut always helped kill the blues.

1

CHARLIE

My eyes were fixed on the screen so intently that I grabbed a pencil instead of my fork. I caught myself before I stabbed another piece of microwave macaroni and brought it to my lips.

"Jesus, Charlie," I mumbled under my breath. "Way to go. Give yourself lead poisoning and you'll definitely lose the project."

I wasn't even sure if it was supposed to be breakfast, lunch, or dinnertime. I was pretty sure it was evening—people around me in the office had come and gone, but I was still here, trying to match the client's exacting specs.

Thank God the building regulations in Singapore were much better than Hong Kong. I'd just come out of a few months of tearing my hair out. Another project like that and I wouldn't have much left by my fortieth birthday.

Not that it was a problem. Unlike many of my peers with trophy wives or cute boyfriends and dogs waiting at home, I was… well, the singleton of the office. They'd long since given up making fun of me for it, at least. A few well-timed comments about my past and everyone had shut up, which suited me fine.

My current project was my baby, just as they all were. An architect had to be good at letting go once it was out the door and grabbing the next opportunity with both hands.

I was in that wrestling stage of trying to see not only what the client wanted to be there, but what *wasn't* there, and what was there but *shouldn't* be.

And that meant a lot of microwave mac and cheese, staring at notebooks and computer programs and material samples, and pacing around the office, staring into space. I did that best when the office was empty of other people talking and walking around and being generally annoyingly present.

I shoved the pencil safely into the pencil cup near the back of my desk, found my fork, and kept mindlessly eating my pasta.

My eyes were getting heavy, so maybe I was adjusting to this time zone after a day back in the city. I largely ignored my computer clock—God only knew what time zone it was set to at any given time. I wasn't constantly on the road like some of my colleagues, but I often used it to keep track of the time zone in another state or country where I had a project.

I looked around to give my eyes a break, but they were still tired, and now I was just staring aimlessly at my coworker's framed picture of his kids and cats. Ugh. Even if it wasn't like seeing kid photos, it was still something else that normal people had. But even cats needed company, and I was always in the office.

I knew myself pretty damn well after five years at this firm. Staying too late at night when my creative well ran dry would only make me burn out and need a few days off. It was smarter to go home, rest, and get back to it in the morning. Or evening. Whatever.

"Done," I told myself and shut the laptop. I'd leave it at the office for once and treat myself to a whole eight hours without it.

Maybe I'd stop by somewhere for a bite to eat on the way back. The mac and cheese wasn't hitting the spot; I wanted comfort food, but not this kind. Singapore had spoiled me. Now I wanted hawker food from a cart. Bah kut teh, or maybe durian. God, I really had no idea what I wanted, did I?

That was the jet lag talking, then, and I needed sleep.

I pushed myself back from the desk, shrugging on my jacket automatically. April was still chilly at night in New York City. The edge of spring, green creeping back into the parks and cracks of sidewalks, but biting at night for the unsuspecting tourist.

I'd lived here since I was eighteen and fresh-faced, off to college for my architecture degree. By now I was used to the rhythms of the seasons, and I wore a light jacket through May. Outfit choices aside—and those mainly mattered because of client first impressions—I tried not to bore myself with many details of mundane life. That was easier when I had no such life to speak of.

There were advantages to my strategy—like being able to do my job. I didn't like to take risks, and my safety was one thing I refused to compromise. Too many countries were already off-limits to me. I'd relented on Singapore, but Dubai? Moscow? No way.

Even if it meant passing up the incredible project in Dubai. They'd only wanted me, and my boss had tried to tell me that there was a thriving underground gay scene in Dubai that would make it safe for me to travel to, as long as I didn't...

And there was the rub. *As long as I didn't.* As long as they didn't spot me and want an excuse to execute me, I told her. She hadn't had an argument for that. They did give a shit about me here at the company, at least.

All these extra considerations straight people didn't have to take into account before traveling the globe for business. Thank God my firm was understanding, and it hadn't held me back, but...

Well, being gay was more of a theory for me than reality after this many years.

I took an Uber home, so tired I barely registered it. I only snapped to when I walked through the door and caught myself wondering for a moment what it would be like to come home to someone again.

I hadn't had those kinds of thoughts in a long time.

I cut those thoughts off as I closed the door. The living room stretched out to the right, flowing into an open-plan kitchen and dining room. A cute little powder room and a study completed the downstairs, and upstairs were two bedrooms and a huge bath.

Everything was the right size and look for me, though I could live pretty much anywhere. A cozy, brightly-painted cabin? High-rise in Manhattan? Meh, same difference.

Brooklyn suited me pretty well. There was an up-and-coming little gayborhood here—cafes, bookshop, bar, diner, and all. I felt safe and comfortable in the neighborhood as well as my home.

Man, I needed to dust. This was a gorgeous little place, but I mostly kept it for meetings with clients, dinner parties, occasional cocktails with the few friends who put up with me—that kind of stuff. I certainly didn't sleep here as much as I ought to, and not because I was sleeping in anyone else's bed, either. Long days at the office blurred into one long... week? Month? Season?

I could probably do with more sleep. I didn't want to end up looking fifty before I even turned forty.

Not that I needed a reminder of how many years I'd spent drifting along, ignoring my romantic life, pouring everything into work.

"Enough of this thinking crap," I muttered to myself, rubbing my forehead. I still didn't even know what I wanted to eat, but the pizza place around the corner sounded awfully tempting. Why my craving was for cheese on a pizza and not in macaroni form was an unimportant question.

I turned around and headed back out, ducking through the jangling shop door a minute later. Late evening or not, this place was always open and always a little haven. It wasn't like anyone wanted to hang out in a pizza place, but when nothing seemed appealing?

Yeah, pizza was what I'd been craving. Nowhere else in the world was quite like New York. Sure, there was great pizza in Chicago, but deep dish always felt like eating a tire filled with tomato sauce. Flat, thin, foldable crust was the way to go. Big as a man's head. Cheap as a MTA ticket.

"What can I get for you?" The kid behind the counter had already started moving for the cheese pizza even as she asked. Hey, there was nothing wrong with routine. Routine had flown me around the world ten times or more by now, and gotten my name attached to big projects.

And, apparently, had gotten me known in at least a couple places in the city. Brooklyn could be big and lonely without anyone to know your name. Not that she even knew that, but my order was kind of my name.

"Cheese pizza, can of Coke," I said automatically. "Thanks." I handed over the cash in exchange for the flimsy paper plate. I was already licking my lips at the grease that soaked through and onto my hand.

The pizza was gone within two minutes flat, even if my burnt tongue was going to be pissed off at me for a few days. Wasn't like I had any better use for it. My job was a whole lot of "shut up and do crap on the computer" sometimes, and this project phase was one such time.

But I wasn't at work, and goddamn it, I was going to try to go eight hours without thinking about it. So I shelved work in my head and dragged my thoughts to the only other interesting thing in my life: who was going to drag me out for my monthly socialization.

I was pretty sure Hugh's family and my college buddies had all set up some secret group to make sure someone was taking me out every month.

I couldn't have asked for a better second family than my late boyfriend's. Hugh's parents were the kind of parents who'd known their son was gay before he'd even told them, and they'd welcomed me like a second son. Even after the fatal single-car wreck that had taken him from us, they'd been as close as my own family—closer, in many ways.

Once I was back in my own house, I checked my texts, and sure enough, there it was.

It's been a while! Wanna hang out?

I appreciated the check-ins from Ben, my college roommate. His All-American sporty look had contrasted my nerdy engineer type, making us great wingmen for each other our freshman year. We covered a great range of guys, so if they weren't interested in one of us, they might want the other. Many a gay bar in the New York City area had seen us in action.

That was, until I met Hugh.

Five years after his death, I could have dated again, but… why bother? I had too much else going on in my life to devote proper care and attention to a relationship. Plus, the idea of meeting someone new sounded awful right now.

On the other hand, I reflected, it wouldn't be a bad thing to hear someone else's breathing in the dark when I crashed in bed. The silence of my house was almost maddening. But loneliness was a bad fucking reason to start dating someone.

At least I had a new problem to figure out… in the morning, when the jet lag didn't make me want to simultaneously run a marathon and sleep for a year.

Thankfully, sleep won.

2

KEV

"Don't you think it's weird that the neighbors haven't robbed us yet?"

I cracked up as I stretched out along the couch, looking past my laptop on my stomach at Adam. I was waiting for my new photos to upload on my profile, so I kept the laptop turned away from him and he didn't look too closely. He knew better by now.

"Really?"

"Really!" It wasn't the Pabst talking, either. He was sincere in the way he waved his beer can at me. It made a change from him making fun of my career, at least. "I mean, your clothes are always... well, nice."

"Not always," I disagreed with a snort. "Just most of the time." I wanted to be able to take a short-notice out-call appointment if I was out and about, and I didn't want to scare away any repeat clients I happened to bump into. Living in New York—or, to be precise, Brooklyn—made that less likely, but not impossible.

Plus, dressing well was a perk of the job. I'd never gotten to wear nice stuff before. I was hooked now.

"And then there's the wash-and-press. Not that I'm complaining," Adam added, holding out one open palm and his beer can. He knew which side his bread was buttered, and he enjoyed having his boxers pressed and folded.

"I'm not trusting these," I waved up and down myself, even though I was wearing my slobby old t-shirt and ripped jeans, "to any old laundromat's high-rev torture machine. And if they wanna break in, fine. I've got insurance, and I can handle a shotgun." I was a Tennessee boy still and it snuck through, as much as I toned it down for my big city clients.

"If only we had one," Adam lamented. I knew he missed Tennessee sometimes, but he only let it sneak out in half-jokes like that. After all the shit he'd been through with his parents, no wonder he had mixed feelings.

I grabbed my crotch. "Who says I don't?"

"Ew," Adam laughed and flipped me off.

"Such a prude," I teased him, which couldn't be further from the truth. I sipped tea from one of my favorite cups—it had elaborate rose designs and a real pretty gold rim. I'd picked it up at my favorite thrift store last week, bringing my collection to… seven? Eight? I wasn't sure now.

Adam choked on his beer and nearly sprayed it across the chair. He clapped his hand over his mouth just in time to manage to keep it down, although he was coughing. "As if!"

For a guy who'd barely hooked up so far as I could tell in the four months we'd lived together before we relocated here, he'd sure as hell hit the ground running. At least my own work often kept me out of the house overnight.

We had our own code for the situation: *watermelon*. That meant I planned to stay out for the night with a client. He could do whatever he wanted, as long as I could stroll in sometime after dawn and not be greeted with any scarring sights. If he sent it to me, it meant he wanted some space, and we'd negotiate a time.

My own dating life was pretty nonexistent. Not because nobody wanted to date a hooker, but because I hadn't met anyone I thought was good enough for me.

It sounded egotistical, but it was also true. The guys who wanted me just because of my line of work… well, what if I saved up, went to school, and became an accountant? That wasn't love, that was lust. And the guys who claimed not to care what I did for work? Jealousy would creep in sooner or later. Easier to avoid the whole mess.

Besides, I was young, single, and carefree, living in New York City. In my shoes, who the hell wanted to get tied down?

Not me.

"You done charging your phones?" Adam wiggled his own phone, indicating that he needed to top off.

"I dunno. The work phone, probably. You can check," I shrugged. I had two, with different ring tones, but I tended to keep them in the same pocket. They were both usually kept on silent, except when I was free and able to text with prospective clients without interrupting anything with a current date.

Adam made a face. "I might see… *things.*"

"Ignore the sexts. I probably will, too," I advised him, biting back my grin. He could be so overdramatic. He'd settled down a lot since we'd met, right after he'd done something really stupid and nearly paid for it.

We'd met on a ranch in Tennessee, and he'd been employed there until he'd gotten lazy and stopped showing up for work. They'd fired him and he'd tried some kind of stupid retaliation stunt.

In the end, the owners had hired both him and me, gave us a cabin to live in, and taught us a lot of valuable life skills. We could never pay Josh and Evan back for everything. I'd learned a lot about how to handle people who wanted to start a fight—kill 'em with kindness. Although Adam could still be hot-headed, he'd grown up since that incident.

Aww. I was so proud of him, like a hen with her chick... even though we were both pretty much the same age, and both parent-free. Me more so—he kept in touch with his occasionally, but they didn't seem to want to know much about him or his new life.

"You're good." He tossed my phone and I caught it, then cussed him out. Last thing I needed was to replace a goddamn iPhone X. "I'm not made of money, you know."

Adam smirked. "Sorry." That much was genuine, even if he acted like it wasn't—I knew him well enough now to tell.

My profile was updated. With a lot of the major sites closing, it was harder and harder to find work without working the street corners again. If need be, I could go back to hustling in bars. It would be a lot less safe, and I'd probably make less money, but I knew what bars my target clients frequented. I wouldn't be able to gauge whether they could listen to me or follow instructions ahead of time nearly as easily, but... everyone did what they had to in order to survive.

And at least I was on PrEP—a pill a day to stay HIV-negative. This way, if anyone didn't take no for an answer, I wasn't at risk of HIV. Other STIs could put me out of work for a few weeks, but they'd be treatable with antibiotics.

HIV was no longer a death sentence as long as it was detected and treated early, but it required expensive meds. Sure, they were the kind New York City covered, but being positive would also mean a lifetime of testing. And like I needed more risk of being jailed, being charged with a crime if I didn't disclose my status to someone I slept with and they later found out—even if my blood levels made the virus intransmissible to other people.

Law hadn't caught up with the modern world. Hell, most people hadn't, either.

"If they rob us because I look too fancy, I'll replace your shit," I offered, which was magnanimous of me since I paid for the renter's insurance myself. He hadn't seen the need and he wanted a couple extra beers a month.

He rolled his eyes and flipped me off, but I ignored him as I opened Grindr.

"Goddamn it."

"What?" Adam mumbled, paying more attention to his own phone.

I shook my head as I quit the app and deleted it. A reinstall, another email address, and I'd be back in business. "Nothing."

Technically, solicitation wasn't allowed on Grindr. But where the hell else was I gonna find work these days? The one site meant for us was pretty damn expensive to use, though I got a bit of work from them.

"I keep telling you, get a real job." Adam's casual insistence on not calling my job *real* grated on me, as it had for months.

I shook my head, refusing to get into it right now with him. "I happen to love mine. I'll find a way to make it work."

The idea of selling my body to a retail store for minimum wage, then having to smile and mentally chant *the customer is always right* when some asshole decided they were having a bad day and took it out on me? Gross. At least in my line of work, I got to choose what I did, which clients I'd accept, and what I charged.

Or, at least, I *had*. Things were different now that the law had changed. FOSTA/SESTA meant that I was walking a fine line. The laws protected some people; but for me, my relatively safe options for finding work were now gone. I was left with a few choices: I could try to sneak onto apps that weren't made for my line of work, like Grindr, and deal with having my profile shut down and potentially reported, and keep reopening new profiles. Or I could work street corners and bars, which was much more dangerous and didn't give me the chance to vet clients and see if they were planning to kill me beforehand.

I did a combination of the above, and I kind of got by. I wanted something more stable and less likely to get me arrested, so I was still thinking about going back to school.

That meant banking away enough to cover rent and expenses while I started studying something that would make me a profit quickly. Massage was the obvious choice, since I could segue from my existing line of work into offering the kind without happy endings, so it was my current goal.

I'd picked up a little of everything at my last job. If massage didn't work out, I could try accounting or something boring like that. Apparently, I had more of a head for numbers than I'd given myself credit for.

None of that changed the fact that I needed work now, though. I sighed and created a new email address as the silence between us stretched out. From there, I registered on Grindr again and started uploading my new photos.

Eventually, Adam stretched and yawned. "I guess you'll be out again tonight?"

"Yep," I answered, keeping half my attention on him as I copied and pasted my profile from my phone notes into Grindr and set my vital stats. "Unless there's a better offer."

I didn't have any bookings, but I planned to hit up a bar and see what happened. Best case scenario, someone would find me, pass my screening test, and I'd have a short-notice out-call. Worst case, I'd find a hot guy of my own for off-the-clock action. I was far enough ahead this month that I could afford a few freebies.

"I was just gonna crash early," Adam told me, and I glanced up at him. He was looking awfully tired lately. Those "real jobs" he praised did so much to drain him—especially going back and forth between them all part-time. But I bit my tongue, just as he normally refrained from criticizing my job, and frowned sympathetically. I couldn't help him change if he wasn't ready.

"Yeah, you look like crap."

Adam snorted and flipped me off. "Thanks, dude."

"Welcome." I winked and saved my profile, then pocketed my phone to feel any incoming notifications. Laundry day was the most exciting evening to go out, because I could get the most creative with my outfits. Not that I had anyone to show them off to.

Friends were lacking in my life. I knew a few other guys in my business, but we didn't tend to socialize much. We shared info about bad clients, but weren't hired to work together as often as female sex workers, I'd gathered.

Maybe that was what I needed to feel unstuck: friends. But how the hell could I meet them in this crazy, star-studded, boom-and-bust city of dreams?

3

―――――――

CHARLIE

I couldn't sleep.

Of course I couldn't sleep. It was two o'clock in the morning here in New York City, which meant it was just past lunchtime in Singapore.

After a day of adjustment, my body was willing to accept that it was morning, but the rule of thumb held true—an hour per day. It seemed to be thinking "after lunchtime" and not "so late only cabs were running."

God, I hated jet lag. It left me spinning for days.

I'd gotten up at midnight and taken a hot bath. That was my usual time-killing activity when I couldn't sleep. It had almost worked, but not quite. After another hour of tossing and turning, I was forced to admit defeat.

These pre-dawn hours were rarely good to me. If I had my laptop, I usually dragged it to bed and started working on whatever my current project demanded. If I was getting up, that meant finding something else to do, though. I'd left work at the office for once.

"Fine," I grumbled as I pushed myself out of bed, the silky sheets dragging against my smooth skin. I was tired of lying here and telling myself I had to be more awake. Tomorrow, I'd push through and fix this jet lag with a long, awful day if I had to.

I pulled on fresh clothes, making a mental note to do laundry this weekend, when it was daylight hours. That was the best part of my house apart from the resale value—I'd hauled my stuff three blocks to a laundromat in the dead of winter as a college kid. A washer and dryer had been a must-have in a new home of my own.

A casual shirt and jeans would do, but where the hell could I go in the city at this hour without getting shot or stabbed?

Friction, of course. I'd be set until four AM at that rate, and then I could hit up Bubbles—the nearby all-night diner—until six, then coffee and the office. Sounded like a plan. A lame, grown-up, sensible plan, but still a plan. God, I was going to gain ten pounds if I kept eating this much junk food.

My buddies would be happy I was getting out, at least. I didn't have to tell them it was only to stop me dying of boredom or, worse, turning on late-night TV.

I did the sensible thing and grabbed an Uber to the bar. One of the best parts of living in New York City was avoiding getting charged an arm and a leg for a quick cab ride, or worse, having to haggle… or worst of all, living in a rural dead zone with no Uber at all. Uber charged an upfront price, no negotiation, and no wasting time fiddling with my wallet when I arrived. I liked that. It was efficient.

At least there was no line to get into Friction this late at night. It wasn't even that busy—of course. It was a weeknight. The weekends didn't seem much different when I was traveling and away for work during them. Only when I was based here did weekends become those few precious days that I only spent half my day working or thinking about work.

"Coke, please," I told the bartender.

He slid it over and I handed him money, then leaned against the bar. I didn't want to start drinking this late and then have to deal with the foggy head later. And I was okay being the sober designated driver at parties. Alcohol didn't make me happy by any means, and I wasn't dumb enough to try harder and make sure.

Some of my colleagues had issues that couldn't quite fit in their recycling bins, but I wasn't going to go that route. Too stereotypical, and too easy to lose everything I'd worked for the five years since my internship to build—literally and figuratively.

It was one of those weird evenings where everything familiar seemed strange. Not just because I'd been away for days, or the late-night fog that set in when I couldn't sleep, but there was something else.

Too much thinking and not enough doing.

I turned to the guy next to me and checked my gaydar. Some straight guys in New York City didn't mind going to a gay bar, and I didn't want to waste anyone's time.

"You look like the most sober person in the room," I said with a grin.

The other guy grinned. "Oh, thank God. The only decent conversation I've had tonight." He stuck out his hand. "Darren."

"Charlie."

He seemed friendly enough, but there wasn't an immediate spark. I hadn't felt that with anyone in some time, so it didn't surprise me.

"Been here all night?" I asked.

"Nah. I was working on a job site late, just got here at midnight. You?" Darren sipped what looked like orange juice and Sprite.

I shook my head. "Jet lag. I was trying to sleep and it wasn't working."

"Getting laid helps with that," he said, then chuckled. "Or so I've heard. It's been long enough. Oh, God. I said that out loud."

Darren's honesty and self-deprecation were refreshing. I'd met way too many guys who were desperate to impress me, even if they didn't want to fuck me. Clients who bragged about their trophy wives and houses, old college friends who bragged about their career trajectories… hell, my few gay friends often bragged about how many guys they'd had.

"Me too," I told him. "I only bend over and take it from work these days."

I didn't have a problem being blunt about my lack of a sex life, even if it surprised and worried people around me. Hell, some people had implied that if I fucked some guys, I'd get over Hugh faster.

Like I needed to get over him. The hole had long since healed in my heart. I just hadn't met someone else worth handing it over to.

Darren laughed richly. "I know that feeling." He nodded toward the rest of the bar. "Every time I try to hook up, I end up with someone I'm not clicking with, and I cut it off. Some people say that means I need to give it a chance."

"Some people are wrong," I told him firmly. "Not that I'm biased."

"Of course not."

"What do you do?" Darren looked genuinely interested in the answer.

"Architecture. You?"

"Electrician."

"Neat," I answered, my attention caught by the guy moving up behind Darren. A handsome one, too—definitely not a bad looker.

In fact, the longer I looked, the more I found to like. The guy had wavy chin-length hair, and the beautiful, dark kind of eyes that showed his soul. He looked calm and centered.

He had pretty pink lips, and the kind of cheekbones that could kill a man. He knew exactly what he was doing, judging by the way he swiveled his hips to face me, though his hand was braced on the bar next to Darren.

"Evening," he greeted us both. He sounded surprisingly sober considering the time of night.

I wasn't expecting Darren's amused smile. "I'm not paying, baby."

It took my brain a few seconds to catch up. I'd been propositioned by women like this before, when I was out for drinks with some of my better-dressed and straighter coworkers, but never a man.

"Even if I flutter my eyelashes?" He wasn't looking at Darren, though—he was looking at me, his voice light and teasing, but his gaze intense.

It had been a long damn time since anyone had looked at me like that.

"Even if," I repeated, but my voice sounded hoarse even to my ears.

It had been just as long since my dick had reacted to anyone like this.

I had to briefly relearn how to keep it at bay—thinking of baseball usually did the trick, but I found myself suddenly wondering how this guy kept in such good shape. His arms were bulging in all the right places, like he'd come straight from a ranch.

And, weirdly enough, he sounded like it. His drawl became even more apparent when he said, "Shame. I'll keep trying." I'd heard that accent before, but I wasn't sure in which part of the South.

"You do that, baby," Darren told him and squeezed his shoulder with a smile. "My friend and I aren't looking."

"Looks like I got here too late." He clicked his tongue in disappointment, but he winked at me anyway, and I felt my cheeks flush hotter than the sun.

Fuck. I wasn't equipped for this conversation. I hadn't flirted in years. "Too late and charging too much," I said with a regretful smile. No way was I gonna get caught out by some hot cop.

"Unless..." He held my eyes for long enough to suggest he'd been thinking of a freebie, then grinned. "Fair enough." His pocket chirped, and he pulled out his phone a moment later. "Pardon me," he added, waving slightly as he headed off.

I caught the glint of a black loading screen in the background, and even I knew it had to be Grindr.

"You know him?" I made myself ask instead of staring after that perky ass, the broad shoulders, and the unmistakably flirtatious toss of his hair that he gave as he left, glancing over his shoulder.

"Yeah, he's tried to pick me up a few times. Or... have me pick him up, I guess I should say," Darren added.

"You don't think he's a cop?"

Darren thought for a moment and then shook his head. "Nah.

He's been coming here for a couple months now. Just a normal kid hustling."

I immediately felt bad for thinking incredibly dirty things about his lips. "Kid?" I questioned, frowning toward the bouncer. Now that I'd hit my thirties, anyone in their twenties was a kid as far as I was concerned, but if he weren't of age? There was a moral obligation to help him out.

Darren shrugged. "His Grindr age is exactly twenty-one, so he's probably like, twenty-four."

I half-smiled. That was something of a relief. Plus, the age difference wasn't as bad.

Not that there was any reason at all for me to be thinking about the age difference between us. I couldn't afford to have my career go down in flames if I got arrested.

But something about meeting the young guy's gaze made me feel alive in a way I hadn't before, and he *was* offering a convenient solution to my problem—wanting to date, or at least learn how to date again, but not having the time for a boyfriend.

I nodded vaguely and finished my drink. "I think I'm gonna get something from the greasy spoon next door. Wanna come?"

"Nah," Darren said with a smile, but he took out his phone. "Gimme your number and we can hang out sometime. You have WhatsApp?"

"Of course," I said and laughed. "I'm old, not dead."

"Old," Darren repeated with a snort and shook his head.

"Out of the scene, then," I corrected myself, and he gave me a quizzical look, but sensed enough not to question. No way was I explaining I had a dead boyfriend, but I was over him now and looking to date. Not even telling him that it had been years ago.

That made me sound like I had unresolved issues. I'd killed conversations that way before.

After we swapped numbers, I shook hands and waved slightly. "Good luck tonight."

"Thanks," Darren said with a chuckle, his eye already on the dance floor. "I'll need it."

The evening air was cool—crisp, even. I shivered and pulled my sweater tighter around myself, glad I'd brought that. Gone were the days I'd dress myself in a t-shirt so thin it could double as plastic-wrap and make my way to a club, shivering all the way. I still hated coat-checks, but I'd add a sweater, at least.

Now I was happy to plonk myself into a window-seat booth at Bubbles, the diner the next door down. I didn't care how many calories were in the breakfast scramble. Didn't even care whether any hot guys saw me eating it. It was gonna be mine.

"Coffee?" the waitress asked, gesturing with her pot toward my cup.

"Please." I flipped the cup over and slid it to the end of the table.

"Long night or early morning?" she asked as she poured, and I glanced at her name tag. Tara.

"Both," I answered. Deciding to make conversation, I added, "You?"

Tara winced sympathetically. "Late night for me. Sunrise means time to sleep, like a vampire."

I toasted her with my coffee cup, my lip quirking as I glanced toward the curved counter of the diner. "To the night owls."

She grinned in recognition. "You betcha, honey."

After she left, I settled back into the cracked seats and smiled.

Gentrification—and I knew damn well I had some small part in it —had touched nearly everywhere in midtown Manhattan, but here by my favorite old haunt, there were still hidden treasures.

New Yorkers were a stubborn bunch. We weren't just gonna give up. I was certain this place had its regulars and a heartbeat of its own as people woke up for early shifts, stayed late, grabbed sober-up food or hangover brunches. And in its way, more than my shiny creations, it was the heartbeat of the city. I was way more interested in the diners than the clubs of New York City. Did that make me old?

Lost in thought, I fidgeted with my phone. I only realized when I'd opened the app store on my phone that I was looking at Grindr.

Fuck. Just because that *one* guy was on Grindr didn't mean I needed to jump back on there. If I'd wanted meaningless sex, I could have gotten it a hundred times in the last few years.

But I wasn't downloading it to look for that. I wanted him.

Which was weird, because wasn't paying a sex worker the defini-tion of meaningless sex? What the hell was I even paying him for, then?

Do we have to have sex?

It sounded like a dumb question. Who the hell would hire a sex worker and then not have sex? Me, apparently. God, my friends would never let it go if they heard about this.

Hell, even *thinking* about this was the most exciting thing that had happened since the pizza delivery guy showed up at my house instead of the next-door neighbors'. I'd sent him over to them and they'd brought me the garlic fingers to say thanks for not shutting up and taking the free pizza.

I just wanted someone to talk to, and maybe I could find that.

I held my breath, hit Download, and stared into my coffee cup for a few minutes before I screwed up enough courage to actually open it and register. I left my profile blank and started browsing nearby profiles.

The number of guys within a few hundred feet surprised me, and for a moment, I found myself dismayed. What if I couldn't find—

There. He'd carefully cropped the photo so it didn't show his whole face, but it was unmistakably the same outfit he'd worn tonight. Clever. I wondered idly how much effort he put into avoiding legal sticky situations.

Before I knew it, I was fumbling my way through finding a message button and typing out a greeting. This was probably a stupid idea. At least it was exciting. Whatever happened, I'd have a story to tell later.

I didn't know if it was my heart, my gut instinct, my dick, or some sixth sense that was kicking in. Something told me I had to know more about him.

4

KEV

So far, none of the messages I'd received tonight had even remotely come close to passing my little test.

It was simple. I'd dropped a few hints as to my profession and rates in my profile, and told them to use a code word if they understood what I was saying.

How damn hard was it to read? Some guys swiped from profile to profile without stopping to read a word, though. The last thing I wanted was someone getting so angry at me trying to charge that they reported me to the cops, especially in today's climate.

Then my phone went off, and I paid attention. The guy's profile was blank, but his message made it unmistakable who he was.

Hi, I'm new on this app. We met earlier and I had a few questions, but my friend shooed you away.

He might not be using my codeword, but I knew who that had to be. Darren had been firm in telling me he wasn't interested in paying—so far, he never had been, but we'd had several great conversations over drinks.

His friend? He was new. At least, I hadn't spotted him here in the four months I'd been cruising this place. The owners didn't care much what I did, as long as I wasn't a nuisance and I didn't hook up on their property. I was always cautious who I approached, and I usually used this place as a convenient place to show up on nearby Grindr profiles.

This was the cutie with the dark hair and tentative smile, looking a little out of place. He looked like he belonged in a catalog, or maybe a movie about a gay potluck club.

Whatever he did, he was set for money—he had nice brand names on, but inconspicuous. Not like the guys with their Diesel jeans and Versace underwear.

I'd stake my life on it, but still, not literally. I answered, telling him to send me a picture of himself flipping off the camera.

A little insurance for me. If he threatened to go to the cops, it was just naughty enough that he wouldn't want it sent to his mom by an anonymous Facebook account. I might have been pretty new to this way of drumming up business, but I was quickly learning the tricks to turning tricks.

His answer came quickly.

I've never taken a photo like that. How about smiling?

I chuckled under my breath and waived a rule. I knew he was a real person, after all, if this was who I thought it was.

Something taken right now will do.

I knew exactly where the photo he sent back a minute later had been taken. It was at Bubbles—the diner next door.

With a warm lead, I didn't think twice about ditching Friction and going to meet him. When they had something to hide, startling them worked well. If someone wasn't expecting me to show up where they were, they were thrown off-balance. Nobody wanted to be caught on security camera with the guy they planned to dispose of later.

Not that I was paranoid, but it paid to be careful.

But although he blinked several times at me when I walked into the diner, his next reaction was a smile. "Hey." He looked like he'd just finished breakfast, and when I slid into the booth, the waitress approached.

"Coffee?"

I looked at him, and he nodded.

"Yeah. Coffee for my friend here."

She didn't say anything as she poured it, which was lucky. She'd seen me in here sobering up after an unsuccessful night—or a successful one—more than once.

I smiled at her, and she turned away and headed for the kitchen. A tiny red flag went up in my brain, so I made a mental note for later.

"Hi," I greeted. My worry was instantly forgotten when I saw the way he watched me. It was impossible to fake that blend of enthusiasm and trepidation, like a giant kid trapped in a man's body. He didn't seem quite sure of what he was doing. That always meant it was my job to put him at ease.

And he was beautiful, too. I hadn't had a chance to appreciate it back in Friction, but in the diner light, he melted my knees. A man in business casual knew the way to my heart. When he had those blue eyes that just seemed to see my soul? Yeah, sold.

"Hey," he answered, glancing outside and then back at me. "I didn't expect you to be hanging out right here still. I mean, Grindr tells me you are. But still." His cheeks flushed and he buried his nose in his coffee cup.

He came off as genuine, and I'd met worse. I'd give him a chance.

"I got a feeling you were interested," I told him with a smile. I knew how to turn the charm on instantly. I always had—it was a useful skill in life, being able to flirt with anyone. But it was more than that. I could easily find something interesting or charismatic about people. Chemistry was possible with anyone if you just worked hard enough.

This kind of magnetism, though, took me aback. I wasn't used to feeling it before I even *tried*.

I was intrigued, despite myself. Enough to give him a freebie? I didn't know, but maybe. I didn't want to devalue my product, but a boy had to have fun off the clock sometimes.

"I—I think I am." His hesitance caught my attention. It was more than shyness or nervousness about legal trouble.

"Spill." I winked. I was happy to answer questions. Sometimes people just wanted to make sure I wasn't being pimped out.

He leaned in, his knuckles white on the handle of his coffee cup. His voice was low. "Do we have to have sex?"

It took me a few moments before the words sank in, and I grinned. "No. I'm not gonna make anyone do anything they don't want to do. Can we start with your name, though?" I teased. "I like to know what to yell out, whether in bed or in the street."

"Oh! Sorry! My goodness. Where are my manners?" The guy stuck out his hand. "Charlie."

"Kev." Normally it was a good idea to use a different name for sex work, but mine wasn't my legal name anyway. Everyone had called me Kev for so long that I happily used it instead of the much grosser Kenneth Taylor. Most importantly, it didn't remind me of home. Besides, Kev sounded like a typical gay guy's name. Generic enough to be forgettable.

"Nice to meet you, Kev." Charlie looked somehow at home here in the diner, even if he looked like he belonged in a Macy's catalog.

It was that air of quiet confidence and the real strength that came from life experience that drew me to him.

"You, too," I said, and I meant it.

I think Charlie heard what I meant, because he gave me the kind of smile that put me at ease. "So, if I wanted to go out for dinner sometime…"

"We can do that," I told him. It might still lead to sex; fairly often it did when men were testing the ground and wanted to make sure I wasn't a cop.

"Oh." He sounded surprised, and perhaps a bit relieved.

"That reassure you?" I drawled, letting my accent come through just a hint.

Charlie nodded, his lips curving up. "You're southern?"

"Born and bred. Moved here three months ago," I told him. I didn't even have to fake a backstory for my clients—yet. They liked fresh meat, and a new, starry-eyed country boy fit many of their fantasies. I planned to keep it at "three months ago" for another three months before I started telling the *whole* truth.

"How are you liking the city so far?"

Everyone asked me this. It was kind of weird. Was I really gonna say *it's awful, I can't wait to leave* to a New Yorker? Especially one I was doing business with? His gaze didn't say business, but I had to remind myself that that was all it was.

"It's great," I said, and luckily, that was also the truth. Overwhelming and frantically busy 24/7, yes. But nobody gave a damn if you held another man's hand in Midtown, or sat across from him at a table for two. That alone made New York City worth the move. "There's always something happening, always someone to talk to."

He paused for a moment as he took me in, and I realized what I'd just said. The way he was looking at me, I was starting to think he didn't always have someone to talk to. A lot of my clients didn't. I wasn't gonna act like they were all just in need of a listening ear, but some of them? Yeah, they needed to talk to someone about their life who didn't judge them, who wouldn't spill their secrets to all their friends and family.

Instead of the life story I half-expected, he shook his head. "I remember moving here," he told me. "For college. It's a heady thrill. So, how does this work? Do we set up a time and date? Do you take PayPal?"

He was joking to hide his nervousness, but I appreciated it. He was trying to put us both at ease, even if he was a bit abrupt. Lots of New Yorkers were. It had taken me two months to realize the cashier at the bodega under Adam's and my apartment didn't actually hate me. I tried to make conversation with everyone in the city at first, and I'd wondered how many people were having really bad days.

"Cash only, at the beginning of the date," I told him. "A hundred an hour." It was a discount, but was I willing to give a discount to a hot, professional guy who could hold a conversation and didn't even seem to want sex yet? Hell yeah, I was.

Part of me wanted to offer him a freebie, but I resisted the urge. I might be an awful businessman when my dick did the thinking, but I still had rent to pay. Hot guys were dime a dozen here. I owed it to Adam to do my job if I was gonna rub his face in the fact that I had more freedom in mine.

"Only a hundred?" he questioned, his brows furrowing.

I blinked at him. "This ain't your first time at the rodeo?"

"That sounded *very* Southern," he said with a teasing gleam in his eye. "I've never hired a…" he looked around, and then lowered his voice. "I've never done this before, but I have straight friends."

"Ah." I smiled. "Women tend to charge more. Especially here."

"God bless… well, dick," Charlie murmured and drained his coffee cup.

"Cheap dick?" I teased.

Charlie blushed. "I didn't want to offend you." He was sweet, but if he'd been a friend, he would have quickly learned I had a raunchy sense of humor. I toned it down for clients who lived an upscale life and turned up their noses at dick jokes, but Charlie seemed like he had an interesting edge to him. He wasn't all suits and Financial Times talk.

"It's hard to do that," I told him.

The waitress gave us coffee refills, and I waited until she was out of earshot before I spoke up again. "When are you free? My schedule's looking pretty clear."

"This evening?" Charlie suggested, and there was a barely suppressed eager note in his voice.

That, I was familiar with.

I smiled. "Tonight works. Where do you want to meet? I do outcalls only."

It took him a few seconds to parse that, which backed up his claim that he hadn't done this before. "Oh. Um... I thought dinner? I could pick you up?"

"How about we meet here?" I countered. We could take a cab together to the place. No way was I telling him where I lived, however nice he looked.

"Sure. At six?"

"Six works." I was surprised this time—I'd expected it to be later. Guys like him tended to stay in the office until stupid hours, avoiding their wives. He had no ring on, though, and he'd just been at a gay bar. That helped my chances.

Don't get ahead of yourself, Kev. This is business, I reminded myself. Still, a boy could daydream.

"Tonight, outside here, at six," Charlie repeated to himself, softly, as if committing it to memory—or second-guessing himself. I held my breath until he looked up and made eye contact, his jaw firm and eyes resolute. "Done. Here's my number."

I entered it into my phone quickly and sent a text so he had mine. There was the confidence I was attracted to. It took all I had not to crawl into his side of the booth and rub my cheek against his, just to try to pick up some of that for myself.

"I look forward to it," I said instead with a casual smile, not wanting to dial up the pressure.

He reached over the table to take my hand for a moment and drained the rest of his refill. "Me, too." He squeezed and let go gradually, his fingertips trailing across the back of my hand all the way to the fingertips. "See you later."

I gave him an encouraging smile to hide the reaction my body was having: my hair stood on end in a pleasurable way. I wanted those hands all over me and now I was gonna need a minute in the booth before leaving so I wasn't standing at attention.

On the way out, he flagged down the waitress and paid, then winked at me—presumably to indicate he'd grabbed the bill.

I blushed and waved, and I even caught myself watching him walk down the street. Though the waitress was brisker with me than she had been with him, she still indulged me when I stayed there for another hour, just thinking over that meeting until pre-dawn started to touch the edges of the dark sky.

Dog walkers weren't yet out, but a couple of the craziest early-morning runners were starting their days as others ended them. It was time for me to join the first group, not the second, for today.

Sleep was for later.

5

CHARLIE

What the hell had I gotten myself into?

Thinking about my date that night with Kev was incredibly distracting. I sleepwalked through the morning until a couple more coffees jolted me into action.

God, I was gonna need to take off early and nap today. But this conference call was dragging on, and I was so clearly spaced out that it wasn't even funny. But it was all engineers arguing about the practicalities right now, which meant I didn't really have to pay attention.

I tuned back in just in time to hear, "We need to add a load-bearing wall."

That made it my job to figure out how it could be done without ruining the open concept of the ground floor of this hotel. I sighed and scribbled a note to myself, already planning how I'd do it. "Fine."

"What? No arguments? No sassy *In my vision, I'm working with engineers who find a way to do it?*" Fred was only sitting one row of desks away from me, so he looked up over his computer and gave me a shit-eating grin. Luckily for him, I liked him.

I wadded up a Post-It note and chucked it toward him. Still had that Little League baseball arm, because it hit him square in the nose. "Very funny," I said as the rest of the conference call participants chuckled. "No, I'll go back to the drawing board on that, if you're not gonna argue the vaulted ceiling."

"It's a cool idea," Fred surprised me by admitting. "But you know I can't do it as-is. We'll keep the concept and make it work."

Weird. For once, an engineer and an architect agreeing on practical matters. That didn't happen often.

"I'll leave you two to come up with a way to make that work." That was the client's project manager. He had an exacting vision, but in some ways, it was better to work with people who did. It gave me a strong framework. Without my background, he didn't know the impossible things he was asking, which pushed me to find a way to do them. No coasting for my paycheck, which would be a miserable damn life.

Every damn time I pulled it off, it was a heady high, and I remembered why I loved the hell out of my job.

"When's your meeting?" I asked. He had to present the vision to the rest of the board to approve.

"Tomorrow at three."

I glanced at Fred, who nodded at me. "We can get you the final proposal by tonight."

Once we'd hung up, Fred looked over at me and pulled a face. I knew that meant *by tonight?* and I beckoned him over.

"What's got into you?" was the first question Fred greeted me with.

I knew my coworkers were listening now. There was no privacy in an office. I sure as hell wasn't gonna tell him I'd barely slept last night, and then I'd met a male escort…

"A surprising spirit of tolerance. Peace on Earth, joy to men, and all that."

"Dude, it's April."

"Don't be a Grinch," I told him and wagged a finger. "That's not very Christmassy of you." I was too tired to waste time on joking around, so I kept on going. "Okay, here's what I'm thinking."

He pushed back against my first suggestion, but we came to a compromise on a wall that would maintain the airy feeling, but bear enough load to make the ceiling not collapse in a minor earthquake. This building was a small boutique hotel in LA, and that was one of the unique geographical requirements of the area.

"Okay, I'll model that," I told him. "And I'll send you the final files at the end of the afternoon." 3D modeling a complex building took a long time, and we'd already passed the artistic stage where an artist could add a few brushstrokes to put in another wall.

"Better to exceed deadlines than fly past them."

It looked like this project was sailing by smoothly, so I asked, "Anything else on our plate?"

"Not for today."

"Thank God. I might take off early and nap."

Fred shook his head. "No kidding. Early for you is, what, five? You worked a full day after a twenty-hour flight? Go sleep, for crying out loud."

I shook my head and rubbed my face. "Yeah, but this paper tray won't do itself." Most of my incoming work was digital rather than paper, but the point still stood.

"And nobody expects you to do things at the speed you do them," Fred countered. "You just set yourself up as a machine that way, until everyone starts to expect it from now on."

We'd had this disagreement before. Fred was a big fan of slow and steady work, and while I liked a bit of caution and wanted to be sure I got my work right the first time, if I was capable of working fast, why not? Valerie, our boss, was flexible on how we worked so long as we got the damn work done.

He smiled as I eyed him, then held up his hands. "Fine, fine. But I'm just saying, when's the last time you left the office before eight PM?"

"Today," I countered with a grin.

"To nap."

"Maybe I have a hot date afterward," I challenged him, folding my arms.

He burst out laughing and I had to work hard not to be offended. "Sorry," he added after a moment and raised his brow. "I'd just figured you had some secret hubby you were never gonna talk about."

It took me a minute to figure out what he meant. "Huh?"

"You never talk about a family, but you never talk about dating, either. But you said you were gay. A couple of us figured you were asexual or, I dunno, you've got a sugar baby… I said it's none of our business, but I figured you didn't want to talk about it and risk, you know…"

"Bad reactions?" Despite myself, I started smiling. "Man, if I had a sugar baby, I wouldn't be hiding him."

There was a certain prickle in my chest. *He still never asked if I was serious about having a date. Wow. My love life* is *dire, then.*

I casually waved him away to get back to my work, but the rest of my day was just as subdued with that thought hanging over my head.

By the time I skipped out of work, I was determined to make the most of this date. Sure, I was paying for the privilege, but that meant I could really practice how to get to know someone all over again. He could give me feedback. I'd optimize my first-date self.

Whatever engineers said, architects did the same basic thing, but with more style. And I was going to succeed at this—in style.

I mentally chose my outfit before I even got home. I hung it up before I set my alarm for one sleep cycle—an hour and forty-five minutes, by my body clock. A light lunch, workout, and shower later, I fell into bed for my nap. This time, I had no trouble at all closing my eyes and drifting off. Kev's beautiful eyes were the last thing I thought about before blissful sleep claimed me.

I barely knew what city I was in when I opened my eyes, but I knew I had something very important and expensive to do.

Right.

It took me a few seconds to put myself together. Knots of anxiety I hadn't experienced since my first date with Hugh were tying me up. God, that was so long ago, and I was such a different person now.

How the hell did I talk about myself? Did I mention my dead boyfriend before or after drinks? Did I not mention him at all? Was I supposed to focus conversation on Kev and not myself? I hadn't even dated in the modern era, it felt like. Maybe it was all automatically filtered out on Grindr and Tinder and whatnot these days.

What if he didn't like me?

"Get it together," I told myself with a scowl. That was the point of paying, wasn't it? So someone would put up with you, even if you were an anxious, inexperienced mess?

I sighed and slipped on my shirt, turning to check myself out in the mirror. These dark jeans highlighted my ass, and the shirt brought out my eyes. I knew what made me look good, at least. I wouldn't be the ugliest guy he'd dated. And I could bring him to a nice place for a meal. That was enough to make it an okay evening for us both, I hoped.

I took trains and Ubers way more than my car within Brooklyn and Manhattan, only driving anywhere outside of the metropolitan area. I didn't want to worry about parking, and traffic was always a nightmare. As usual, I grabbed an Uber to the diner. It was strange seeing the front of the club, closed up tightly in the early evening, not open yet. When did it open? I'd never tried to go before nighttime.

Kev stood there, his hands casually folded behind his back, looking for all the world like he was supposed to be there. And, oh man, did he ever look good.

A cardigan and a collared shirt made him look like... well, like he belonged on my arm in the student cafeteria.

Where did that come from? I hesitated as I stood up and climbed out of the Uber with a short thanks to the driver, but it was too late. He'd spotted me.

I had to do this. For me. I wasn't used to thinking of me.

Still off-balance from my own thoughts, it took me a moment to awkwardly wave. By that time, he'd approached and he caught my hand to pull me in for a hug. "Hi."

God, he smelled good. He *felt* good. When was the last time I'd been hugged like this? Not by a relative, or a buddy slapping my back, but like a lover.

I'd stopped by the ATM that morning, so I had an envelope ready in my pocket. Four hours ought to be enough for dinner and drinks afterward, I figured. And hell, at a hundred an hour, I'd spent more on bachelor parties for my goddamn coworkers. Buying a few rounds at New York City prices added up fast.

He took it with a smile and pocketed it, then laced his fingers with mine. "Hi, Charlie. You could have waited until we were off the street." His grin was broad and teasing, though, rather than annoyed.

"O-Oh." I cleared my throat. "Sorry! I wasn't sure."

He kissed my cheek and slid his arm around my waist. He seemed brashly confident all of a sudden, not even looking around to see who was nearby. It was the gayborhood, and I'd never had a problem in New York, but it was still an amusing little signal of a small-town boy who thought the city was a haven for guys like us. "No problem. Uber or a cab?"

"Uber." I could do something with my hands, then, since I wasn't sure if I should touch him or back away or hold hands or what.

"And when we're waiting for the Uber, we can talk about what you want," he told me with an amused smile, taking half a step away. Maybe he sensed my nervousness.

I cast him an appreciative smile. Another car was already on its way to us. "Yeah. Sorry." I pocketed the phone. "I just haven't done this in ages."

"Dry spell?" he asked. "We can take it slow." Instead of wrapping his arm around my waist, he edged away a little more, and then took my hand. "If anything I do feels like too much, just let me know."

Actually, that was nice. I tightened my grip on his hand. I liked a man who wasn't afraid to be confident and affectionate in public. And it was nice not to have to second-guess how far he wanted to go on a first date, whether I was insulting him or being too pushy, and so on.

He might have been younger, but he radiated confidence. Maybe a little naïveté, but that was adorable in its own way.

"So, how old are you?" I asked.

He chuckled. "Wise question. I used to say nineteen..." he started, then cut himself off and looked up at me.

I raised my eyebrow. "You can give me the Grindr answer or the real answer. I'm thirty-two, so I'm definitely older. I don't care. And I don't want a guy as young as possible, that's gross."

"In that case, I like you," he chuckled. "If anyone else asks, I'm twenty-one."

"And if your ID falls out of your pocket?"

He laughed again, louder. "Twenty-three."

"That's not a big difference."

Kev winked at me. "You'd be surprised." He didn't seem to mind questions, so I plunged ahead.

"Do guys really focus that much on age?"

Kev shook his head. "Not as much as they do for women in my industry, I don't think. But it fits my image better. Just barely legal to drink, barely out of Tennessee… they didn't care if I wasn't legal to drink there."

"So I was right about Tennessee." I felt a moment of triumph. "I did a job down in Nashville a couple years ago. Whole different pace of life."

"It sure is," he said with a rueful smile.

Our car arrived, so I ushered him in and slid in after him for the quick drive. He peppered me with casual questions about my day and how long I'd been in the city, but he was obviously steering clear of asking what I did for work yet.

Made sense. Some guys wouldn't want this transaction known in their industry. Hell, I could be in just as much trouble as him, but I didn't think I was in much danger by telling him. "I work as an architect," I told him as we walked into the restaurant.

"Aha! I thought I detected that vibe." He grinned. "Smart, well-dressed, an eye for lines…"

I winked. "And curves."

The musical laugh he gave after all of my jokes? God, it was magic to my ears. He had to know how pretty he was, but I had to tell him anyway. "You're gorgeous. It's a little intimidating," I admitted under my breath as we waited to talk to the maitre-d'.

His smile was sweet. "Thank you," he said graciously, but he didn't act cocky about it. He knew how to act under pressure, and I felt bad for being surprised by it. He was clearly quick to pick up new situations. Somehow, the amount he was charging, I'd expected less.

God, that was a dick move of me. I was glad I'd never said a word to that effect beyond our initial conversation yesterday.

"This way, gentlemen." The table by the window had a view of some fairy lights and a pretty typical street scene, but it also had a small bowl of water with a floating rose candle. Definitely a date night spot.

For a moment, Kev looked shy as he picked up the menu and settled himself in his chair. When he looked over his menu at me, he took a moment to compose himself.

What was going on in his head? I would have paid a lot more to know that.

"Do you recommend anything in particular here?" was all he asked.

I shook my head. "No. Everything I've had here is good."

That seemed to relax him, and he raised his menu again. He looked more confident already. "Great." It felt like I'd just passed a test, but I wasn't sure what.

"The chicken's particularly great, though," I offered. "That's what I'm having."

Kev laughed. "I'd better hurry up and choose something, then! Hm. That looks good…" He put down his menu. "Okay, let's test your taste. I'll get the same."

I found myself suddenly worried that he wouldn't like it—as if that would reflect on me. "Time to sweat," I muttered.

He laughed. "I'll try to distract you with my stunning conversational skills."

"That was a missed opportunity to discuss your oral skills." I said, straight-faced.

Kev choked on air and laughed as the waiter approached to ask about the wine list.

"Do you drink?" I asked. I wasn't going to push it tonight—just a bottle between us. But if he wanted to stay sober, I was fine with that. I caught his hesitation and interrupted myself. "Actually, let's stick with something lighter. Sparkling water?"

"Please," Kev agreed.

"And we're ready to order, I believe," I added. I ordered first so he'd know what to get, in case he'd forgotten and he still planned to copy me.

Sure enough, he added, "And the same for me, please." When the waiter left, he looked back at me. "Thanks for skipping the wine. I don't love drinking on a first date, but most people seem to need to."

I nodded. I'd noticed that in other social situations myself. "It settles the nerves, I guess. But if you need a drug to be more like yourself…" I shook my head. "Well, I won't lecture anyone, but it doesn't seem healthy."

"I agree. It's always a little red flag, but then, I don't have much problem being me whether or not people like it." He grinned. "So are you a fitness, outdoorsy kind of guy?" he guessed.

I grinned. "If I lived anywhere else, I might be. But you couldn't pay me enough to wrap myself in spandex and play target practice with cabs here at five in the morning."

"Hm. Yeah, I see your point."

After a few more minutes of idle conversation, he excused himself to head for the bathroom, and I had a minute to compose myself.

This was already the best first date I'd been on in ages, and it had only just started. Mind you, it was the only first date I'd had in, like, a decade. Okay, maybe not quite that long, but even so…

As long as I didn't screw anything up, I'd be happy. Maybe I'd have the confidence for more. Except there was one little problem: I wanted my next date to be with *Kev* again.

This was not how the plan was supposed to go.

6

KEV

I rinsed my hands in the sink and thumbed my phone to check that Adam had gotten my safety text. The cash was tucked securely in my wallet, and all there. He was paying me for four hours. That was enough for dinner and a trip to a hotel, if he really wanted.

There was the snarky reply from Adam. Yep, he knew not to call the cops.

Couldn't be too careful, so I always did safety check-ins. This was a legit restaurant, and better yet, it was a regular haunt of Charlie's, which meant he wasn't planning to bring me to some abandoned alley afterward and knife me.

With that taken care of, I could focus on prettying up. When my hair looked just right, I toweled off my hands and headed out to the restaurant to rejoin my dinner companion. Charlie had clearly made an effort to dress up, so I was glad I'd trusted my instincts and overdressed just a touch. I looked perfect on Charlie's arm at a fancy place like this.

"Hey," Charlie greeted. Our water had already arrived. Damn, I hadn't been able to keep an eye on it. I'd take it slowly just in case. Water was the best, though. Very hard to sneak anything into water.

"Hi," I answered and gave him a breathless smile. Normally I had to fake being interested in a guy until he said something interesting that I could seize upon and milk, but there were too many interesting subjects to choose from with Charlie already. "So, you were saying about the outdoors… not your thing?"

"Oh, no," Charlie chuckled. He sipped his water. "I'm more of an urbanite, but more by career than choice. I'm not often needed in forests."

I nodded. "That makes sense. Any other hobbies, then? Or does your career take over your life?"

"Yep," Charlie said succinctly. "Unfortunately."

I reminded myself again that he was blunt not to be rude, but because that was what people here were like. "I get out to Central Park a lot, and when I find another park, I explore. It's the closest I get to… well, where I came from."

I didn't love inviting questions about it, but I had the feeling he would be tactful.

Sure enough, he chose his words carefully. "Any particular reason you came here?"

"The usual," I told him with a rueful grin. "To get away from anyone who knows me."

I steered the conversation back to his work to avoid any further prying, and before long, he was telling funny work stories. Even though I had to laugh at them, it wasn't a chore. He was a lot cleverer than he seemed to know, and I liked his humor. Subtle and quick, not in-your-face, but he wasn't afraid of a dirty joke.

He'd be a lot of fun in bed. It was a shame he wasn't thinking of that.

Our main courses turned out absolutely delicious, and I complimented his taste. The white wine garlic sauce and parsley brought out all the juicy chicken flavors, and the vegetables on the side had been roasted until they were sweet. I loved every bite.

"You should see my taste in men," he deadpanned.

I couldn't resist a laugh. He had a way of taking me by surprise, but not to try to prove how funny he was, either. Nothing about him seemed egotistical, which was a surprise. Most men in the city were on some quest to be the best, smartest, funniest, richest guy out there.

But his humor was self-deprecating, too. He added after a moment, "Good thing they don't reciprocate."

"Don't put yourself down," I immediately told him, leaning over the table. "You'd be a catch by anyone's standards, and I should know."

He opened his mouth for a moment, and then that shy attitude came back. He blushed and looked down at his empty plate. Now I had to get him to believe it, didn't I? But if he didn't want to believe, there wasn't anything anyone could tell him to change his mind. It was a struggle I constantly had: whether to try to compliment people who clearly had insecurities, knowing that it might not do any good.

I just wished I could show everyone how I saw them, in all their interesting quirks and foibles, and the beauty that came from being real people, not the porn stars and actors they compared themselves to.

Saved by the waiter, who came to check on us. Charlie recovered his composure, asked for the bill, handed over his card, and made small talk.

Only after we left the restaurant did he wrap his arm around me. "Thanks. It's been a long time since my last date, like I said. It's easy to start believing that I'm… you know, not a good candidate."

"Just because you weren't the right candidate for other people's positions doesn't mean there isn't a kama sutra of options out there," I told him.

Charlie grinned, as I'd hoped. "That makes me feel better, but slightly horny," he admitted. "Sorry."

"I'd be insulted if it didn't," I teased, licking my lips. With the charge between us, I wasn't sure if we were going for coffee or to his place.

"Would you like to…" he trailed off, seemingly genuinely conflicted.

"Probably, but you can ask," I told him, taking both his hands as I turned to face him.

He squeezed my hands and composed himself again, then let out his breath. "Right. Would you like to come back to my place? I told myself I wouldn't, but… things have changed."

It's amazing how often one date can change them. I bit back my smirk and nodded eagerly. Good news for me. All that time shaving wasn't going to go to waste. "I'd love that."

"Good." He looked relieved. "Even if we just have coffee… we can't really talk openly in public, can we?"

"I think we'd be more comfortable somewhere private," I agreed. As the Uber pulled up, I checked out the license plate and texted it to Adam, then climbed in after Charlie, who didn't even seem to have noticed the safety precaution.

He really was sheltered. God, he was going to be so much fun.

Surprisingly, the car ride wasn't the kind we tuned out and waited to end. He kept asking questions about what TV I liked, where I'd been in New York City, and offering suggestions about places that were must-see sights.

By the time we got to the brick townhouse, I felt like I knew him enough not to assume he was a snob for owning one. A well-paid nice guy was a rarity. One who wanted me inside his own house, not even a hotel? It felt more and more like a date, even if I had to remind myself it wasn't.

A discreet, quick text of his address to Adam, and I double-checked the time. Technically, we had an hour left. It was bad practice to let customers overrun the time—they start to feel like they're something… well, exceptional. I had to fight every instinct that told me that maybe Charlie *was*.

A guy like him wasn't still on the market for no reason.

Maybe Charlie wasn't a serial killer, but he was horrible in bed. Or he hated puppies. Or he stayed late at work every night. Or he put his milk in the bowl before cereal. Yeah, that much sounded true. I couldn't see him being bad at sex or hating puppies, and definitely not putting the milk in first. Although I couldn't wait for him to put the milk in me.

"Welcome," he told me, ushering me into the foyer. "It's not cozy, but it's mine."

When I could speak again, I scoffed. "Nonsense." It was definitely the kind of showy home you'd invite your clients to, nothing like I'd expected from the outside. Not ornate and old-fashioned and pretentious, but young and hip. Was this really the same house, or had I entered a warp portal?

"I get that reaction a lot." Charlie grinned, gesturing at my face. "I designed this myself, and hand-picked my favorite contractors."

Suddenly my own apartment seemed that much shabbier in comparison, and I blushed. "Right," I agreed. "Makes sense, in your line of work."

"All I do here is cocktail parties and dinner parties and that stuff," Charlie sighed. "I've been meaning to add a few more personal touches."

The whole lower floor seemed ideal for entertaining: a large living room looking out into the small but well-landscaped back yard, an open-plan kitchen with an island, and a full bathroom.

These glimpses into strangers' lives were always fascinating. My curiosity was engaged about what the upstairs looked like, and whether it was equally impersonal, but I might never find out. God, I hoped I did. Watching him walk in those tight pants did things to me.

"So, workaholic?" I asked, settling on the couch as he brought us glasses of sparkling water again. "That's why you haven't been dating?"

"That's half of it," he admitted. He handed me a glass and sipped. "I… had a boyfriend five years ago," he said slowly, his expression fixed on mine. I knew something was coming, so I waited.

I'd heard several variations of this story, and my heart already ached as I wondered which it would be.

"He died suddenly. Car accident."

Oh, *shit.* I hadn't expected that from a guy his age, and his expression told me that he knew exactly what my reaction was. He must have had a million people tell him the usual useless condolences.

"Sorry," I said simply and frowned. No use going over the top when I hadn't known about it at all. It always came off as fake when strangers were *oh so sorry* that my family were useless pieces of shit. I was still bitter, but having random strangers wish them harm always felt weird.

"It's all right." His response was automatic. Years of practice. "I'm over him, I think. How can you really tell if you're over someone?"

"When they're not always on your mind," I said without hesitation. "When you don't catch yourself thinking about them obsessively, or torturing yourself with memories."

His gaze was far too perceptive for my liking, but he didn't ask. He just nodded. "There was a day I woke up and realized that the day before, I hadn't even really thought about him. I knew I'd turned a corner then."

"Good for you," I told him.

"But I threw myself into work to get through. So, even though I feel ready to date? Have been for years? Still don't know how."

I nodded. "Were you together long?" I didn't mind asking since it sounded like it wasn't a sore point anymore.

"A few years. College boyfriends."

So he hadn't dated as an adult, really. College was a whole different ballgame, and a different set of social rules, and it made it much easier to meet people.

I suddenly understood why he'd looked overwhelmed and clueless when I greeted him with a pretty standard hug and not even a butt squeeze. It was a serious moment, though. Not the time to think about butt squeezes.

I put a hand on his knee. "Right. So it must be hard to get back in the game."

"It is, but that's what I'm hoping to do," he agreed. "I didn't really want to, but then… I don't know. I saw you, and it suddenly seemed like it was worth a try."

I'd had plenty of guys tell me that I was different, or too good for sex work, or they could rescue me. My speech was prepared in the back of my mind, but I hoped I didn't have to use it. "Yeah?"

"I was hoping today to learn… more about dating, and what I like these days. And what I can do better." Charlie looked at me, his eyes shining with hope. "Would you help me?"

I couldn't exactly say no. "Of course," I told him. "That's what I'm here for. What do you mean, help you?"

"Is there anything I could have done better?"

I stopped for a moment. It was all I could do not to break out laughing. "You want me to… to give you a report card?"

"Yes."

"I can't," I grinned. "I enjoyed it too much. And I'm not even fibbing a little," I added before he protested. "Honestly, that felt the most like a real perfect first date than most of my dates ever have."

"And you say that to most guys, right?" Charlie winked.

I grinned and held up my hands. "Maybe. But I mean it. I walked up to you and Darren at the bar because I was interested in you. And you turned out to be more interesting when I got to know you more. I think you're gonna do just fine when you get out on the prowl."

I was already jealous of the lucky man who would get this guy. He was kind, intelligent, smart, and hard-working. As long as he could learn to stay at home now and then and pamper his boyfriend, he'd be a damn lucky guy.

"There's only one section of the report card we haven't filled out yet," I added. When he blinked at me, I grinned again. "The bedroom."

"Ah, right." Charlie's blush was adorable. He nodded, his eyes fixed on mine.

"So… what do you say?" I tried not to plead. He bit his lip, and I couldn't breathe. If he was going to let me down, I hoped he'd do it quickly, because I needed the answer right now.

"How much time do we have left?"

God, I'd gotten so sucked into spending time talking to him that I hadn't even kept track of the time. I checked my watch. "Half an hour."

"That's not much time," Charlie hummed quietly.

I would stop my watch if that was what it took to get him in bed with me, but I bit back my comment before I sounded too desperate. "There's lots we can do in half an hour. So, is that a yes?"

I didn't want to coax anyone into something they didn't want. But goddamn did I want to see this man with his clothes off, and I didn't care if he was a top or a bottom or a side or oral-only or even if he had the weirdest fetishes out there.

I just wanted him.

Shit. I wasn't supposed to feel like that about a client. I wasn't supposed to be hanging on, waiting for his answer. And I shouldn't be crossing every finger and toe that the answer was *yes*. Whatever he answered in a few moments' time, I was screwed, because now I knew I was into him.

What the hell had I done?

7

―――

CHARLIE

I wanted to say yes.

It felt like every single cell in my body vibrated with that desire. But my brain was telling me otherwise, questioning the logic of my decision. I wished that, for once, I could shut it off. But the problem with seeing the world in grids and rulers was that I couldn't just walk away from my brain.

I closed my eyes for a few moments, focusing on how right that touch felt. The hand on my knee grounded me, made me remember what it was like to be held like a lover.

Just like the hug at the beginning of our date, but potentially so much better.

I didn't want sex. That much hadn't changed. I wasn't exactly saving myself for Mr. Right, and I certainly didn't want Kev to feel like I was avoiding him. I didn't think he was dirty because of what he did for a living, and I knew damn well some guys treated him like that.

It was none of that. It was a lot harder to explain. I wanted more of a connection. More time to relax and get to know the other guy first. More… well, more *romance*. And I wanted Kev to look at me like that, without the money I'd paid making me question myself.

On the other hand, I wanted to keep our arrangement monetary. It meant I could walk away at any time, and that made me safe.

I was safe right now, I reminded myself. I could try this, and if I didn't like it, I could just walk away.

I already knew I would like it, though. There was no way my body would have been this on-edge all night, in a way I'd forgotten, if we'd had a lousy connection.

"Yes," I whispered. "Kiss me."

The eager grin of relief that Kev gave me was impossible to fake. "God, I was hoping you'd say that," he whispered, and he scooted closer until our thighs touched. He kept his hand on my knee, and his other hand rested on my shoulder to gently turn me to face him.

I knew how to do this. Just because I hadn't in so long didn't mean I didn't remember.

My own desperation surprised me as I leaned into his touch, my whole body flaring up with need. *Yes*, I wanted to say. *Yes, please.* I barely bit back the words.

He read my body language, though. He didn't make me beg for it. He just closed the distance between us, gently pressing his lips against mine for a few long seconds.

For a few seconds, I froze, almost unsure what to do. Then my body relaxed and remembered.

It was like letting go of one language and embracing another, with its whole new way of thinking, its gestures and unspoken move-ments, its history and shared culture.

Just for a minute, I wasn't the uptight architect everyone saw. I was a man who loved men again—who loved holding and touching them, looking at them, kissing them, breathing in their scent. Loved the way they walked and talked and fucked. Loved their passion and cattiness and distance and warmth and all the myriad contrasts of the whole damn lot of us.

In that moment, I loved him, and for the first time in a long time, I loved *me*.

The kiss and its significance took my breath away, and made me press close for more. My arm slid around his shoulders, pressing his body into mine and breathing him in deeply.

The soft gasp he gave against my lips made me feel stronger now, in charge of this. The fear had passed. All that was left was desire.

I shivered with pleasure at the way he eagerly pressed into me, his hands roaming over my chest and shoulders. He felt like a man starving for attention, and I reacted well to that. I needed to make him feel as precious, as fascinating, as gorgeous, as I found him.

In the privacy of my own thoughts, I could daydream about being the one to sweep him off his feet, even if I knew it wasn't reality.

That finally made me pull away from him, my lips sensitive. God, I hadn't kissed anyone in so long that I'd almost forgotten what the scrape of stubble against my chin felt like, or the way I still tasted him on my lips. A hint of peppermint, from the restaurant's complimentary mints.

"Well?" Kev murmured, his hands still on my shoulders. His gaze grew more intense as he waited for an answer.

It was impossible to sum up everything that had gone through my head. It felt like I'd just put down a box of thoughts and anxieties I'd been carrying on my shoulder for miles. "That was good," I breathed out.

Kev let out a breath of relieved laughter. "I was worried for a moment."

"But I need some time alone now," I told him apologetically, biting my lip. It sounded like a brush-off, but I didn't mean it that way. It was true. I had to figure out what the hell this meant for me, and I had no idea what might come up once I let my thoughts start rolling. I wasn't going to subject him to that.

He smiled softly, like he'd expected it. "All right. You have my number. Text me if you want to meet up again," he told me.

"Thank you for a great night," I told him, and I meant it. I tried not to seem over-eager as I touched his knee to show my sincerity.

"No, thank you."

I rose to my feet and offered him a hand getting up, then steered him to the door. God, my hand itself seemed to automatically find his lower back—like it was meant to be there. I dropped it quickly, like I'd been burned, and slid my hands into my pockets.

It was all so strange. It looked like a date, felt like a date, but it wasn't. Or was it? My lines were getting blurry. I didn't know what I'd expected, but it had been something... *other* than this. Something that felt like a cold, commercial transaction. Something like I expected a Grindr hookup to be.

But even though this was technically commercial, he wasn't faking the warmth of his smile as he reached out. "Do I get a good night hug?"

"You get a good night kiss, if you give me those eyes," I told him with a grin as I embraced him. This time, it felt natural to press our bodies together and relax into Kev's warm, strong hug.

He pulled back just enough to press his lips against mine for a long, slow, and undeniably sensual kiss. His tongue and lips worked along mine, like he was gently trying to tease every nerve in my body awake.

It worked, too. I shifted, my pants suddenly that much tighter, and finally pulled back.

I could barely breathe as I murmured, "Good night, Kev."

"Good night, Charlie." Kev squeezed my shoulder and finally turned to head out the door.

The moment he reached the front porch, I wanted to call him back. I wanted to say *we've still got fifteen minutes, haven't we?* I wanted to wring out every last moment of his company, like a refreshing drink after a long, hot summer's day.

What the hell had come over me?

I raised my hand in a silent wave when he reached the sidewalk and turned for another look. He waved back, smiled, and then he was gone.

I shut the door, turned my back to it, and slid down it. I sat in the entrance hall for a few minutes, staring at nothing in particular, trying to get a handle on my emotions. To handle them, though, I needed to name them. I wasn't sure I could do that.

The date was everything I'd expected and so much more, and so much deeper. But it was also my first date in so long that anything was going to be amazing, like water after a whole day on a construction site when you forgot your water bottle. How the hell was I supposed to deal with that?

Eventually, I coaxed myself into getting up again and tidying up the place. I moved on autopilot as I took our half-full glasses to the kitchen, set them on the counter, and then folded my arms and stared at the glasses like they contained the answers to his heart, or mine.

The glass half-full was a metaphor for optimism, but what about two glasses half-full? If you put them together, there was enough for one full glass.

That seemed like a metaphor, but I resisted it.

I was taking this to heart because it was my first date in ages, not because he was *the one* for me. And what the hell did *the one* mean, anyway? Hugh had been *the one*, and now look.

Dating other men would mean admitting that there wasn't a soulmate for everyone, wouldn't it? Or did it mean that there were multiple soulmates? Or that the whole thing was a crock of shit, and you were just supposed to find someone who put up with you for a lifetime?

I had no idea. Back when I'd been just the widower Charlie, everything was simpler. Now that I was back on the market, nothing made sense anymore.

"Back to normal," I told myself. This was just like the disorientation of landing in another continent after a long time away. I needed a routine.

So I checked my voicemail as I grabbed a glass of water for bed.

"Hey, Charlie."

I nearly dropped the glass in the sink. Goddamn, of course it was Chris. Hugh's dad.

"Hope you're doing well. I think you're back in the country now, huh? Linda and I were wondering if you wanted to come over for dinner on Saturday. Let us know if you're free."

I hung up and shut off the tap, then brought my glass upstairs to bed.

It was nothing new. I spent plenty of time around Hugh's family. They'd basically taken me in as another son, after all, even if I'd never become their son-in-law.

What the hell would they say if they knew I'd gone on a date with an escort tonight, and now I was fantasizing about dating him so I didn't have to be emotionally vulnerable ever again? God, that made me a loser.

I needed to talk to Ben. If anyone could help, it was him.

As soon as I was naked under the sheets in bed, I dialed.

As usual, he picked up. "Ben," I greeted. "I've got a dilemma." I wanted to say the words fast enough that I couldn't back out.

He was never taken aback by me anymore, however blunt I was. It seemed hard to get him angry in general, which I liked. It was a valuable trait in someone living here, where the choice every morning was road rage or MTA rage. "This is the help desk, go ahead."

I chuckled grimly. "Love life help desk?"

"*Ohhhhh.* What's going on?" Ben sounded excited, and it wasn't surprising. It had been years since I'd even shown an interest in having one.

"I went on a date and I kind of liked it."

Ben caught his breath. His voice squeaked when he said, "Whoa!"

"I know," I assured him with a quiet chuckle.

He'd been there for me through the rough nights when I woke up at one o'clock and wished with everything I had that I could roll over into Hugh and hug him against me. He'd seen me keep my composure until I walked into the house, and then sit on the floor and cry my eyes out, unable to even stand for long enough to get to the couch. He'd seen me lose interest in men, and in the rest of my life, and run on autopilot. He'd seen me get back up, but never out there again.

He knew damn well that I wouldn't say this lightly.

"Who? When? Gimme more!" Ben prompted. "Holy shit."

I hesitated. I could tell him anything—but this seemed like a step too far. Would he judge me? Or, worse, Kev?

When I didn't answer immediately, Ben's voice turned serious as he added, "Charlie? Tell me what's going on."

I let a long sigh out. I had to trust in someone here, and it sure as hell wasn't gonna be my family or Hugh's family or my coworkers. It had to be Ben. "I kind of accidentally hired an escort."

Ben's noise of reaction was something between a choked laugh and a gasp. "Charlie!"

"I know," I groaned. "I just wanted a date, with no strings, where I couldn't hurt the other guy's feelings if I turned out to be... you know, stuck in the past."

"And?"

"What? No *that's illegal, dipshit?*" I asked, frowning.

"You're a dumbass if you think I care about that," Ben snorted. "Unless—wait, he wasn't a cop, was he? Are you calling me to bail you out?"

"No! God. He wasn't. I just thought..." I trailed off, my cheeks flushing. I knew Ben. So why was I so worried? "You're right, sorry. I've made such a big deal of it in my head, that's all."

"How was it accidental? Did you accidentally click on a Craigslist link?" Ben teased.

I groaned. "Shut up. No, I went to a bar last night—"

"—Goddamn, you'll be telling me you're hitting up swingers' parties at this rate—"

"—and a guy approached us. The guy I was talking to said he's an escort. I found him on Grindr and… well, messaged him…"

Ben gasped again. "You're on Grindr? Jesus! Are you okay, dude?"

I sighed. I could see how it looked like I'd just had a personality swap with an alien. "I saw the guy open Grindr when he walked away."

"Aha. And you were hoping to meet him again," Ben surmised.

"Right."

"Are you into him? You know, not just in bed."

I wished I could punch his shoulder. He was grinning now. I could hear it. "Asshole. We didn't even fuck, I'll have you know."

"What? You paid an escort and you didn't even…" Ben laughed. "Charlie, oh my God."

"He's not just… I wasn't looking for…" I trailed off, my cheeks flushed. "All of this is beside the point. Hugh's dad called me and they want me over for dinner on Saturday. But I was gonna ask him out for another date instead, this weekend."

"A *paid* date," Ben emphasized. "It's not the same, baby."

I didn't appreciate the patronizing tone, even if I knew why he was saying it. He didn't want me getting my heart broken by the first guy I'd seen in half a decade. "Yeah. I know. That's what's so appealing."

"That you can see him whenever you want, do whatever you want, and not have to worry about losing him?"

Fucking ouch. I considered hanging up, but Ben would only call me back right away. I sighed and put the phone back to my ear. He ought to have been right, and it wasn't his fault that my heart had suddenly gotten involved. "We're not that serious yet. I wanted a date where he can tell me if I'm doing a good job before I go make an idiot of myself in the dating world. You forget what it's like not to date for so damn long."

Looking eligible and attractive to other guys was suddenly the least of my worries, but Ben didn't have to know that.

It was just a stupid attraction that came from sudden exposure to human contact after years of isolation. It would go away once I started going on regular old dates with plain old guys. Guys who would inevitably be less interesting, attractive, smart, or smooth.

Fuck. I was already doing the comparison thing. Maybe it had been a long time since I'd felt a crush, but I recognized it.

"Okay, babe," Ben said, trying on his soothing voice. "Tell Chris and Linda yes. No point in upsetting them and shutting yourself away. And tomorrow night, you and me. Mandatory drinks. We'll figure this out. You don't need to pay someone for it."

I didn't mind paying Kev for his company, but at least Ben was trying to calm me down. It would be good to have some help figuring out what the hell was going on with me.

"Fine," I agreed. "Text me when you're off work."

"Will do. Get some sleep," Ben told me.

I doubted it, but I said, "Thanks. Night," anyway before I hung up. I had just enough time to think, *How the hell am I gonna get through this one?* before my eyes shut.

8

KEV

"You're fucking kidding," I grumbled, tossing my phone on my bed. Another goddamn Grindr profile shut down overnight. As I swallowed my daily PrEP pill with the glass of water on my bedside table, I tried to brainstorm other solutions.

This was getting tedious, and I was starting to worry that they might report me to the police. The last thing I needed was to have some cops on my ass. That really *would* drive me to working street corners, and I would never do that again.

Not only would Adam kick my ass, but so would the closest thing I had to big brothers.

I'd stumbled on a gay-run dude ranch in Tennessee last autumn, and decided to drop by for some quick cash. I'd just assumed the place would be easy money if I could hide out from the owners.

Instead of the easy hookups I'd expected, I'd run into the owner right away. Josh was only a few years older than me but way wiser. He had taken me in, offered me the job and a place to live, and... well, the rest was history.

Josh and Evan—the owner's boyfriend—had taken the time to give both Adam and me as much work experience as we could handle. In our short but intense internship with them on their ranch, I'd driven tractors, done accounting, and everything in between.

It had given me a taste for other jobs. Not crappy retail jobs, but jobs where I could do different kinds of interesting things.

Not that I hated escorting, but all the bullshit that had sprung up around it, making it harder and harder to do safely and with any measure of dignity? It started to make other lines of work look more attractive, and I was goddamn lucky that I had some other experience, a roommate, and a credit card.

"Bad luck again?" Adam called from the kitchen, where he was pouring us coffee and bowls of cereal.

I sighed. "Yeah. Another profile shut down. No way can I make it work with just my paid ad sites, though." Some people used them, but not enough. All the guys who might want to hire me were on Grindr. It was easy pickings… or it had been, anyway.

"I keep telling you, they're always looking for employees at my place. Or any old convenience store. It's reliable hours," Adam said.

"And I keep saying no."

Adam was juggling bowls and cups as he pushed past the blanket in my makeshift doorway to bring me cereal and coffee. The lack of privacy was getting old, but whatever. Adam plopped on the bed with his own bowl and mug, shoveling cereal into his face. "Yeah, but you should try it out," he said around a mouthful.

"Gross," I told him—both the prospect of working retail and his idea of table manners.

For starters, I'd need clothes I didn't mind getting ruined. Wearing my thrift store Armani to work at a corner store was a recipe for mugging, dry-cleaning, or both.

But it would be predictable income, he was right. And when my last job before Charlie had been several days prior, and paid less than I was used to…

"What's wrong with me? Am I getting old?"

Adam paused and then choked with laughter, which answered my question.

"Never mind," I mumbled, blushing.

"If your job's making you question whether *twenty-three* is *old*, there might be a problem," Adam pointed out.

I made a face. I hated to admit it, but he had a point there, too. I spent so much time obsessing over details of my skincare regimen, my clothing, and how old I should tell people I was.

I didn't mind reading newspapers to stay current on world events, taking online courses so I could understand enough to ask smart questions, that kind of stuff. It didn't make me feel bad like staring at myself in the mirror did.

"Every job has its perks and pitfalls," I told him. "But bring in a job application, I guess."

"One step ahead of you!" Adam scrambled to his feet so fast he flipped his cereal bowl and spilled milk and soggy Lucky Charms all over the foot of my bed.

"Adam!" I grabbed his spoon and chucked it after him as he raced for his room. "You asshole!"

He brought back a sheet of paper and waved it in my face. "Yeah, but I got you this."

"And now I have to do laundry!"

Adam shrugged. "Oops. So, I'll help you fill this out." He didn't let me grab the sheet, which was just as well, because I was pissed off enough that I would have torn up the job application and need to get another.

"Jesus. I don't even know that I want the damn job," I grumbled, picking soggy cereal off the bed and flipping the bowl over. "Grab me a towel."

When I glared at him, Adam relented and brought a dry towel to sop up some of the milk, at least. "Sorry."

That was rare enough to stop my anger in its tracks. I sighed instead and shook my head at him. "Someday you'll learn to move with more grace than a charging buffalo."

"I doubt it," he told me. "Not at this rate. I think I've reached peak grace. I dropped a case of cans the other day at work, you know. Burst two open." He sounded almost proud of his own clumsiness.

"Well, I can't suck worse than you do at working there, then," I told him.

It was far from my dream job, but if I took part-time hours, maybe I could supplement my income. Might be a crappy fourteen bucks an hour or something, but diversifying income streams was just a smart maneuver.

"And while you work, you can study—" Adam started.

I held up my hands. "Whoa, whoa. Ain't nobody talking about studying here."

Adam huffed a sigh of frustration. "You're the one with all the money, Kev. Spend it on your future instead of your wardrobe. Pay your way through, like, law school or med school. Isn't that what hookers are supposed to do?"

My jaw dropped. He knew damn well that I didn't like that word.

God, I wished he'd grow up a little. He could stand to actually show some feelings once in a while without throwing jabs into his sentences. I knew he came from a shitty family background, but so did I, and I managed not to piss off everyone I talked to within three sentences.

"Sorry," he muttered, holding up his hands. "You get the point."

"That you think I'm a cheap whore," I threw back at him. "Who's supposed to be working my way toward, what, a free future?"

He shrugged and pressed his lips together tightly, clearly holding back what he really wanted to say. That was a change.

"Well, newsflash. I'll apply for your shitty job, *for now*, until I get a better balance of regular clients," I told him, unable to keep the fury out of my voice. "But I'm not gonna follow anyone else's life path. Do you think I wear this stuff because I like it?"

This time, Adam did answer. "Yeah."

I glowered. The fact that he was half-right made it worse. "Yeah, I like to look good. But I can do that in thrift store clothes. I don't give a shit what brand names I have on. I do it for *my* job, like you get those dumb haircuts for *your* job."

"Hey!" Adam frowned at me and patted his hair. It looked lousy short. Back in Tennessee, it had been grown out and he hadn't looked like a dozen other frat boys in our block.

"Oh, no. Did I insult your hair after you insulted my whole damn life?" I grumbled. I grabbed the job application from him and shoved the bowl of soggy cereal bits into his hands instead. "Go on, let me finish cleaning up this mess you made, as usual."

He huffed and stormed out of my room, which was a bit silly since he couldn't slam the door. He flourished the blanket in the doorway instead, and I had to bite back my laughter at his attempt to dramatically exit.

God, Adam pissed me off sometimes, but despite my natural impulse to dig my heels in, he had a point about getting an education. I didn't want to go get some useless degree that I didn't need, but practical training in another career could pay off.

Look at Charlie. It took five years in school to become an architect, he said, but it was a practical set of skills that made him employable anywhere, however old he was and however he dressed.

What could I do in a year or two? I'd dabbled in so many different things at the dude ranch that I barely knew what I was interested in anymore. I liked a bit of everything.

That was one perk to escorting: lots of free time and exposure to a hundred different types of lives. They skewed to the middle-class or rich guy jobs like lawyers, politicians, and bankers, but there were plenty of boring accountants and middle managers who needed to get laid, too.

I liked to keep things running, but I had the feeling being in an office would just crush my spirits. I wasn't going to put myself through that hell just to make someone like Adam feel better about his own existence.

"Fuck," I mumbled under my breath and flopped onto my back on the bed. My legs touched the wet, milky patch and I moaned to myself with the awfulness of it all. It was too late to get wash-and-press back in time for tonight without some exorbitant fee.

First stop: laundromat. Maybe a few hours of staring at the machines would give me a flash of inspiration about what I was supposed to do next.

As it turned out, watching the shapes of my clothing blur into circles in the aggressive coin washer didn't give me the answers to the mystery of life. The laundromat did, however, give me free wi-fi. That was a perk of spending the extra couple bucks and going to an upmarket laundromat, as much as Brooklyn contained such a thing. Another was not having my clothes ruined by a shitty machine, of course.

The wi-fi let me log into Scruff, where my profile had flown under the radar for now. It was a little easier to bury my job description in the text description, even though they said explicitly at the top of the description box that paid solicitation wasn't allowed.

And I had a new message.

Hey handsome, looking for company this weekend. Yes, I read your profile. Extra gifts for discretion.

That perked my interest, and I thumbed to his profile. It was blank.

I typed back a quick message to tell him to WhatsApp me, and sent another message with my phone number. That was the first sign of trustworthiness—when they didn't hesitate to give me their number. WhatsApp was encrypted, too, so neither of us had to worry about the cops.

It took a few minutes, but I got a WhatsApp message not long afterward from him.

I work in Washington so I don't want this getting out. Do you understand?

Oh. That answered too many of my questions at once. I bit back my first few responses, and instead settled on a simple question.

Does your wife know?

I was completely unsurprised when I glanced down to see a one-word answer.

No.

I gritted my teeth. May as well go the whole way.

How did you vote on FOSTA/SESTA?

His response was quick.

How about I give you a fat gift, you shut up and do what you do best?

I rolled my eyes, but I couldn't stop the laugh that burst out of me.

What's that?

Suck my dick and look pretty. Does that turn you on? Or is it the money?

If he thought the alpha-male politician thing was gonna turn me on, he had another think coming. Guys like him didn't even want to admit that guys like me were human, much less worthy of protection. Why the hell would I trust them in bed?

I actually felt kind of sad for him. He really didn't understand how human beings functioned, yet he was trying to govern them. And I might agree with his policies otherwise, but who knew? He wasn't going to sit down and talk with me, or try to listen.

It didn't feel like there was any safe place for me anymore in politics, or in life.

I blocked him and chewed my nails. He'd probably get pissy and report me in retaliation. Wasn't the first time, wouldn't be the last.

Maybe, as much as I hated to admit it, Adam was right. And he did give a shit about me, even if he had a backhanded way of showing it.

The dryer's soothing white noise stopped, and I was finally free to head back to the apartment and make amends. Clients were great, but I wasn't going to lose a friendship for a few careless words. Fine, I'd pick up a bottle of wine on the way back.

I bundled all my sheets into my hamper, turned off my work phone, and headed for home.

9

CHARLIE

Walking into the bar, I spotted Ben immediately. He'd barely changed throughout the years since senior year of college, when we'd spent half our time in places like this.

Well, we'd hung out in "student-friendly" (cheap) dive bars, and we went to cocktail places now. He was just as comfortable in a sports bar or an upmarket lounge, but the sudden raucous cheering that tended to break out in sports bars at seemingly random moments unnerved me.

"Over here, Charlie!" Ben called, oblivious to the attention he drew to himself from other people here who looked like they'd like to be over there with him.

I bit back my grin. It wasn't his fault he was unreasonably attractive. It was always hard to compete against that boyish smile and the size of his biceps, but we catered to very different tastes when we went out on the town together, so it had worked.

Maybe being hot made it hard to settle in a relationship, though. From what Ben had hinted through texts, his relationship status was back up in the air. Again.

"Hey," I greeted and hugged him tightly. It was always good to see one of the few guys who'd stuck with me through thick and thin. "Oof!"

He squeezed the life out of me, as he always did, and I always complained it was unfair. "Hey, pipsqueak," he greeted affectionately. "I got you a drink. Guess what kind?"

I had to stare at it for a few moments before I identified it. "Sex on the Beach? Funny."

"Hey. Better to enjoy some free Sex on the Beach than paying for a Blowjob."

I flipped him off, but the ungraceful snort of laughter I gave betrayed me. "Thanks for thinking of me," I told him and sipped the sweet drink through its pink paper straw. Brooklyn was such a hipster place now, but little details like the straw made me appreciate it.

"Anytime." Ben smirked and winked at me, then scooted his chair closer to the tiny round table. "So! Spill. More juicy details, please." He tapped his wrist and the table.

It did nothing to raise my stress levels. I'd long since gotten over feeling pressured by anything Ben said or did. I worked at my own efficient pace—no slower or faster. And I'd already carefully planned what to say.

"I want to see him again."

Ben stared at me for a few moments and then nudged my drink closer to me, like a good stiff drink would make me come to my senses.

I sighed and sipped it again as I gathered my courage. "I know he's just doing a job, and I'm okay with that."

"Are you really? Will you *stay* okay with that?" Ben asked. As usual, he cut right to the chase. He knew better than to try to lead me through a tangled emotional conversation. It was a waste of time.

"Dunno yet," I shrugged. "I'll find out, won't I?"

Ben frowned and drained the rest of his cocktail, staying silent for a good minute while watching me. He didn't say anything yet.

The silence was unnerving enough to prompt me to speak a little more. "I like him. He's fun to hang out with. He's been patient with me. If I jump on Tinder or whatever, I could just find some guy who's willing to date me, sure. But it's not like I'm the average twenty-something young professional in the city. I've got baggage."

"So does everyone," Ben pointed out.

I stuck my lip out for a moment and gazed into the distance as I considered this. He had a point. "Okay. But some guys don't want to date people like me. They'll always feel like they're competing for affection with someone who they can't beat."

"Are they?"

I knew the answer to this one, at least. "No. If I'd been dating a few years ago, maybe. But not now. He's like any other ex. We were separated by... death, rather than choice, but it's still a past relationship."

"He isn't, though, is he? If you're worried about telling Hugh's family that you're meeting another guy?"

Ben had me there. I realized that he was at least partly right. "I'll have to think about that," I admitted. "But I'm not stopping seeing him."

"You're putting an imaginary guy's needs above your own," Ben told me. "Let *him* decide if you're dateable. Don't stop yourself dating someone, just in case you find out you're not up for it and hurt him."

Still, it sat wrong with me. Going into something not knowing if I wanted it was a waste of everyone's time. I shook my head. "It's better this way. Besides… I want to see *him* again. It's not just the safety, or whatever."

Ben looked doubtful, but he nodded. "If that's what it takes to get you back on the market." He toasted me. "To your rekindled love life."

I clinked glasses and drained mine, then got up to get the next round. By the time I made it back to the table, Ben was looking around the room in a very prowling way.

"Someone's looking," I teased, clapping his shoulder once I set down the drinks. I slid into the chair again and raised my eyebrows. "So?"

"Ivan dumped me," Ben put it succinctly.

I winced. I'd figured it was a bad idea for him to date his boss, but I'd kept my opinion to myself, and… there it was. "Sorry, man."

Ben snorted. "Nah. It was long overdue. He was just bored, and I was there, all starry-eyed and fuckable…"

"As long as he's not being a dick on the job," I told him.

"Nah. And you know what? I'm free to go to parties. I'll be at the Cock every weekend. You should join me and get some," Ben told me with a wink.

I'd half-expected this. "Me? In a foam pit? Or a darkroom?"

"Come on. You've got the whole hot nerd thing going on." Ben sat back and assessed me with a critical eye. "Your shoulders are definitely broad. That's a great silhouette to cover in foam. Artfully dab foam on your cheeks."

"Oh, shut up," I laughed to hide the blush. I would never fit in at that kind of place. Ben might be right at home in himself, but I was barely able to drag myself to a nice restaurant with a date. "I'll do my thing, you do yours."

"Is this a race?" Ben smirked. "First to get a new boyfriend?"

"I'll lose that any day," I shook my head.

Ben gasped and clutched his chest. "Are you calling me easy?"

"Um…" I smirked at him. "You used the word, I want it on the record."

It was Ben's turn to flip me off.

"Only compared to me?" I added.

Ben eyed me. "You're making it worse. Stop while you're only a few steps behind."

"Okay, okay." I nudged him. "So, catch me up on your life apart from Ivan not being good enough for you."

I did my best to keep up with the information dump he treated me to over the next hour or so, asking questions at the appropriate times, but my mind was still on Kev. I wanted to tell Ben all about him. I wanted to tell him about the way he smiled gently at me, or the way he'd held my hand with such confidence, or the way he'd asked the right questions to get me to open up about everything— even Hugh.

Or the way he'd kissed me.

A few drinks later, Ben called me out. "You're daydreaming about him."

"No…" I blushed, averting my gaze. Suddenly, the mirrored back-drop of the bar was fascinating to me. "Just planning my weekend."

"So, daydreaming about being with him."

I opened my mouth and then shut it again.

"Fine," Ben smirked. "Since I can't talk you out of this, you have to keep me up to date. It's the law, you know. And I'm going to take every chance I can to tease you. I've been waiting long enough for my chance."

"Oh, God." I rolled my eyes and pushed myself to my feet. "I can't stop you. And I'm gonna call an Uber. I'm still not back in this time zone, you know."

"No kidding. You must be wiped." Ben stood up too, and pulled me in for a hug. "I'm gonna hang out here. There's a guy over in the corner, by himself…"

I cast a quick sideways glance and caught him looking at Ben. "Yeah, you're in. Have fun with that."

Ben smirked. "I plan to."

It didn't take long for me to get home—or maybe that was the cocktails talking. By the time I got there, though, I'd made up my mind.

I opened my WhatsApp conversation with Kev and tapped out a new message.

Free tomorrow afternoon? Let's do lunch? 2-3 hrs?

I wanted to make it clear I still expected to pay, in case he thought I was trying to get a freebie. I knew some guys tried to pull that stunt and date women in the industry so they could get sex for free… but it usually ended when they realized the sex was just like any other relationship.

Then, in the evening, I could go talk to Hugh's family. They didn't have to know I was dating anyone yet. I might bring up that I was interested in seeing guys again, or maybe not.

I hummed to myself and grabbed my laptop to check my work emails. Only after I'd done that, responded to a few, and added to my Monday to-do list did I realize I was literally trying to soothe my dating anxiety with work.

"God, Ben was right," I mumbled, pushing my laptop to the other side of the bed. It wasn't the worst addiction I could have, but it was still something I was using to numb my feelings. And it wouldn't help me get my life balance back to some semblance of normal.

But was it worth cutting back on work before I had anyone to cut back *for*?

I flopped onto the bed. The bar had actually been surprisingly nice to spend time in with someone I knew, but being home alone suddenly emphasized how damn quiet it was here all the time.

No wonder I spent as little time in my own bed as I could.

All my thoughts nearly distracted me from the fact that I hadn't yet heard back from Kev. Maybe he was with another client, I reasoned, but I still worried that that wasn't it. Maybe he didn't want to see me again. Maybe I was so undateable that I couldn't even pay for it.

I fell asleep without getting an answer.

10

KEV

"What makes you a good candidate for the job?"

The manager—Dirk—who was sitting across from me looked like he couldn't care less what I said in reply. He wasn't even looking at me, just staring down at the back of my job application form as he hand-wrote notes on it. Well, most of the notes seemed to be tick marks.

I fumbled for the answers. "Um, I'm used to working with people. I like to work hard and treat people fairly. I think making people smile is a great thing, but I value efficiency, too." Did that sound good? It had been a long time since I'd worked in a crappy retail job—and a gas station in the middle of nowhere as a fifteen-year-old wasn't quite the same experience.

"Fine," Dirk told me, and made another tick mark. Even his voice was bored. "What hours are you free?"

Is that it? I stuttered for a moment. I'd expected to have to wait to hear back. "Uh, I mean… anytime. I don't have anything else planned right now."

Another tick mark. "Can you start right away? Monday?"

I wasn't sure whether to be flattered or insulted. They hadn't even checked my high school diploma that I'd lied about on the application, like Josh had once advised me to do. I was pretty sure that Adam was right, and all they wanted was a warm body.

Compared to the qualifications it took to be successful in my other line of work? It *was* an insult. In that job, I had to be conversant in arts and culture, politics, science… a little of everything. I had to know how to blend into any social environment, whether the rough humor of a mechanic's garage or the snobbery of a black-tie ball. I had to know a hundred unwritten social codes. I hadn't done a lot of upscale work, but I had to present myself as if I had in order to get more of it. That was how you climbed the career ladder.

But I was here for steady hours and a legal career. I swallowed my pride and resigned myself to feeling cheaper than I ever had on a date with a client.

"Yes, sir."

"You're hired."

The paperwork didn't take long. There was barely any. Just my name and SSN, and my bank account number. After I wrote it all down, he took the paper and grunted in approval. "Two weeks for your first check, son."

No contract, no formal agreement of any kind. I just had to trust that I had a job now, because some random guy told me I was hired. "Thanks, sir. I look forward to Monday."

"Great." He stood up, a clear sign of dismissal.

I left the office, still dazed and half-considering just disappearing before Monday. One look around the little grocery store and I already felt trepidation. I kinda felt crappy. I'd be stuck here for at least twenty hours each week, and for all that time? Maybe three hundred bucks. That made maybe twelve hundred a month, but that was before taxes…

Fuck, this stung. Retail was not going to be my future.

If I had to suck it up and go back to school, maybe it was worth it. Even a community college to learn some useful office skills. I didn't care what—it had to be better than this.

"Hey." Adam caught me before I reached the door. He was working today, so I'd dropped off my resume. I hadn't even let on that we knew each other before getting pulled in for an interview, so I knew it wasn't nepotism. It was straight-up desperation for workers.

Which was always a good sign.

"I got it."

Adam fist-bumped me. "Knew it. I'll get the good wine tonight."

"The five-buck bottle, not the two-buck chuck?" I joked.

He grinned. "You know it."

"What time are you off?"

"Four. I'll make dinner," Adam offered, which was unusually generous. I kind of wanted to be able to eat my meal without having to rescue it with copious amounts of chili powder tonight, though.

"Nah, I've got it. You bring the wine, I'll figure out something to make. See you later, man."

We'd both been extra-nice to each other since the fight. Even though we'd both apologized in our own ways, we'd never really backed down, either.

I sighed as I headed around the block to our apartment, my mind a hundred miles away.

If I was making an abrupt transition, this was going to be rough. I had emergency savings, but it definitely meant no more laundry pickup, no more tailoring, no more steak for dinner. All of that stuff I could live without. It was just an abrupt change, which made it feel like a sharp fall.

There was no harm in checking to see if I'd gotten any interest, was there? It would make the new job sting a lot less if I had more of a safety cushion. *Lifestyle creep*, they called it when someone got used to making a lot of money and spending it, too. But I couldn't quite stop myself yet.

I switched on my phone and eyed the messages that came in all at once. I could already see a few offers, but only one interested me.

Charlie.

I'd spent a lot of time over the last couple days thinking about our date, so opening his message was an easy decision.

And then my heart dropped. He'd wanted lunch today, and… well, it was already just past lunch.

"Fuck," I whispered as I let myself into my apartment. I knew that quitting my current career meant missing out on seeing regular clients, but… there was something else about Charlie.

Lots of guys wanted to hire an escort to get over their hangups. Lots of guys were nice, smart, funny, and incredibly dateable. Lots of guys respected me and what I did.

But something about Charlie spoke to me. It was intuition, and I'd spent years learning to trust mine. I wasn't going to start ignoring it now.

Maybe I was quitting, but I could keep going with regular clients pretty safely, surely.

Or…

"It's a dumb idea," I told myself out loud as I heated up a mug of milk for hot chocolate. I deserved a reward for getting a job, after all. "You don't let clients get close." That was an amateur mistake.

Unless I wasn't in the industry anymore.

Before I could talk myself out of it, I dug my phone out, my thumbs flying over the surface of the screen.

Sorry I missed your text. I'd love to meet for a date when you're free. No gifts this time—just enjoying each other's company. I had a great time.

Was that too forward? Maybe, but I didn't care. I had nothing to lose.

I put my phone on the counter face-up and jabbed the screen every minute when it darkened, waiting for a reply. But even after I made my hot chocolate and brought my phone to the kitchen table to keep staring at it like I was about to receive the winning lottery numbers, he didn't answer.

Fuck. Maybe I'd already screwed up by keeping my work phone off.

Speaking of which, I had an angry message on Scruff from that politician.

Enjoy sucking cop dick, you stupid fucking whore—

As expected, my Scruff profile had been reported, so I couldn't even open the conversation to see if there was more to the notification. He'd probably reported me to the cops, too, but what could they do? I was careful to send my photos on WhatsApp, not the app. All they had was my phone number and one body shot that I used everywhere.

I grimaced and muted everything but the conversation with Charlie, and then pocketed this phone alongside my personal phone. In comparison, it usually barely saw any use.

Fine. I'd keep myself distracted by cooking supper, which meant buying ingredients. Probably vegetables and things. God help me, I was going to try something fancy, and it was either going to be spectacularly good or a huge mess in the kitchen.

But, for the first time in a while, either possibility seemed fun.

"Let's do this."

"Lord," Adam concluded as he put his fork down and pushed his plate back. "You're getting better every fucking day."

I couldn't resist. "That's what he said." I picked at the last few grains of risotto, determined to enjoy every morsel of it. I'd stood still, stirring the goddamn pot until my feet ached, after all.

Adam groaned and waved me off. "I don't wanna think about that. Can't we have one moment without your sex life being shoved in my face?"

"Hey, some guys pay good money…" I trailed off, laughing as Adam threw a tea towel at me. "Okay, okay."

"You've got a real job now," Adam told me, and then he seemed to sense his mistake before I could even begin to glower. "I mean, another job."

"Smooth," I muttered. "Yeah, can't wait to see how this goes."

"Have you done it before?"

"Nope."

"Did you tell them you had?"

I snorted. "Obviously." I'd learned how to do whatever it took to get what I needed, but as it turned out, that hadn't been necessary. "Dirk didn't seem to care about anything I wrote down, or even said. I think he was just making sure I could answer a question and breathe at the same time."

"Hey," Adam retorted. "I represent that remark."

"I'd have thought your lungs would be better after a few months here," I said with a wicked smirk. When he raised an eyebrow, I poked my tongue against the inside of my cheek and mimed a blowjob.

"Oh, you sick bastard." Adam laughed and blushed from his neck to his hairline.

"Mmm." I didn't relent for a moment. I could give as good as I got. "I know you're running free now that you can. I'll watch for you on the next Farm Boys Gone Wild."

Adam grunted and poured me another glass of wine. "I'll take my shitty paycheck and dignity, thanks. Speaking of which, Bobby said he's training you. He's a good guy. Accidentally had twins with a girl and stayed with her, and now he's trying to provide for them. He's covering my shift next week so I can go to a pool-cleaning gig. You'll learn fast from him."

I sighed as I grabbed the bottle and my glass, elbowing him and nodding to the couch. It was tucked in a long, narrow slice of the apartment that had once been the dining room portion of the combination living room and dining area. With the living room turned into a bedroom, it was all we had for lounging, but it was fine by me.

"We should talk about this." I wasn't gonna let Adam escape this time.

"Talk?" Adam looked horrified, like I'd just asked him to clean the drain. "About...?"

"The way you treat sex work like it's dirty, and by extension, like *I'm* dirty." I'd had just enough wine to loosen my tongue.

Adam gaped for a moment. "No!"

"Dude, when you say stuff like *dignity* about appearing in porn? That makes it sound kinda shame-y." I wasn't going to go into technical language like *slut-shaming*, but he might not give me much choice. "If I weren't getting paid for sex, would you still be so uncomfortable about me hooking up with guys all the time?"

"Yes," Adam muttered, but it sounded more like stubbornness than truth. He wasn't meeting my gaze.

I raised my eyebrows and waited.

"Maybe not," Adam finally concluded, then drew a heavy sigh. "It just seems so... *wrong* that you feel like you have to do that."

Back to familiar territory we'd trod a hundred times. I decided to take a different approach. "So, every time you're on a date, the other guy pays for dinner, and you give him a handjob even if you're not super into him because you feel like you owe him? That's technically sex work."

Adam looked like I'd slapped him with a cod. His mouth opened and closed, and his nose crinkled. When he found words again, he protested, "But it's not!"

He was getting hot under the collar, but I knew him well enough not to let that scare me. Even his raised voice didn't get to me anymore. The first month or two had been tricky, but I'd dealt with those associations pretty well, I thought.

"But it is," I responded evenly, not letting him get away from this. "It's sex for paid compensation of one kind or another. Hell, whenever you flutter your eyelashes at your boyfriend to buy you something—the general *you*, since you're a single loser..." He threw a pillow at me and I caught it and carried on without interruption. "It's sex work when you have an expectation of money being spent and sex being given."

"I don't like thinking about that," Adam told me, making a face. I appreciated his honesty, at least. "It's not... that's not what I was taught."

"We all think about *twenty bucks for a blowjob* hookers in the truck stop bathroom—like they aren't people, too, but whatever," I muttered, pushing that anger aside for now, "like that's the only kind of sex work there is. Escorts are rarer in the gay world than the straight world, I think, but we see them as classier, right? But what about porn? Phone sex? Sugar daddies? When your laptop breaks and you ask your man to buy you a new one and suck him off while he's browsing the Apple website?"

Adam covered his ears and rocked back and forth. "Dude. Uncomfortably specific."

"Whatever," I laughed and tossed the pillow back at him. "It's a good laptop."

"Oh, God! *That* laptop? I've touched that laptop!" Adam shook his hands like he needed to disinfect them, but I could see it—there were gears turning in his head that I hadn't seen before. "Man, so I guess that's right. It's all kind of one big industry."

"And I give freebies sometimes," I added. "I hook up, too. You treat it all just as weirdly."

Adam tilted his head, and I appreciated that he was thinking about it. "I guess cause you're giving away something you sell?"

"You help me move heavy things sometimes when you wanna be nice. Same thing." He didn't get to pretend he was heartless. "People are allowed to do the thing they do for work for fun, didn't you know?"

Adam blushed, and then he snorted. "Fine. Fair point." He didn't even have an insult to come back with, which meant I'd really hit home. Why he was embarrassed about being a pretty decent guy under all that bluster, I didn't know.

"You watch porn? You don't get to make fun of sex workers," I told him with a grin.

He hummed and leaned back, hugging the pillow to his chest and picking up the glass of wine again. "I guess you're right, man. Sorry."

Whoa. An actual apology. It was tossed out there casually, like he didn't really care, but he was watching me closely.

I shook my head. I was never gonna get used to Adam's quirks and his bluntness, but the weird vulnerability in places, and the way he acted like he didn't care but still got het up over the littlest shit. "Yeah. Thanks." It would have been nice to come to this understanding *before* quitting sex work, but... "Oh, right. That's the other thing. I'll be working a lot less now. Maybe not at all."

"What?" Adam gaped at me. "But I still need the apartment to myself sometimes."

I snorted. "I can still go on dates, loser. In fact..." I trailed off.

"Oh?" He raised an eyebrow. "You're not Pretty Womaning this shit, are you?"

I laughed. Nothing could be further from the truth. "He's a cool guy, but no. I'm quitting because I don't wanna end up in jail, man. I can't afford that shit. If I get a date out of it, whatever."

It only sank in later, after we finished the bottle of wine and I still hadn't heard back from Charlie and I'd checked half a dozen times, that I'd never sounded more like Adam than when I'd said that. Acting like I didn't care, when for reasons I didn't understand, I really did.

Had I fucked up my chance before I even knew about it?

11

CHARLIE

I stared at my phone, my jaw dropping. "A real date?" Kev's offer was the last thing I'd expected, and getting it now—on my way to Hugh's parents' house for dinner—didn't make it any easier.

This was way outside the bounds of what I'd been expecting, and I wasn't great at dealing with surprises like that sneaking up on me.

No, the message would have to wait for a response. I tucked my phone into the cradle and started up my car, trying to ignore the thrill that had coursed through me at the mere sight of a message from Kev.

I wanted to see him again, but then he'd sort of ignored my message. I couldn't believe he'd only seen it now. His business relied on seeing customers' messages as soon as possible, especially over the weekend. Was he uncomfortable with taking my money? Was he trying to make it romantic? Or just be friends?

"I hate trusting people," I mumbled under my breath. It was such a risk, and there didn't seem to be much reward. But I knew that attitude came with time and isolation, too, and just as much as my attitude toward friends, I had to work to counter it.

I'd just focus on Hugh's family and figure out what to do about Kev later. Why the hell he was hanging around in my thoughts was a problem for later, too.

What with those thoughts, and trying to avoid them, and then noticing when they snuck back in again, the drive went quickly. I blinked when I found myself outside their house. God, I was out of it. I couldn't even blame the jet lag.

"Hi, Charlie," Linda called out as soon as I was out of the car, poking her head out the kitchen window. "Come on in."

I could hear country music drifting out the window, and I grinned. They were down-to-earth South Carolina natives who had moved to the city and had refused to give some things up.

Oh, yeah. Kev's accent kind of reminded me of Hugh's. That was an uncomfortable realization. Was that even okay? Did it make me weird? But I put that aside. It wasn't like they were anything alike otherwise.

"Hi," I greeted once I pushed open the door.

Their little place was as familiar to me now as my own parents' home, but it had never had quite the same warmth and love that it once had, with Hugh filling every room he was in. We'd all survived the awful experience together—them losing their only son, me losing my boyfriend—and we were firmly friends, but I didn't want to rub it in.

No way could I bring up anything to do with Kev.

"Come through!" Chris called, and when I headed to the kitchen, I found them working together to cut shapes in the top of a pie. "I'm afraid we're running a bit late. Sorry," he apologized.

"No problem. Good things are worth the wait." I hung back and let them get the pie into the oven before they gave me hugs and handshakes. We all headed to the kitchen table together to wait for the pie to bake.

The familiar conversations helped. "So, how's work going?"

I got to chat about my current projects, although I focused on the most interesting before long. "We're doing some pro bono work for a LGBT hotline that's losing its tenancy to a real dick of a landlord. They've bought land and they want to build an office that reflects their needs."

"Oh, that must be rewarding," Linda said, smiling at me. They were always supportive of whatever I did, which only twisted the guilt knife about what I was hiding a little harder.

Not that I was hiding it. I just wasn't telling them.

"It is. They're so excited to get construction started. Their office is a tiny place." One section of the office had to be reserved for the counselors working phone lines. Everyone else was basically jammed into corners, sharing desks.

"Like a crisis counseling line?" Chris asked, and when I nodded, he hummed. "That might be a good place for our donations this year."

"I was thinking of it, too," I admitted. "They seem to be doing good work with what they have."

"Well, you could always do something to help them in person," Linda said, and there was no way to avoid feeling like she'd been waiting to suggest that in some way for some time now.

God almighty, I felt like I was going to my first day of school. *Make friends, Charlie.* "I'm trying to make friends," I said. The defensive tone in my voice was clear even to me. "I even got chatting to a guy at a bar."

"Ooh." Linda looked intrigued. "Tell us more about him. Is he cute?"

Oh, no. No, now they're going to think I'm into that Darren guy. "No, I'm not—*friends*, Linda."

"Oh. Okay." She looked strangely… disappointed?

I had to figure out how I felt about that. They weren't just okay with me dating someone else, they *wanted* me to? Was I their only son now? That was a lot to take in all of a sudden, and I felt angry, but I didn't quite know why.

I put that firmly on my *think about later* shelf, which was getting crowded. Instead, I kept going. "Met a couple guys in the last week or two who seem interesting. I'm going to try to work a little less and socialize more."

Linda lit up again. "That's great news, Charlie. I've been worried for a while now, you know that."

"I'm fine," I told her automatically. I'd said the phrase so often throughout the years that I wasn't sure what it meant anymore. *Fine with this situation? I hate it but I'll live? I don't want to live, but I have to because he'd want me to?* It had meant so many different things throughout the years.

She hesitated, but apparently she didn't want to push it.

And why was I so against everyone trying to set me up or get me out of my shell, anyway? Just because it felt like everyone was suddenly nagging me at the same time? If it was the spur I needed to kick into action and make new friends at last, wasn't that a good thing?

As we chatted about the headlines, Linda's quilting club, Chris's watercolors, and all the mundane events of everyday life, I kept coming back to it in my head. Maybe what I needed was to talk to my own parents. Or maybe that would just screw me up even more.

I was an adult, goddamn it. I could figure out what I wanted to do with my life—and who I wanted in it—without consulting the whole world.

When I stepped away for the bathroom, I paused for a minute after washing my hands and took out my phone.

I sent Kev a text.

If it's not business, we should start out as friends and make sure we're both interested in spending time together. That's a big change.

I hadn't even pocketed my phone before I got a response.

Yes. When and where?

I smiled. Someone else was eager, then. That made me feel better.

Tuesday night?

If I was going to try this "go home from work on time" thing, having a date in the evening was the best possible motivator to shut off my computer and get out the door.

I'm free anytime after 6 Tuesday.

I resisted thinking about what he might be doing up until six o'clock that day. Surely giving up his evening was actually a big deal. It made sense that most of his work would happen in that time, right?

The prickle of jealousy was weird, and the cause clear: I hadn't spent enough time around him yet. I needed a little more, to satiate my curiosity. That was an easy solution.

How about 7, outside the usual diner? I tried not to laugh. At this rate, we'd be the best-known customers who never entered the diner.

Perfect. See you then :)

The emoji made me smile, too. I sent one back. Then I pocketed my phone and got out of there before they thought I was having a sneaky jerk. With that awkward thought and a date on my calendar, I left the bathroom to face the fire once again.

12

KEV

Retail was the lowest common denominator of jobs. Not only were my coworkers either dumb or lazy—and I excluded Adam from this, even though from his stories, he did the bare minimum required to keep his job—but the customers.

Man, the customers.

I kept a polite smile throughout my first shift as I learned the cash register. I was working a four-hour shift from noon to four that day. I had to do everything in my power to forget that I was making less than sixty bucks before taxes.

That was how the rest of the world worked, and it sucked. Working poverty sounded awful, but at least I wouldn't get arrested. Adam's fixation on getting me into school suddenly made much more sense, and by the end of my shift, I was already considering how much I had in savings.

"Excuse me?" The snotty tone preceded the woman who looked around the end of the aisle, and then strode up to me like she'd expected me to be standing to attention. "I want a discount."

I wasn't sure how to handle this, and dammit, Bobby had left me alone for three seconds. I tried to fall back on my training. Everyone knew the customer was always right.

"I'm sorry—for what, ma'am?"

That only served to piss her off. "A discount for the damage to this can!" She shoved it in my face. "You can't sell this to anyone else, you know. Breaking food safety laws. New York laws. Lots of them."

"I—I'll call my manager to authorize it," I managed when I'd overcome the urge to get her hand—and the can—out of my face. But my hands had already started to shake. I felt threatened, and there wasn't a damn thing I could do about it.

And she knew that. She smirked triumphantly and plopped her basket on the counter. "Cashiers can authorize up to a ten percent discount on a single item without a manager's authorization code."

I didn't bother asking her how she knew the rules better than me, but my warning flags were going up. Before I could say another word, Bobby strolled back.

"Afternoon, ma'am." It was obvious from their expressions that they recognized each other.

"I want a discount, and none of your smart-ass, back-talking, gap-toothed, pimple-ridden attitude," she sneered at him.

My jaw dropped. I looked at him, then her, and then around. Nobody else was within earshot. The manager wasn't in. He'd gone for a long lunch break and never came back.

Bobby was a supervisor, so he could do the discount, but why would he?

"Of course, ma'am." He scanned the can, examined it, and then looked toward the aisle where it came from.

"What?" she snapped. "I didn't dent it. It was sitting on the shelf like that. I oughta turn you in to the Health Department. They'd have your ass fired so fast. Shut this place down. Then you'd have to get some other greasy job with that greasy smile."

"There's your twenty percent off." He gestured for me to start scanning the rest of her basket.

I couldn't understand why he was taking it. Sure, the customer was right, but this was just personal abuse.

"Good," she snapped, then flicked her fingers at me. "Hurry up. I've got places to be. I can't just stand around arguing with the supermarket boys."

I bristled but kept my focus on scanning, since that still took most of my attention to do right. It didn't stop me overhearing what she was saying, though.

And then I spotted the cart behind her, which was so full of toilet paper rolls that it was almost overflowing. My jaw dropped, and I swapped looks with Bobby.

"I'm afraid there's a limit of ten per promotional item…"

"What if I'm buying ten for me, and ten for my husband, and ten for my sister—"

"If you're by yourself, I'm afraid that's a limit of ten."

"Ten items per transaction? Ring them up separately."

"Per person."

"Fine. I'll leave and come back," she hissed. "See how you like that, moron. Or is that too much math for your simple brain?"

I shook my head as I finished scanning her basket and loading things into bags. "You're still the same person, though," I said, looking at Bobby for confirmation.

Bobby had left from behind the counter and looked down the toilet paper aisle. "That's… the entire contents of the shelf."

"It's a free country. You can't stop me buying things. The customer is always right, even when you're too stupid to understand." She got in his face. "I. Buy." He raised his eyebrows but said nothing and she persisted, "You. Sell. Me. Things."

"Please don't treat him disrespectfully, ma'am," I spoke up.

Apparently, that was the wrong thing to say.

"This stupid fuckface has cost me *hundreds* of dollars before," she hissed, folding her arms. "I can't believe he's still employed here."

"Okay, I'm not comfortable dealing with someone who can verbally abuse staff," I said, shaking my head. "That's what this is, ma'am. You can ask for a discount without insulting him."

"Oh yeah?" She rounded on me. "And what about you? New here? Don't you get it? They can't stop me. I'm not hurting anyone. I'm just demanding my rights. My rights as an American citizen."

"Right," I snorted. "The right to bear arms, not *be an ass*."

Oops. The door rattled and I looked up, only to see Dirk standing there, his mouth hanging open.

She pushed her shopping basket off the counter in my direction, and I was shaking so hard I couldn't even grab it. It felt like she could come over the counter at me and everyone was too afraid to stand up to her that they wouldn't lift a finger.

"I can't believe you'd treat me with such disrespect!" she howled in my face.

"And I can't believe you'd treat us with such disrespect," I countered.

Dirk stepped in. "Kev, take a break. Bobby, ring up the basket."

Ring up the basket case, I barely refrained from saying. I was glad to escape to the break room and calm my nerves before I said something I actually regretted.

It didn't stop me hearing her ranting as I left. "I don't want any of this shit. I'm never shopping here again!"

The break room was tiny—more of a break closet—but I flopped on the single chair in there and breathed deeply.

The relief was short-lived. When Dirk followed me in, I could read on his face what was about to happen. Fuck. What the hell?

"Sir..."

"I realize this was a frustrating incident to deal with, but you were out of line. Don't come to work tomorrow."

"She called Bobby all kinds of names. Bobby could have called the cops," I protested, standing up and unlacing my apron.

Goddamn, I'd be glad to get out of this place. I could still feel her spittle hitting my bare arms as she screeched.

"And he wouldn't, because the customer..."

"—is always right," I interrupted with a snort. "Except when they're harassing, abusing, and intimidating your staff. You should be ashamed to protect her and not us."

Dirk didn't even seem to know what to say. He opened and closed his mouth before pointing at the door.

"Don't bother paying me," I added with a snort. "Take the fifty bucks and buy a conscience."

I stormed out without a second look, and Bobby avoided looking at me. I knew why. He couldn't risk it, even if I'd stood up for him.

My eyes pricked with tears, and I swallowed my anger. Not for myself—I was going to be fine financially. I could make it work somehow or another. But someone like Bobby? He couldn't just fire a bad client or go find another job. He had to put up with this shit, and smile while he took it.

It made me feel too sick to look back at him, and I stormed down the street without a second look.

Thank God they hadn't even asked Adam to vouch for me. Whatever I screwed up from being unable to hold a normal job without getting angry about the universe being unfair, it wouldn't fuck him up.

But if I couldn't even swallow a coworker being yelled at by a customer, fast food was completely out. Starbucks? No way. People were grumpy before their morning caffeine. Maybe I was spoiled after being treated like a real person at my last job, working on the ranch, but I didn't want to compromise my own humanity to survive.

I bit my lip hard to keep myself from crying as I walked home. I felt like crap, even if I also felt like I'd done the right thing. How was that fair? I ought to feel good about having principles, but instead, I just felt like I was letting everyone down around me.

It was easier to be on my own in some ways. I could do stupid shit and not affect anyone else. But it was too late to go back to that state, unless... well, unless I ran away.

But no. I was done running away. I didn't have to stand still and let people hit me, but I couldn't just leave every time something went a little bit wrong. My friends from the ranch—the significant brothers, they called themselves—and Adam would miss me. I had people who cared. I couldn't throw that away.

The dread that built in the pit of my stomach only got worse as I approached the door. I had no idea if Adam was home or not. He was probably out cutting lawns or doing odd jobs for cash. He was a scrapper, and I felt like a loser in comparison.

Sex work was hard work, but if it was all I could do… he was tougher than me, hands-down.

I carefully opened the door and let a breath of relief escape. Adam's boots were gone. I had time to figure out what I was going to tell him. It made me almost chuckle, because it was like having a spouse… but not, thank God. I wished strength to whoever had to put up with Adam in matrimonial bliss someday.

"Lunch," I told myself. I hadn't been hungry before I left, and I hadn't even gotten a break today. I wasn't used to not being able to eat when I wanted, even if I was working and it was just a salad.

Ramen sounded great right now. Although I was making—had been making—way more now than my twenty-buck blowjob days, I hadn't lost my taste for cheap food. Something about it had reprogrammed my taste buds, I was pretty sure. I could appreciate a good steak or caviar, but when I wanted to feel good? Ramen, Spam and rice, cheesy tuna noodle casserole, stewed chicken… cheap and easy foods.

I didn't even try a battle of willpower—I headed right for the stove and threw a brick of noodles into water.

I grabbed a pitcher of tea from the fridge and poured it into my favorite pretty teacup from the shelf. I usually drank it cold and sweet from a glass, but the winter here had introduced me to the idea of hot tea, and now I used the cups for any drink when I wanted to feel better. Even wine sometimes.

Only when I was curled up on the couch with the bowl cradled against my chest did I let myself think about what I was going to do next.

It stung, but maybe Adam was right and I needed to use those skills that Josh had been so careful to teach me. Sure, it wasn't like professional certifications in anything, but enough to know what I liked and was good at.

Details: I was surprisingly good at those, after years of managing my own life. Listening to people. Smoothing out disagreements. Maybe an office job would be better than I'd thought.

I grabbed my laptop, grinning again at the memory of Adam learning how I'd gotten it, and searched for New York community colleges. I sure wasn't going to get into debt going to a four-year college when a trade would serve me better.

A massage school popped up near the top of the results. I eyed the page and then sat back on my heels and spread my arms along the back of the couch, digging my heels into the crack between the cushions.

It wasn't a bad idea at all. But how much would it cost?

I'd expected to rack up debt no matter what program I chose, but a little Googling had me staring at about a ten-grand bill, depending on what school I chose. That wasn't unaffordable, especially if I was able to start using my skills before I'd graduated.

Of course, I could do it cheaper by taking classes without certification, but then I'd be limited to erotic massage rather than actual massage therapy. But I could at least see if I liked it before I threw myself into a program.

A lot of Googling later, I'd chosen a taster session and booked it, trying to ignore the pounding of my heart and the way it felt like every little decision I made was a crossroads I could never come back from.

"Hey!" The door banged shut, making me nearly jump out of my skin.

"Fuck! Dude," I groaned. "You could give me a second of warning."

"Are you naked? You're not, are you?" Adam poked his head around the corner and grimaced. "Oh, thank God."

I snorted with laughter and shut the laptop. "Dude, if you thought I was naked… well, you just looked."

Adam flipped me off. "Pizza for dinner?"

"Sure."

"How was your first day?" He bounced into the armchair and looked expectantly at me, and… fuck. I had no idea how he was going to react, but I had to come out with it.

I mumbled, "I might have gotten fired."

Adam blinked a few times and leaned forward. "What?"

"Some asshole customer came in and cursed out Bobby. I stood up for him. The boss didn't like it."

"I—what did you say?" Adam's expression was a curious mix of anxiety and amusement. "Did you mention me to him?"

"No way, dude. Your secret's safe. I just can't visit you at work anymore, ever," I snorted. "I didn't even say anything that bad! Told her she should respect people."

Adam's shoulders shook with laughter. "Oh, man. You can't just say that to a customer, dude."

I threw my hands in the air. "But why not? She should!"

"The customer—"

"—is always right," I snapped. "Yeah, so I've heard. If they think you're a disgusting piece of shit, they're right? Where's *your* self-respect?"

He glowered at me. "Self-respect don't pay the rent."

"Well, neither does minimum wage."

Adam froze for a second and then cracked up. "Touché." He dug around in his pocket and flashed a wad of cash. "Today was good, though."

"Nice! You hit up a bank?" I grinned.

"Just a couple houses that needed work done, all in a row." Adam shrugged. "When you have the balls to walk up and ask for work, it's amazing what you find."

I couldn't help but feel that was aimed at me. Sure, it worked for him—a strapping American farm boy with a charming smile—but me? Not a chance.

"I'm going back to school," I announced. "Order the damn pizza."

Adam stared at me and then shrugged, a grin spreading across his face. I let him have his moment of obnoxious triumph, since he didn't rub my face in it for once. "Pizza and beer it is."

13

______

CHARLIE

I fidgeted and shifted from foot to foot, checking the buttons on my sleeves. It was hard not to look suspicious while loitering outside a greasy spoon next to a closed gay bar. At least the work clothes helped.

I hadn't had the chance to get home and change after work, as I'd just darted out of the office after a conference call. Nobody had cast me a second look or even said good night, which underscored the point: they were all so used to me working late that it didn't even register on their radar that I might be going home, not out for dinner and straight back to the office.

But it was Tuesday, and I had a very good reason for ditching work only slightly late: Kev.

This was my chance with him, and I didn't want to fuck it up. The idea that he might be interested in me as a friend without money involved seemed crazy, but I was willing to believe it. As long as he didn't let me down.

"Hey!"

Kev startled me by approaching from behind, but when I turned to take him in, I was even more surprised.

Fucking hell, he looked *good*. He'd chosen dark, clingy jeans and a casual t-shirt that seemed equally clingy, showing off his lean, yet muscled body. His hair was just as perfectly styled as it had been on our first date. And did I have the right to call it that? I wasn't worrying yet, since this totally wasn't a second date.

"H-Hi," I managed with a breathless smile. The moment I saw him again, it just reminded me how damn hard it had been to keep my hands off him last time.

And he treated me the same, sweeping in for a tight hug and a kiss on the cheek.

The intimacy reminded me all too well of our date. Fuck. Staying friends with him was going to be impossible, wasn't it?

"Hey, Charlie," he murmured back into my ear, and my knees just about melted at the way he said my name.

Don't get carried away, I tried to tell myself. *Just because he's gorgeous and friendly doesn't mean you have a future together.*

"How was your day? Where should we go? I can choose a place," I offered, trying not to ramble. Even that much was weird. I wasn't a rambler. That was about as far from me as it was possible to be.

He didn't seem to notice, luckily. "I had a pretty crazy day. I'll tell you about it over supper. Have you eaten at all today?"

I smiled at the Southern word and then scrunched my nose in thought before deciding that I must have eaten lunch. It was hard to remember, but the stock of microwave meals in my desk had been steadily depleting since I got back from Singapore. "I... probably have?"

Kev clicked his tongue and took me by the arm. "That's no good. Italian. Follow me."

I smirked. It was kind of hot when he got bossy, and being touched… well, that made everything worse. Hopefully these trousers could contain the rising situation. "Yes, sir."

We chatted about the weather until we got to the restaurant. It didn't look like much from the outside—most restaurants outside the trendy Midtown places didn't—but the inside was nice. Not impressive, not fancy, but also not shabby. Just a comfortable place to hang out and have a meal. They were quick to take our orders, too, which was a plus.

The waiter greeted us warmly and I smiled, relaxing already. I was pretty sure I'd be safe to have a date in most restaurants in Manhattan and Brooklyn without getting glares, but I was out of touch with dating reality. Once we placed our orders, we had plenty of time to talk.

"So, tell me about your day." I just hoped he hadn't run into any problem clients. He was a grown adult capable of handling his own shit, but I might not be able to contain the urge to go after them on his behalf.

"I got hired for a crappy cashier job, fired on the first day, and I spent today putting together a list of careers."

"Oh." I blinked several times, wondering if I'd heard that right. "Careers?"

"As in, outside this job. Which is why this is us just hanging out," Kev told me.

"You're quitting?"

Kev grimaced. "I don't know. I'd like to, I think… for now, at least. It's too dangerous right now."

"There are always assholes out there," I agreed with a frown. I admitted to myself that I'd be glad to see him a little safer in a city like this.

"Oh, it's not the clients I'm worried about. I haven't had many bad dates," Kev told me with a shrug. "It's the cops."

"Oh." I blushed, sorry for a moment for my ignorance. "You mean, the legal risks?"

"Yeah. They're hunting us down online, and the internet lets me screen clients." He talked about it so frankly that even I could understand. "My only other options are agencies, which are bullshit, or the streets, which are dangerous. Independent contractors are disappearing."

I bit my lip and nodded. "What color is your parachute, then?" He blinked at me a few times and I grinned sheepishly. "Sorry. That might be an outdated reference now. I don't know what the kids these days use in career planning class."

He snorted. "I didn't finish high school, so I don't know, either."

That took me aback. He seemed smart as hell to me, and then I winced at my own bias creeping up on me again. "Why not?"

"Full of questions today, aren't you?" he teased. The waiter approached and poured sparkling water for us both. Kev waited to thank him before he spoke up.

"Sorry—" I started as soon as we were alone again, but he shook his head.

"No, it's a fair question. I don't tell a lot of people that. I'm supposed to lie, I think. That's what I've been told. Probably got me the grocery store job. Usually nobody would hire me."

That surprised me even more, because he looked gorgeous and approachable and friendly. "What? Really?"

"A spotty employment history and no diploma?" Kev pointed out, and I winced again.

"Right. Sorry." My middle-class background was showing.

He never seemed to take my clumsy words to heart, though. He just smiled back at me. "I like that you're curious. It makes a change."

That made a change for me, too. I wasn't used to taking an interest in a guy, especially one I'd only seen once. "Do people not usually ask?"

"Some do," Kev said, sipping his water. "I can't really generalize. I've had lots of different experiences. Some are just normal guys who want to make small talk. Some want to know as little as possible about me, so they can objectify me. Some want to know my whole life history, so they can exploit me."

I felt even more inexperienced and naive sitting across from this guy. It wasn't something I was used to feeling, either—especially about a guy who was about a decade younger. "You're wise for your age."

"Oh, God. Don't tell me I'm enlightened just because of what I do," he said with a grin.

I blinked a few times. "I..." Yeah, I had been about to go there. "Oh."

"I want it treated like any other job. And I want more protection for everyone," he added firmly. "Like, at least I'm a freelancer and I can pick and choose clients. But Adam—my roommate? He's stuck working at a shitty grocery store with a shitty boss, and customers who yell at him. And he has to smile and agree or he loses his job."

I sighed and nodded. He was right about that. I wasn't so isolated that I didn't know what service workers went through every day. I tried to be nice, but I'd seen people—even supposed professionals from our partner companies—be dicks for no good reason.

"But that's me getting defensive again," Kev admitted and smiled. "I'd rather not talk about work right now. I've been thinking way too much about it."

"Fair enough," I agreed. "I'd rather not think about mine, either." The less time I spent thinking about that goddamn construction meeting this morning, the better. The client from Dubai had come back insisting they only wanted me, and my boss had given an excuse—that I was on another project. They'd offered a ton more money to get me assigned to this instead.

But tonight I didn't want to stress about work. I had some fabulous gayness to indulge in.

He leaned in. "So, what interests you? What are you passionate about?"

Well, that was one way to kickstart conversation. I respected his cutting right to the chase, but I had to think about it for a few moments. "I... I'm not sure. As you know—me and my job..."

"Right," he agreed. "But what catches your eye? What do you love about architecture?"

"The feeling of space," I said without hesitation. "That's one thing that comes at a premium here. Aside from Central Park—and even that doesn't feel spacious in the summer with hordes of tourists."

He cracked a grin and nodded, gesturing for me to go on.

I felt a little awkward rambling, but I tried to let go of my self-consciousness about possibly saying something he didn't agree with. "I like that feeling of being together when you're alone. Not lonely together, but the opposite. Bringing people together in a way that makes us appreciate each other."

Kev's smile widened. "Yeah. I know what you mean. New York City is…" he trailed off, then settled on just, "big."

I sensed he meant more than space-wise, though, or population-wise. "It feels big?"

"Yes!" Kev leaned in again. "The energy between people, it just multiplies. I go out and I feel recharged, just seeing everyone around me doing their thing. Doing things they love. I love it when people do things they love."

I smiled. "What about you? What do you love?"

"So much." Kev's passion spilled over in his words. He was talking with far less restraint or grace than he'd shown on the date, and I loved it. This was a raw side of him that he seemed all too eager to share. "I love the city, like I just said, and everyone being so free to be *them*. I love old things, things with history. I love testing myself and seeing what I like, when I'm not being pushed into doing or liking anything in particular. I love quiet mornings in, and late nights out. I just want to experience things now, while I can, like I might never have the chance again."

"You never know when you won't," I agreed. I didn't want to bring down the mood, but I didn't think the lesson was necessarily somber. Still, he reached over the table to touch my hand and left his hand there. I didn't mind that one bit. "So you're an explorer."

Kev thought about it for a minute before smiling. "I never heard it put like that, but sure, if you like. I like learning more about the world and people in it. And I like supporting people."

"You sound like an idealist," I said, and then hastily added, "not that it's bad."

Kev still eyed me before laughing. "I only ever hear it used badly. That's what Adam told me when I got fired…"

"Your roommate, right?" When he nodded, I shrugged. "Well, you did walk out on principle."

"Technically I walked out because they told me to get out. I just told the lady to respect people," Kev scoffed, throwing his hands up and nearly knocking over the waiter who was approaching with our food. "Oh, shit. Sorry!"

I tried to stifle my amusement, but it was in vain. Giggles slipped out.

"Th-Thanks," Kev stuttered, trying to cover up the moment. "Much appreciated."

When the waiter set the dishes in front of us and fled, my giggles turned into full-fledged laughter.

"Stop," Kev protested, his cheeks flushed as he buried his head in his hands. "My timing is the worst."

"Normally *mine* is the worst," I explained, grinning around my giggles. "It's just nice to see I'm not alone on that front."

"You're definitely not alone. If I've learned one thing so far in life, that's it," Kev told me.

Whatever he said, he was wise. I was a little worried about what he could have experienced to be this smart and tuned-in, but I'd learn that in time, maybe.

We both lapsed into periods of silence and small talk as we ate, and by the time the meal was over, I felt closer to him than ever before. It was like every little thing he said resonated with some internal sensor that I hadn't known I had.

Something that was looking for a partner—an equal match.

"Is this a date?" The waiter approached us again with a lighter in his hand, a smirk on his face as Kev avoided eye contact and blushed. "Let me just get that for you…" He lit the extinguished candle in the bowl on the table.

I didn't want to hastily say *no* and make Kev think I wasn't interested, but saying yes would also be presumptuous, wouldn't it? Kev and I made eye contact.

A few seconds of stammering from both of us later, the waiter waved it off. "In any case, you two made the chef smile today, and that's rare. Dessert's on the house."

"Th-Thanks," Kev managed. "Sorry about punching you."

"Oh, don't worry about it. That's probably what made him smile." He grinned at us and retreated.

Kev put his face in his hands again while I laughed.

A couple minutes later, a large chocolate brownie with ice cream, whipped cream, chocolate sauce, raspberries, and two spoons arrived. The waiter winked and high-tailed it out of there.

"This is very…" I trailed off, my own cheeks heating up.

"Romantic?" Kev teased. "Only if you want to see it that way."

I didn't say anything, but I picked up a spoon and offered him the other one. My heart pounded as the cool metal heated under my touch and he gazed at me.

After what felt like an eternity, he reached out and plucked it from my fingers, and then dug into the ice cream on his side of the plate.

A smile spread across my face. It was hard to contain the giddiness that swept through me, but I did my best to stay cool and collected. Inwardly, though, I was squealing. *He wants me! This isn't just a friendship!*

"I don't know what I can promise yet," Kev said slowly as we worked our way through the brownie. He kept watching me, though, like he couldn't quite take his eyes off me.

God, did I ever know the feeling. Especially when he was dressed up in clingy jeans and that gorgeous shirt that highlighted his eye color. The top half was thoroughly impractical for April, but I couldn't wait until it grew a bit later, darker, and cooler tonight, so I could offer him my jacket on the way home.

Maybe he'd let me walk him home? Was that still a thing people did?

"I don't want promises," I told him with a firm shake of my head. "I want action. It's easy to promise the world."

He regarded me closely over his water glass, running his thumb around the droplets that had formed on the outside. "That sounds jaded."

"I don't think it is. It's realistic." I grimaced. "My boyfriend promised to be there for me forever, and look what happened." Before he could jump in and apologize, I hastily added, "Don't be sorry. It is what it is. But… life takes you in weird directions, and if you start counting on anything, that's the pride cometh before the fall moment."

"Hm," Kev murmured. "You don't think that's a convenient excuse to act like you're too independent to need anyone, in case you lose them?"

I opened and shut my mouth for a few moments, my cheeks suddenly hot. I wasn't sure what to make of this man in the first place, but now that he was picking me apart so effortlessly? It was almost terrifying, but I was a moth to a flame. "Maybe it is. But maybe your exploration is, too. If you lose someone, or something —a person, a career you love—you can call it exploration."

"Touché," he murmured and offered a smile. "As long as it serves you well, I don't see anything wrong with having that kind of belief."

"It doesn't always," I admitted. "If I can't count on anyone, well… I can never plan for the future. And the past suddenly seems more gray than it was back then."

"I don't want to count on anyone," Kev shook his head. "But I've learned to. The alternative is miserable. We need each other, as people."

I frowned. "A relationship based on need isn't healthy."

"No, not if it's codependent," Kev agreed. "But isn't that what most marriages are? It's an arrangement set up because you each need something from the other person. Different things or the same thing."

I nodded slowly. I'd never been terribly romantic compared to Hugh. "But there's more, too."

"Oh, sure," Kev agreed. "But romance comes and goes."

"Do you believe in true love?" I wasn't even sure what I was asking now. I wasn't examining it or planning ahead of time. It was just spontaneous conversation, and the intimacy drew me in like the candle on the table that I kept fidgeting with.

I didn't expect him to lean back and fold his arms, examining me like he was deciding whether to trust me. I held my breath like I was trying not to startle a fawn.

"I don't know how I feel about that question. I'll be right back." He excused himself for the bathroom, and I was left staring at him, biting my thumbnail.

Fuck. Had I just pissed him off? All I could do was wait in silence until I found out.

14

KEV

I patted my cheeks with cool water and stared in the mirror for a minute, listening for the sound of footsteps approaching the bathroom. That was the definition of gay problems: worrying that your date would interrupt your moment of simultaneous vanity and self-reflection.

On the other hand, going to the bathroom with another guy meant you could sneak a kiss or a glimpse, although I had the feeling Charlie was way too sheltered for that.

I smiled as I dried my hands and pushed them through my hair to rearrange it just so. Now that I'd texted Adam to let him know I was alive and might or might not be home tonight—not a full *watermelon*, but just a *strawberry*—I had to figure out where the hell this was going.

I could walk out there and cool things down, treat him like a buddy, and try to make friends. But what would be the fun in that?

I wanted him. I knew that much. I wasn't entirely sure why, except that I was horny and he was hot, and I knew damn well there was more behind my attraction that I was trying to avoid. It was way too quick to know if I liked the guy as more than a friend, wasn't it?

I'd heard a lot about my clients' lives. Many of them had fallen in love just as quickly, and that had led to happy marriages. What made it work was the determination to work things out and talk instead of trying to inflict hurt when you felt hurt. Whatever people told me about their lives, I took in and arranged in my head, adding to my mental database of the world. Without many people to give me guidance, it was what I had to do.

What would Josh and Evan say?

I knew that much already. I'd triggered jealousy when I'd come to the farm just as they were figuring their relationship out. Maybe I needed to get him jealous… but no, that was just playing games. What had worked for all of their friends? From the sounds of it, just talking things out.

Okay. I'd tell him I liked him.

I marched back out to the restaurant and sat down, my head spinning already. "I don't believe in true love, but I want to. But I don't want it to be with some guy who goes *I can replace your job, so stop being slutty and independent and then I'll respect you,* because I'm sick of that. Pretty Woman is bullshit, and I want to make my own way in the world, but I don't want to be alone."

Charlie stared at me for a few moments and then laughed. "I was worried you'd forgotten the question. Wow. Okay." He leaned back slowly and then smiled. "Do you want to talk about this over coffee at my place?"

"Hell, yeah." I drew a breath and let it out to get the nerve to say it. "Especially if coffee is a euphemism."

The excited grin that flitted across Charlie's face was adorable.

Then it was replaced with a familiar nervous expression. "I'm probably the worst you'll have had in a while."

"I doubt that," I teased and leaned in. "You care about me, right? As a friend, or whatever?" There was a lot contained in that *whatever*, but I didn't want to scare him off yet by suggesting romance was blossoming. That wasn't supposed to be the deal between us.

Charlie paused, and he seemed almost surprised by himself when he nodded. "I... do. Why?"

"Then you'll be better in bed than a lot of guys, whether or not you bring my work into it. And I like you," I told him. "You should know that."

Charlie went pale for a moment and opened his mouth, not saying anything for a few long moments. Shit. I started to fear I'd said the wrong thing, but before I could try to smooth that out, he nodded. "That's... flattering, but then there's my baggage, and..." He frowned and looked around at the waiter who was nearby and clearly trying not to listen in on the date. "I definitely feel like we should bring this conversation somewhere more private."

"Back to your place," I agreed.

Although I tried to split the check, he wouldn't let me. It set my teeth on edge a bit—like I owed him—but I knew him better now. He wouldn't think I owed him, right? I had to trust that.

At least I booked the Uber, which also gave me a trip history and address in case anything went wrong. It was a safety precaution I hoped not to have to take anymore.

"Five minutes," I told him as I scanned the info of the Uber on its way. "A nondescript black car, of course."

He chuckled and put his arm around my waist as we stood outside the restaurant. "Still easier than hailing a cab."

"I've never managed to," I admitted, blushing. It didn't sound very worldly, and yeah, it had gotten me into trouble before—but then, some guys liked jumping in to my rescue. Native New Yorkers just seemed to be able to detect when they were coming and how to get them to stop. "I'm good at hitchhiking, but I can't get a damn taxi."

He laughed. "Hitchhiking? Brave."

The memory that swamped me for a moment was less than pleasant. It hadn't exactly been a choice—I'd needed to leave town and get to the "big city" of Knoxville as soon as possible. Once I left my parents' house, I got more familiar with making money stretch than I'd ever been before.

Luckily, I'd stayed safe on those first few trips, but pretty soon, I'd run out of money. The hustling I did these days was nothing like those first few jobs. That was survival sex work, where I didn't get much of a say in how much I charged or what I did.

I was lucky I'd gotten out of that unscathed. Well, not just lucky—Josh and Evan, and their friends, had stepped in to make sure I'd never be in that position again. And I could have been left with triggers, but sex these days—even with clients—didn't give me any unpleasant reminders.

There were guys who'd had way less ideal times, I knew. For all the money, we didn't have much protection out there. No way would I go to the cops if anything ever went wrong. It was just as well I was walking away now, before… well.

"Sorry," Charlie murmured, and I snapped back to reality. I was dizzy, and he had his arm around me tighter now. "That looked like a bad place to go."

"I ran away from home by hitchhiking," was the best I could sum it up. "Stereotypical, huh? Gay kid making his way in the world, selling his body?" I wanted to put a lid on the bitterness, but I'd so rarely been able to express it for one reason or another. I was either defending my right to exist or work, and I didn't want to make my own life harder.

But it wasn't all sunshine and roses, and... he was warm and comforting and right here, listening and not judging me. Not even feeling pity, which I hated. Just sympathy and concern for my wellbeing.

"I think we're all stereotypes in one way or another," he offered. "The single gay professional without time to date? I could have gone down a different stereotypical path very easily, too."

The Uber arrived before I had a chance to think up a way to ask more about that. He'd tell me when he was ready.

Luckily, the driver seemed to sense we needed space and didn't chat much on the drive back to Charlie's house. Instead, I was able to keep chatting casually with him about Tennessee and what Knoxville was like. By the time we arrived, he even knew that I'd worked on a ranch, though I was careful not to identify it as a gay dude ranch. That would make it way too easy to find the closest thing I had to family. And I didn't trust Charlie *that* much yet.

But I'd already told him more about my real past than anyone else, and I tried to justify it. He was a friend now, not just a client.

If I were honest? I'd admit to myself that I was lonely, and I liked him, and I was tired of hiding bits and pieces of myself to make myself more... palatable.

"If you don't mind my asking," I finally said when we were settled on the couch with glasses of water again, "when did you lose your... um, boyfriend?" I nearly said *ex* before realizing that would be a dick move. The guy had died, not dumped him.

"Five years ago." Charlie's voice was soft, reminiscent, but I didn't hear the pain in it I'd kind of expected.

I glanced over and then scooted closer, and he put his arm around my shoulders. "That must have been huge."

"Oh, yeah. Yeah, I was a wreck. I was finishing up my degree at that point. I had nothing to spare except keeping going with that, and then coming home to break down."

My heart twisted. God, and I was all cut up when Adam and I had a little disagreement over whose turn it was to do the dishes? "I'm sorry," was all I could say. "I hate to think of you in pain."

He hummed and pressed his cheek against my shoulder, and I rubbed his knee. "It was hard at first, yeah. I wouldn't wish that on anyone. When you think you've found the one, and then you have that ripped away from you, your whole life just… shatters. Worse than a breakup, by far. You never get to say goodbye properly, or see them again, or… anything."

I sensed he hadn't talked about this in a long time. He spoke slowly, like he wasn't sure what words to use next. "Yeah."

We lapsed into silence for a minute as he rested against me. He didn't seem torn apart, but there was a quiet, sweet sadness around him that I didn't dare disturb. God knew how long it had been since he'd let himself be vulnerable. I didn't want to keep comparing him to my clients, but very often, they hired me because they desperately needed someone to listen without criticizing or judging or, God forbid, shutting them down.

"I guess it must be like that for you," he finally murmured, looking over at me.

"Huh? Oh, with…" I grimaced. "My parents."

"If you don't want to talk about it—"

"No," I interrupted firmly. I wasn't upset about it anymore, either. It was just a fact of life, most of the time. Except when it wasn't, but now wasn't one of those moments. "They're dead to me, because I'm dead to them. They held a funeral."

"What?" Charlie yelped.

"Not a real one at a church, like they were collecting the insurance," I managed a joke. "Just a private thing in their living room with their friends. Everyone knew damn well I'm alive, by the way. They were just mourning the Kev they wanted me to be."

"That's still the shittiest thing ever," he growled, his arm tightening around me so much a bone in my shoulder clicked.

I liked being squeezed against him, feeling like his arms around me were a forcefield nothing could get through. I could get dangerously used to this. It was so unfamiliar that I hardly knew where to take it next, but I wanted more.

"You haven't dated at all since?" I asked in a murmur. It was hard to pick up and set down my water glass on the coaster since I wanted to keep looking into his eyes… and I felt like I shouldn't turn away from him at this kind of critical moment.

It was Charlie's turn to blink. "Huh? Oh… no. Not even once." He chuckled.

"Dating: not even once. You might just like it," I warned with a grin. "Though I'm not really an expert. I've tried dating, but guys just reacted weirdly to my career, or Pretty Woman-ed that shit, or I didn't connect with them… all the normal dating stuff. Maybe half a dozen dates since I moved here?" Then I smiled. "Plenty of Grindr dates, though."

Charlie chuckled again, and I picked up a nervous tone. "Yeah, not even that for me. I'm gonna be so damn bad."

I wanted to challenge that idea as soon as I could. "Sooner you start practicing again, the better you'll get," I said with a smirk.

"Oh!" Charlie's eyes lit up as he grinned at me. "That's a good line."

"Is it working?"

"It might be." Charlie was eager, despite his nerves. His breathing was quick, and he held onto me like he didn't want to let me get away without trying something—anything.

I smiled. "How far do you want this to go?" I asked first. I didn't want to get carried away and push him further than he was comfortable going. In some ways, he seemed a little bit traditional. If he wanted to save anything for marriage, I wasn't gonna get in the way of that—although I might be a little jealous of the eventual husband.

"Anything you want," he murmured, hesitation in his voice. That meant there was something he wasn't saying.

"What do you want to do the most, then?" I prodded gently. I'd gotten laid plenty, whatever my dick told me. Relative to him, I was Casanova. I wanted to make *him* feel good.

"I'd love to fuck you," he murmured at last. "It's been... so long. But I don't want to just use you. And when I was paying, that was all I could think."

My heart ached for this beautiful man. It was like he was used to putting his needs in an orderly list and assigning price tags to them. "I'd love that," I assured him, reaching for his cheek to cup it. As I'd hoped, it made him look at me. "And I'm on PrEP, but I'd rather use condoms."

"Oh! Yes." He looked kind of embarrassed. "I didn't know how to ask that, either. I'm negative... I mean, I've been tested years ago, and since then... like I said."

"Once you pop, you can't stop," I warned him with a wink. "Get your protection right from the beginning. It'll keep you from antibiotic resistance in the future." If he was going to go through a phase of rediscovering his sexuality, he might well get carried away otherwise. No need to encourage the superbugs of today.

"Yes, sir." He looked amused. "What if I just want to fuck *you* tonight and think about the future tomorrow?"

Oh. I hadn't expected that to take my breath away quite the way it did. I gulped, lacing my fingers with his. "I'd tell you to touch me, however you want." I dragged his hand onto my thigh, wanting to see what he did and whether he needed to be guided.

But once he was touching me, he didn't act like a beginner anymore. Muscle memory, perhaps, or pure instinct guided him as he ran his hand along my thigh and up my stomach, carefully avoiding my half-hard cock that was straining in my jeans. When his palm was flat on my chest, his other arm still around my shoulders, he leaned in to press our lips together.

I lost myself in that kiss and closed my eyes, letting him take over.

For tonight, everything about me was his. We could worry about the future tomorrow.

15

CHARLIE

Making out with Kev was like finding a missing piece in a puzzle you thought you'd completed. How the hell had I missed that gap in my life for so long? And when I'd acknowledged it, I'd thought it unimportant?

I needed the man's touch on me more than I could express. When he finally started to return the exploration by running his hands along my chest and around to my back, I surprised myself with how goddamn loud I moaned.

There was definitely something going on here I didn't understand.

Kev pulled back for a second, and my lips were suddenly disappointingly cool. "You okay?" he murmured, those dark eyes intently fixed on mine.

I managed a smile. "I—I'm great," I whispered. My tone faltered, though. I wasn't even sure I believed it myself.

"What's going on in here?" He tapped my temple gently with one long finger.

I sighed and closed my eyes for a second, trying to find words for it, and I failed. "I don't know, but I need you. This."

Kev smiled slightly, knowingly. "Have you heard of skin hunger?"

"Sounds like a horror movie. I don't watch horror movies."

That made Kev laugh, a musical sound that lifted my spirits right away. "No, it's a concept. We as people need contact. That's how we evolved. And in America, men don't touch each other unless we're," he rolled his eyes, "*gay*. And even then, only when you're dating another man. It's why straight guys act like they so desperately need women—because they don't get to be intimate with another person. Don't get to touch someone, like this."

His hand slipped up under my shirt, and even though it was sexual, the shiver of *rightness* that passed through me was far deeper than that. His words made sense. They tallied up with the feeling of completion in my chest.

"Oh," I whispered. "Yeah. I *am* hungry."

Kev cuddled close right away, swinging his leg over my lap and pressing himself into me, sliding his hands around my waist and burying his head in my shoulder.

Saying it felt good to hold him didn't do justice to the neurons, or whatever they were, firing in my brain. I felt stronger somehow, even as I showed this vulnerability. "So sleeping with people is more than just sex," I murmured.

"It can be," he murmured. "If you're not hugging and cuddling friends regularly… well, people deprived of contact start to feel isolated. Paranoid. On edge, like you're craving something but you don't know what. Sometimes people seek out addictive habits. But contact? It's not a miracle cure, but I think it would stop a lot of bullshit if we just hugged our friends a little more often."

I buried my nose in his shoulder. "Or fucked them?" I was hard now, my hands slipping under his shirt. I kept my touch light as I trailed my fingers up his back, indulging in the daydreams that had so distracted me during the boring conference calls this week.

"Please," Kev whimpered. "Yes."

"Bed, now," I ordered. "Or I'm not gonna be able to walk."

Kev grinned and peeled himself off my lap like he was in no great hurry. He took my hand immediately, as if sensing I didn't want to break the contact between us, then said, "Which way?"

I jerked my chin toward the stairs and let him lead me through my own house. A parallel to the rest of life. I was only, what, nine years older? It still meant I'd been dating when he was still figuring out who he was.

God, I hoped he'd had the chance to do that before his parents told him it was all wrong and bad. They sounded like the scum of the earth. I preferred to fight with words—or better yet, diagrams —but I wanted to punch them in the face for letting a sweet, extraordinarily smart and kind young man like this slip away.

"You're really amazing, you know that?" I murmured.

Kev half-smiled. "I'm not all amazing. For example, I can't figure out which of these doors holds the prize." He pretended to wave like a game-show host. "And behind one of them, a new car!" Just when I was about to laugh, he leaned in and kissed behind my ear. He flicked his tongue against sensitive skin and whispered, "And I wanna ride it all night."

"Fuck," I moaned, pressing him up against the hallway wall. I knocked one of my framed pictures—a print I'd bought in Singapore—askew, but I didn't care.

Right here, I wanted to taste him and take him. Press him up against the wall and kiss him while I sank deep into him, his hard cock trapped between our stomachs. I wanted to be naked, bare skin against skin, his limbs wrapped around me. Goddamn, he was right. I wasn't just skin hungry—I was *starving*.

He writhed against me, hitching a leg up and running it along the backs of my legs until he nearly got it up to my ass. I responded on pure instinct, grabbing his sexy little ass and taking a moment to enjoy squeezing it before hiking him up and off the ground.

"Oh," Kev gasped into my ear, rolling his head back against the wall as I pressed him there. "You're so fucking hard, baby. It's hot to feel."

"Yeah?" I grinned and kissed his throat. I was loving feeling his own hard-on against mine, even if they were way too confined right now.

My worries from not even ten minutes ago had vanished. I knew how to do this. I could make him feel good. Even if I didn't last long, I could go down on him for as long as he wanted. I'd love to suck dick again.

As I kissed sensitive skin, he rolled his head left and then right to let me at him.

I wanted to suck on his skin, but it had been so damn long that I might go overboard and leave marks. I just nibbled, my fingernails digging into his skin with how much self-control I had to exercise.

"Suck harder," he whispered. "I want you to. It's been ages."

For that, I was gonna need to get his shirt off. I growled and hitched him up against me, holding him firmly before I carried him to the bedroom. My ego got a rise out of hearing him gasp, feeling him wrap his arms and legs even tighter around me as he entrusted his weight to me.

When I gently set him upon the bed, he had to let go, but I was kneeling over him before either of us could forget the heat between us. I helped him sit up so I could yank his shirt off.

"Oh, I'll leave you as many hickies as you want," I promised with a grin. Though I meant it to be wolfish, it was more goofy. I felt like I was eighteen again, messing around and just enjoying what my body could do. Especially against and inside another man's body.

"Good," he giggled. "I always tried to avoid them, but I... I like how it feels."

There. He'd told me something he liked. He always seemed to be neutral, asking *me* what I wanted, but never expressing his own preferences.

I was damn well going to leave him with more splotchy purple marks than a bingo card if that was what he wanted. But first, I knelt back to strip my own shirt off, cursing the buttons.

Kev laughed gently and helped, working his way up from the bottom far more efficiently.

By the time we met in the middle, Kev dropped his hands to wriggle out of his jeans. It took some doing, since they were the skinny kind that clung to his leggy frame, but watching him twist and thrust under me was no hardship.

Best of all, he had no underwear on, so his hard cock sprang straight up across his stomach when his jeans reached his thighs. He moaned as he worked them over his knees, using his toes to help tug them off. "Fucking things. Oh," he laughed when he finally had them off, fishing condoms out of his pocket, and caught me watching.

I grinned. "What? I'm enjoying the show." And I was. The first guy I'd seen naked in years? I was gonna savor every glimpse of his dusky pink nipples, the flushed thick shaft that gave away his excitement, and faintly visible, smooth abs. "You're fucking hot as hell."

"Th-Thanks," Kev murmured, oddly shy for a moment. He looked away and then back at me, his smile growing. "You now?"

"Me what?" I pretended not to notice that my hard-on was throbbing in my jeans.

Kev answered by locking his legs around mine and flipping us over so he was on top. "I'll show you."

The adrenaline rush was incredible. "Oh, fuck," I gasped, not even sure what he'd done there. I liked it, whatever it was.

"Mmm," Kev winked. "That's better." He scooted down the bed, unbuckling my belt and taking his time working with the trouser button and zipper.

"Fucking hurry up," I begged. I was beyond worrying about being pushy. I needed his hand around my shaft, and I needed it now.

"What's the magic word?" he teased.

Damn it, he was in charge right now, and he knew it. I pouted at him, but that didn't change his resolve. "Please," I finally relented, all of two seconds later. "I need you, baby. I… I just… wow."

Kev's expression softened, and he kissed my chest gently before sliding down to help me fight my own trousers off. They came much easier than his jeans, at least, and when he was done, he was conveniently kneeling between my legs.

And looking straight at the line my hard cock made in my underwear.

"I want you to suck me," I whispered. "Just for a minute. I won't last long enough otherwise. Is that okay?"

Kev wiggled a condom between his fingers. "For tonight, we need this."

"Cool," I agreed easily. Whatever the price to feel that hot mouth around me. I appreciated that he was taking such good care of me —and himself. That kind of respect was hot, but completely in character for a guy like he'd proven himself to be already.

"Then I'd be delighted to."

His words were formal but teasing, and there was no hint that he was hamming it up for my sake. I appreciated that. I might be desperate, but I didn't want a pity fuck.

From the way it sounded, neither did he. We might just be the perfect match—at least for one night.

His lips pressed against my underwear, and my cock jolted with pleasure at the pressure. Through fabric, the touch was too soft to do anything useful, but hard enough to get my attention. "Yes," I whimpered, but despite my begging, he took his time.

He kissed the whole length of my shaft before he eased my under-wear down and ran a finger along the slick tip. "So turned on," he whispered.

"Told you so," I mumbled back. "Need you."

The condom was tighter than I'd remembered, but it wasn't enough to kill my desire for this man. Just seeing his slender, naked body perched above me was enough to keep me hard for days. Especially when I imagined being inside him in a few short moments, and then in another way not long afterward.

"How did I get so lucky?" he whispered, and my jaw dropped.

"I was just thinking that."

Kev grinned. "About your big dick?"

That got me blushing. I knew I was on the bigger side of average —thick rather than some ridiculous double-digit length—but I hadn't heard anyone say that to me in so many words.

"Your face is adorable," Kev informed me with a soft giggle and then wrapped his lips around the tip of my cock. A wave of pleasure swept the response straight out of my mind, and all I could do was close my hands around his shoulders and beg for more.

Pressure and heat from tip to base, and best of all, the sight of my cock sliding between the pretty lips I'd admired from the first moment I saw him. Fuck, blowjobs were the best thing ever. How had I lived without them?

He took me in to the very base, and I felt my head touch the back of his throat.

"Fuck," I gasped, scrabbling for grip in his hair. "You're—oh, my God, that's sexy!"

Kev moaned slightly and nodded his head as much as he could once, in a kind of *thank you* that made me giggle. It was still sexy, though, hearing his noises muffled by my dick.

Emboldened by Kev touching my fingers, encouraging me to grip his hair in my fist, I fucked his mouth slowly a few times, watching the slide of smooth, hard, sensitive skin between his lips. I whispered the first thought that came to mind. "I love everything about this view." Then I pulled away, wanting to hold out longer. "I thought you were beautiful the moment you walked up to me at Friction. But if you keep that up, I'm gonna come way too quick."

Kev grinned. "I'm glad you know your limits. We can have a lot more fun that way."

"You like bottoming?" I asked, just to make sure. He'd never really said.

"Baby, I'd bottom for *that* dick seven days a week," Kev groaned. "No, eight."

If I hadn't already been horny as hell for him, I sure would be now. "Then hurry up and get ready," I gasped. "Lube on the bedside table." With nobody else around my house, I didn't need to hide it.

Kev grabbed it and sat back, sliding two slick fingers into himself a few times before he called it done.

"A-Are you sure?" My eyes widened. I'd never fucked anyone without a few minutes of fingering and pillow talk.

Kev just laughed at the expression on my face. "Most people have a little natural lube in there," he informed me. "Some have lots of practice. And some just like it rough. I'll let you guess which applies to me."

"D, all of the above?" I grinned.

Kev gasped. "You're a quick study."

"Oh, I'll study you any time you want," I promised, winking. "You wanna ride me?"

Kev considered it for a moment before he smiled and shook his head. He rolled onto his back, his gaze meeting mine. "Like this."

It was intimate—no question about it—and exactly what I needed. I considered thanking him, but that would be weird.

"Fuck, yeah," I whispered. The other advantage—I could put his knees over my shoulders, and... Oh, yeah, I was gonna need to think about baseball, or I was just gonna embarrass myself.

I slid into position on my knees, scooting up close to him. My lips twitched as I tried not to make a pun, even to myself, about sliding into home base.

"What?" he murmured when he saw the look on my face.

I snorted with laughter, unable to help myself. "I'm hoping to squeeze it in high and tight."

Kev laughed and slapped my ass. "Less baseball, more bouncing balls."

I pressed myself against his entrance, glancing up one more time to make sure it was okay before I was sliding inside.

Fuck, it felt good. My brain almost blanked for a second at the squeeze—tighter than my hand could get without feeling painful. The rings of muscle around me slid down my shaft as I entered him, and both of us were breathing harshly all of a sudden.

"Y-You okay?" I reached for the lube to add more, but he smacked my hand away.

"Just fucking fine. This'll get me off faster."

I loved that he knew himself and what turned him on. That was endlessly attractive, and it made it so much easier for me to please him. "Okay. Let me know," I murmured and kissed him before sliding his knees onto my shoulders.

When I had him arranged the way I wanted, bent in two under me, I paused to admire him for a moment before I started to thrust.

The bed creaked under us as skin slapped skin, my thighs trembling with pleasure within moments. I grabbed him as if I needed to stay grounded to keep from floating up into the sky with the ecstasy that was already coloring every burst of pleasure through me.

From his moans, Kev was enjoying it just as much, though I slowed down just to make sure. Before I could even ask, Kev grabbed my back, his nails digging in. "Yes, Charlie. Don't stop," he breathed out. "Fuck me until you can't hold back anymore."

I obeyed with everything I had, and for the first time since I could remember, I had no walls. No smartass comments. Nothing else to distract me from the intimacy of the two of us, as close together as it was possible to be, gasping into each other's mouths between kisses.

Something in my chest shifted—not physically, but from the sensation, it might as well have been. It was a reminder that I needed to be loved, that need was okay. Good, even. Love had kept me sane in my darkest days, and it would once more.

The only problem was the same unshakable part of me which knew I wanted that not just from my friends, but from this man I was struggling not to make love to. However rough he wanted it, and however he wanted this relationship to go, it might not be enough to satisfy me.

Fuck. I wasn't supposed to fall for him. Realizing this when our bodies were locked together in passion, orgasm sprinting up on me so much faster than I'd hoped, wasn't ideal. But at least I had the chance to satiate myself now.

Like a starving man, I let his knees go and straddled him instead, pressing our bare torsos together and blanketing him with my weight. I needed to feel every inch of his skin pressed against mine, from head to toe.

Kev's arms locked around my waist, and his lips pressed kisses along my collarbone and neck and cheeks. He was whispering to me. "Beautiful. You feel so good, baby. I love this. I'm so hot for you."

This didn't feel like standard patter he might give anyone. He was squirming under me, stroking himself, and part of me wanted to watch. The rest of me was perfectly happy to make him grind against my stomach as he came.

"I'm so close," I moaned, pressing my face into his neck. "I need to come, baby."

"Do it," he whispered. "Come in me, my beautiful Charlie."

I lost control, my hips breaking their smooth, hard rhythm now as I came. "Fuck!" I tilted my head back, gripping his shoulder and the headboard as I released every drop of my passion in shuddering thrusts.

I hadn't even slid out before he came, too, clenching tightly around me and making me gasp in one last burst of pleasure. "Charlie!"

"Yeah, Kev," I moaned, wanting to help him along. "Look at you. Fuck, you're gorgeous!" Watching the strings of milky-white passion coat his stomach was better than any porn I'd ever seen.

Knowing I got him so close to the edge did wonders for me, and getting to watch his expression grow taut with pleasure? Fuck, yes.

I collapsed on him with a groaned laugh when the exertion finally made itself known. My body was weak and shuddery, and I didn't trust my legs enough to try standing anytime soon.

"You good?" Kev murmured, sliding his hand up my chest.

"Yeah. Aren't I supposed to ask that?" I grinned, rolling onto my side as I pulled the condom off. "Are *you* good?"

"Oh, I'm perfect," Kev assured me with a jaunty grin, grabbing towels to clean up.

I looked at him, and suddenly I couldn't look away. "I know." He was so much more perfect than he even knew, and I didn't know how else to express what was in my heart.

Silence fell for a few minutes while we stroked each other's skin, cooling down together.

When Kev finally spoke, he murmured, "Whatcha thinking?"

"I don't know how this conversation is supposed to go," I laughed sheepishly. "But... us."

Kev grinned. "I don't know either. I'm horrible at dating. So, what do you want to do about us?"

I shook my head and smiled. He was doing that thing where he met other people's needs, and I wasn't sure if he knew it or not. "You first."

Kev seemed surprised, but he settled down on his elbow and propped his chin on his fist. After a few moments of thought, I could see the decision cross his face before he ever said a word. *No.* Goddamn it, this was going to be an inconvenient crush, then.

"This would be some bad timing for a relationship. My life is... up in the air."

I wanted to tell him that I didn't care, that I'd put up with whatever the hell was going on in his life, but I had to respect his decision. I swallowed hard and nodded. "Yeah. So is mine, if I'm honest." It was the right call and I knew it, but it didn't make it any easier.

Kev smiled. "We'll figure the future out when it comes," he promised.

I knew damn well he wouldn't want to be with me. He had too much else going on in his life, and even aside from that... he was young and pretty, and he probably wanted to play the field before he committed. It was all perfectly sensible.

So why the hell did it sound so romantic when he said that?

"Yeah," I murmured, rolling over and putting an arm across him as I buried my face in the pillows. "We will."

16

———

KEV

Good thing Adam was banned from touching my precious tea cup collection. He'd managed to break another goddamn mug, which was why we shopped at thrift stores.

Well, I generally went by myself. Anyone seeing him coming would have hidden their china, even if it was a buck apiece.

"Morning," I greeted the checkout clerk at Treasure Aisle with a cheerful smile. Just because New Yorkers weren't used to seeing common courtesy didn't mean I wasn't going to show it. They usually heard the Southern accent and suddenly loosened up if I said anything more than a few syllables, but she gave me a slightly terrified stare like I was a loon.

If I stayed in this neighborhood long enough, eventually they'd get used to my incessant good manners. I raised a hand anyway and grabbed a t-shirt first to wrap up everything until I got home. Then I bypassed the other shelves to head straight for the housewares.

If they had any good mugs, they would be my first priority. If we

147

ran much lower, he'd start using my cups instead of washing the dishes—I knew him. He'd chipped one once.

If I daydreamed about displaying them in a cabinet sometime, in a nice apartment, it was a private daydream.

"Perfect," I murmured, jamming the first couple mugs I saw into my basket. They clinked as they rolled around together. One had a skull and crossbones on it, and the other said WORLD'S BEST DADDY. Adam had said a hookup called him that last week, despite his being my age, so he was back to a smooth-shaven face. He'd kill me for buying him this mug, so how could I resist?

I spotted another mug that was marked up like a thermometer to measure how safe it was to approach the drinker based on how much coffee was left in it. I snickered and grabbed it to add to my basket.

Nothing jumped out at me from their cups and saucers today, though I picked everything up just to make sure. All cheap, chipped, or not to my taste. Chips in themselves weren't a problem—I liked fixing things up that I bought to make them more functional. But combined with garish patterns? No, thanks.

Before I got to the registers, I had to pass the bookshelves, so I stopped for a look. I didn't read a lot outside of work—a couple newspapers, the Economist, and books on general political or social subjects so I could talk about them. Fiction, though? My life was stranger than fiction. I didn't want to read about kids like me, which seemed to be how every gay story ended. I got irrationally jealous when I read about people who didn't have to worry about that shit, and I sure as hell didn't want stories that were even *more* sad.

"Wow," I murmured when I spotted an orange-bound set of encyclopedias. As a kid, I'd loved standing in my dad's office, staring up at the bookshelves and pulling a book at random out.

I'd flip open his old encyclopedias and browse them, trying to learn everything. But there had been so many volumes—ten or twelve or more—that I'd always given up. The sheer quantity of knowledge in the world had always been exciting. Someone out there knew all of these things.

I drew one off the shelves and flipped open the cover. I wasn't disappointed: there was a scrawled signature in there. The spiky, loopy handwriting looked old-fashioned. No doubt the former owner. I checked the other volumes, too, and then stopped and laughed out loud.

Volume three had a signature underneath in loose, blocky printing and lines that went everywhere but where they should. I couldn't even read what the name was supposed to be. Definitely a kid's signature. It was the only book like that.

I slid the last volume back onto the shelf and crouched back to look at them all together. If I were more of a book person, I'd grab these in a heartbeat just for that little quirk.

I wondered about the story behind them. Had a kid defaced the book without being noticed? Or had they gotten in trouble for it?

It stung all the more to realize that I'd lost every connection to my own childhood. Here I was, in a thrift store, looking for the oldest, prettiest things I could find so I could imagine a history for other people in lieu of my own. Most of the time, I was okay with being a blank slate and ignoring everything in my life before sixteen.

As far as anyone who knew me now was concerned, I'd come out of nowhere. To most of the people who'd known me, I'd vanished into nowhere. I was careful not to maintain any links between that past life and the *me* of today, which was why I was such a blank slate.

"Screw that," I mumbled as I stood up, leaving the books behind. I didn't need to cling to any remnants of the past—or others' pasts —to be me.

I found myself in the clothing racks. I could use a few new pieces, but I didn't normally shop here. I looked for brand names and left the rest behind. But without others' scrutiny to be conscious of, surely I could afford to relax a little. Plus, I couldn't afford those brands now. Better get used to my new reality.

I flicked through the racks, making a face at some of the styles that looked like they came straight out of the seventies. At least the nineties were cool again.

Not cool enough to wear a denim jacket, though. Not unless I had Britney herself on my arm. I stifled a laugh and flicked past that hanger.

"My thoughts exactly," said someone near my elbow. Even from my peripheral vision, I could see a bright blue jacket.

I turned to take him in, and smiled. He looked familiar somehow —very snappily dressed, skin like a dark calla lily but even softer, dark eyes glinting with humor. Gorgeous, but not in the way that said *I'm hot, you want me*. Self-assured. I picked up these impressions as fast as that, well-used to judging people at a glance and remembering people by their personalities as much as their faces.

Had I met him? Had we slept together? He wasn't a client—I tried to take particular care to remember them. Oh! That was it! He hung out at the diner next to Friction. I got the feeling he dated the owner, from the little interactions I'd seen.

"I mean, some guys can pull it off," I offered. I'd seen them—they were tall, with even more modelesque figures than mine. They were the men who could make the most ridiculous fashion seem totally normal. That definitely wasn't me. I was way closer to the preppy boy next door with a sweater tied around my shoulders.

He laughed, flashing me a broad smile. "I sure couldn't."

"Me neither."

"This, on the other hand?" He plucked a shirt out of the rack, and I tried not to wince at the pattern. I stuck to things that all combined together well, so I could mix and match no matter what I had in the laundry.

I shook my head. "I'm not as bold as you. I've seen you around. You always look good."

"Thanks." He smiled again. "Shay," he introduced himself, offering his hand to shake. Even that was unusual here. Lots of New Yorkers just swapped names and rushed on with their lives. I felt old-fashioned for always wanting to shake hands.

I took it and squeezed. "Kev," I said. "I come into the diner sometimes."

"So do I." Shay winked. "My boyfriend owns it, so I'm obligated to accept free pancakes. I remember seeing you before. Always dressing nicely, too."

"I'd be diabetic by now," I marveled and shook my head. "Thanks. It's... kind of for work."

"I see." His expression—reserved but amused—told me that he knew more about me than I'd hoped. Damn it. Did that mean the owner did, too? My mind cast around for his name for a second before I remembered: Jared. He'd never been rude to me. A few of the servers were brisk, but most treated me pretty well.

Not all places were like that once they figured out I was going there on dates with different men constantly, all of whom were well-dressed and clearly rich enough to buy my time.

Damn it, that just brought me back to thinking about Charlie. *He* always dressed well, too, but he didn't seem like he was living in his own universe like some rich guys did. He was down-to-earth, and even though he owned a nice house, he clearly wasn't flashing it around like it meant he was a better human being. Some people did that—compensated for acting shitty by telling themselves they were valuable because they made a lot of money.

Not Charlie.

A smile touched my lips a few seconds before I realized that I was now daydreaming about Charlie while in the middle of a conversation with a stranger. Goddammit. That had to mean something.

"Sorry?" I shook my head.

"I said, fun plans this weekend?"

"I'm not sure," I admitted, biting my lip. "Hoping to go out, but it depends what other people want to do." Namely, Charlie. When we'd woken up together on Wednesday morning, he'd muttered something about not knowing what work was going to have him up to, and that he'd get back to me tomorrow—that was today.

I was expecting a text message any time now.

"How about you? I've seen you in Friction, too, haven't I?" I'd put him down as a potential client, but he wasn't a frequent guest there. I'd never gotten around to introducing myself.

"Oh, we don't do the club scene much anymore." He gave a sheepish smile. "So I live vicariously through the youth."

I snorted. "Like you're ancient. You sure don't look it."

"Past the big three-oh."

"That's only ancient in twink world," I informed him. "That's not even daddy territory yet." I shifted the t-shirt in my basket to cover the daddy mug.

Only in this part of Brooklyn could I have this conversation and get no raised eyebrows at all.

He laughed and smoothed his tie down, pretending to bask in the flattery. "Well, then. I accept all compliments. Clever dressing will do that. Try that shirt—or at least something more *you*, won't you?"

I was surprised by the warm smile Shay gave me, and I mirrored it. I wasn't used to people giving a shit around here. Maybe back home they might have, but everyone was too busy to have a conversation like this. He sounded like a transplant from the West Coast. That must be it.

"Maybe," was all I'd give him with a grin.

"A bit of vintage, or a splash of color," Shay said. "That's what I always tell people."

He wasn't wrong. I knew exactly what he meant. I dressed like a catalog model because that was what I'd copied in learning to dress like this. I'd never quite diverged from looks I'd seen on Instagram and my wardrobe staples. I sure couldn't afford quirky mistakes at full prices, but thrift stores... well, it was a chance to explore.

"I will," I finally conceded. "On your expert advice."

It was a thing that I did—I formed bonds with people quickly. I could find chemistry and magic it up from nowhere. Hell, I'd connected to Charlie that first moment in Friction.

Maybe that was what I was afraid of. My stomach lurched as I dared to think it: *what if this is all just playacting? When do I drop the boyfriend experience?*

"See you around," Shay wished me, and he turned around to head to the cash registers with a few shirts in his arms.

"See you," I echoed in a murmur, watching after him. It was a stupid fear to have—worrying that I had *too much* of a spark with Charlie—but now it was starting to take root.

No way. Just because I'd struck up a conversation with a guy who I'd seen around didn't mean I was misleading Charlie somehow, or tricking him into loving me.

Here I was, making excuses for my fear because I really didn't know what I wanted.

I gave up clothes-hunting and grabbed the shirt Shay had pointed out, then headed up to the checkout. I was too distracted to even chat much at the register, but she didn't seem to take it personally.

Brooklyn was good to me sometimes, at least. Walking around in a daydream, as long as I kept out of people's way, was okay. Plenty of other people were on a Thursday, just waiting for the weekend.

I paid and headed back home, dodging a bike courier who nearly mowed me down and shouted something after himself.

"Fuck," I whispered. "Thursday." The admissions deadline for the community college I'd chosen was Friday.

Okay, I put the problems with my fear of the future to one side. I had to get on top of this, or the deadlines would fly by. I didn't have anyone to nag me to get my application in on time. I had to call the community college as soon as I got home.

All these fucking details to keep straight. I ought to be used to adulting and keeping everything running by now, but I really didn't feel like I was competent. I might be organized, but I was faking it until I made it.

Nobody would box me into a corner again. Not even a man who made all the other choices seem that much duller compared to being around him.

"God," I grumbled as I banged into the apartment and slammed the door, the dishes rattling.

I needed to get the fuck over this guy, and I couldn't seem to do it. Everything I'd tried for the last two days hadn't worked. I was over the moon every time I thought about sleeping with him, or holding him in the morning, or talking with him, or even just holding hands. I was grumpy when I thought about not getting to do that again.

My temper cooled enough to let me set the mugs gently in the sink before I tossed the shirt into my room and headed for the living room.

I stared at the ceiling like it had the answers and then gave up and closed my eyes, tapping my phone against my chin. Whatever the hell I was doing, I had to figure it out in a hurry.

You can't live for anyone else. I knew the advice Adam would give me. *Gotta do what you wanna do.*

I wasn't sure massage qualified as "wanted to do" as much as the best legal option, but I didn't hate the idea, unlike nearly every other job. It fit my personality, and I could start building a real employment record. Best of all, I could tell Josh and Evan I had a career path now.

Fine. I wasn't even remotely ready, but I'd make the call. I looked up the admissions number and dialed it, holding my breath until there was an answer.

"Hi. I'd like to talk about admissions to your non-traditional student program."

17

CHARLIE

It was Friday evening, I was done with work for the weekend, *and* I'd gotten the answer I wanted to the text message. *Yes!* Kev had said to hanging out with me in Brooklyn Bridge Park. Not *that sounds too romantic* or *fuck off, weirdo*, but *yes*.

With an exclamation mark, too. That meant he was excited, right? That was a plus. I might win him over yet, without pressuring him or trying some big cheesy movie moment.

My week had gone pretty damn well, too. I'd woken up in conference calls, and the Singapore development was going on time for once. By rights, I ought to be back there and supervising, but my boss had given me the okay to keep monitoring from here since it was ahead of schedule.

Not to mention the highlight of my week, Tuesday night. I'd had sex again for the first time in years, and didn't do too bad a job at it. Kev still wanted to talk to me and everything.

All things considered, I deserved to celebrate a little. However much I felt like crawling into bed and never moving, I coaxed myself into showering and changing. I could spend a couple hours out, and Ben had said he was up for going somewhere.

I texted him again to make sure he was in.

Friction later?

It took about five seconds to get an answer, which was unusual. Ben was one of those guys with a million WhatsApp chats. It was nice that he still prioritized mine.

LOVE IT! SEE YOU THERE!

The all-caps message made me laugh. He wasn't one of those people who typed in capitals because he forgot to turn off the caps lock. He really was that excited to see me going out. To be honest, so was I. I was proud of myself for coming out of my shell so much in just a couple weeks.

Ben would never believe it if I told him what I'd been up to lately.

A grin spread across my face as I left off the tie. I'd been constricted enough all damn week. I wanted to breathe today. I just adjusted my collar and smoothed down my shirt before grabbing my wallet and heading for the door.

Another Uber later, I was standing outside Friction, trying to get a look in through the windows and guess how busy it was. Was it worth getting in, or should I wait for Ben at the diner?

"There you are, darling!" Ben nearly tackled me from behind as he wrapped his arms around me, laughing when he had to pull me to my feet again.

I hadn't actually hit the ground, but I still glared. "You're lucky there's no more ice around, moron."

"Nothing that could cool my fire for you," he teased, slapping my ass. "Come on, I'll buy you a drink."

"Dunno why I'm even friends with you," I grumbled, straightening my jacket. I followed Ben past the bouncer, who exchanged a nod with him.

He smirked. "The free drinks, mostly."

"You've got me there."

When we had drinks, I settled at a table against the wall. I didn't want to be the center of attention any day, but being a little further away from the bar also meant fewer guys would stop and chat to—or hit on—Ben. It was hard being the ugly friend. Not that I cared that I got less attention, but it made it hard to have real conversations.

Speaking of hard to have conversations, as if they'd heard us coming in, the music suddenly went up a few notches and the lights went down. We exchanged looks—mine definitely less pleased than his.

"You wanna dance or talk?" Ben leaned in to make himself heard, clearly reading my expression.

"Talk. I have shit to say."

Ben snorted. "Good luck with that in here. Let's finish these first." He was already casting his gaze around the room, no doubt deciding who to try for later.

"Come on." I drained my Coke in a matter of seconds.

"Chug, chug, chug—nice!" Ben cheered when I finished the drink.

I rolled my eyes and waved toward his rum and Coke, waiting for him to do the same. Once he had, we moved out of the club together before the seats were even warm.

"Diner?" I nodded towards it once we were outside.

"That wasn't long," the bouncer commented.

Ben grinned at him. "My friend here is less about the dancing and more about the intellectual conversation."

I rolled my eyes as they laughed, well used to being the butt of the joke.

"Apparently the diner's where that's at. See you later, though, handsome." Ben fluttered his fingers and we headed into the place next door.

I shook my head. "You have something going on with him, too?"

"I hope to sometime," Ben corrected with a grin. "Can never have my fingers in too many pies."

We grabbed a window booth as I looked around, and just as I did, I made eye contact with someone walking outside. I recognized his sharp nose and large eyes in a second—Darren.

He raised his hand and doubled back to head inside and join us. "Hey! Charlie, right? Didn't expect to see you around again."

"Charlie's figured out how to be sociable," Ben broke in before I could say anything, his gaze focused on Darren. "It sure helps when the crowd's hot."

Darren didn't need to be told that Ben was flirting. He grinned and slid into the booth next to me. "Darren," he introduced himself.

"Ben." At least he didn't try to kiss Darren's hand or anything.

I rolled my eyes. "I dunno if this is where the party's at," I advised Darren. "I have… boy problems to talk through."

"Oh my God!" Darren lit up. "Those are my favorite kind. I thought you were single? The other day you were. Have you met someone?"

Ben gasped and covered his mouth with both hands, and I pointed at him. "Say nothing, or I kill you."

The owner was coming over, a notepad in his hand. "What can I get you boys?"

"Coffee all around," Ben said, looking at Darren to confirm that was okay. "Thanks, Jared." Of course he knew the guy's name.

Darren smirked. "I don't need help staying up all night, but the coffee here's good."

Even the owner rolled his eyes as he scribbled it down. "Anything else?"

"Uh, yeah. Fries, onion rings, wings," I listed off, glancing between the others. "That'll be good to share, right?"

He nodded and scribbled that down, too. "Gotcha." When he got to the back of the diner, I heard him shout, "Enrique! Look lively for three seconds. I don't care how late you were out last night."

I laughed under my breath and turned back to the table only to find both of them staring at me. "What?"

"You need to fill me in pronto," Ben told me.

"I'm getting there! Sheesh! That's why I said we gotta talk here and not in that place," I complained with a laugh.

Darren grinned. "Oh, has it gone into weekend mode already? Damn, it's later than I thought. So, did you meet him last time we were here?"

I opened my mouth and then closed it again, waving a hand. "Kind of on an app, but—"

"Grindr! You met on Grindr? Nobody ever admits that, dude," Darren gasped.

Ben nodded. "You didn't really think I met my last ex at the grocery store, did you?"

"I can't keep track of them, let alone how you met," I told him, rolling my eyes. "Now, if you can stop asking me to tell you for three seconds so I can actually get around to telling you?"

I heard a quiet, "Oh, snap!" from Darren, but he didn't have any sassy comebacks to add to that.

Ben snorted and raised his hands. "Be my guest."

Coffee arrived, and once Jared had left again, I leaned in. "Okay, so. I met this guy, we hung out a couple times. At least one of those was a date. We… uh…"

"Fucked!" Ben exclaimed, making the owner jump and curse before he got to the counter to slide the coffee pot in. "Sorry, darling!" he called after him.

"If you wanna call it that, whatever. Yeah." I waved my hand, trying to play it cool.

Ben, more than Darren, knew how big that was for me. He was just staring at me, his mouth hanging open in some combination of delight and surprise.

"Shut your mouth. You'll let the flies in," I muttered.

Ben leaned over the table to slap my hand. "No, you shut *your* mouth! Good job, bro. Was this a date, or a *date*," he air-quoted with a smirk.

"A date." I felt weirdly defensive about it, and I knew it came through in my voice.

Darren grinned. "That's awesome. You said you wanted to get out more, didn't you?"

Ben let out a sigh and nodded, looking over at Darren. "He's needed to get a life. Ever since his boyfriend—" He broke off and looked at me awkwardly.

I snort-laughed. Ben had never been awesome about thinking before he let words come out of his mouth. "I told him before," I said, shaking my head. "But you may as well go for it."

"Oh, right!" Darren winced and looked at me. "Sorry."

"Ever since then, he's been like the thirty-something virgin," Ben sighed. "I offered to set him up with some big dick, too."

Darren chuckled. "Sometimes it's not big dick you need, it's a big heart."

That's exactly it. I sat up straighter, a smile just starting to form on my face, before the two of them burst out laughing. I was disgruntled now, folding my arms over my chest.

"Like anything beats good dick," Ben said, and Darren high-fived him.

It was Darren who first noticed me and blinked, his expression shifting into concern. "Wait, you meant that," he said.

And it was Ben who knew what that meant. "Oh, *shit.*"

"I know." I buried my face in my hands. My chest seized up as butterflies danced in my stomach. I was so not ready for this conversation—or any of these feelings.

"It's *good,*" Ben said softly. I felt him wrap a hand around my elbow. "Charlie, he would have wanted you to be happy. Don't hold yourself back now."

"It's not that," I insisted. Sure, a bit of it was, but I still didn't know what the real problem here was. He was right—I should have been happy Kev was interested in seeing me again, but instead I was… waiting for something to go wrong.

"What is it, then?" Darren asked. It already felt like we'd known each other for months, the way he seemed to care. He was a good guy. At least after all this, I'd accidentally made a friend, it looked like.

"He doesn't want to date me." That was a good bit of the truth, but nowhere close to all of it. Still, it was enough to give them both pause.

Ben leaned in. "Oh, shit. Like, he's only in it for the sex?"

It had been so long since this kind of confessional, gossiping about boys and figuring out how to navigate the social waters of dating. I felt like I'd been dumped in the deep end without a life preserver. "No…"

Ben looked confused. "Why do you say that, then?"

"Cause we're going on a date on Saturday."

Jared came over to deliver our food, sliding plates in front of us and refilling the coffee with what seemed like more hands than one guy should have available. "Word of advice?"

Oh, God. I hadn't realized he'd been listening in, too. Then again, it was slow so far—everyone was heading straight into the club at this hour, not stopping for food yet. I sighed and looked up at him. "Sure. Throw in your two cents. Between you all, you'll have a betting pool."

While Ben laughed, Jared sobered up, bracing a hand on his hip. "Find other guys you like. Figure out your type. Flirt again and relax. See if it's *him*, or if you're just learning to love again. It's rough being through that kind of stuff—I've seen a lot of guys go through it later in life. Not a lot who are around my age like you, but still."

"That's the sweetest thing I've ever heard you say," Darren gasped.

"Shut up and eat your fries," Jared told him, pretending to cuff him upside the head as we all laughed. He headed back to the counter with the coffee pot.

"No, thanks," I said after him, and only received a grunt and shrug in reply.

It was a great idea—if I didn't feel so damn defensive about my attraction to Kev. I didn't want to challenge or test it, or compare it against anyone else. I didn't want to flirt with other people. I sure as hell didn't want to get over him. I just wanted him to like me back. Was that too much to ask?

"He's got it bad," Ben murmured, taking my hand. "Oh, man."

"I don't even know him that well, really. We've been talking, like, a couple weeks." I was purposely vague, not wanting Darren to put together the pieces—although the way he was watching me, God only knew what he already suspected. "Hung out a few times. And slept together once. That's it."

"Is he single, at least? Looking?"

"Single but not looking. He's got a lot of changes going on in his life."

Ben's eyes lit up. "So it's not hopeless. Not even close, dude. It just means he's not sure how to handle this yet. You take it slow, keep showing him that you're there for him."

Darren grinned. "And you show up on time for your dates and woo him. You don't make him uncomfortable or anything, but you show him what he *can* have with you."

"How long do I hold on?" I asked, pressing my lips together to deal with the unexpected surge of emotion in my chest. The idea of pining after Kev for weeks, months, or even longer, seemed crazy when we'd only just met, but I could all too easily see it happening.

Not even considering the unique circumstances—first guy I was dating in years—I fell for people rarely. That was why Ben was on the edge of his seat, and so was I. Darren might not know me well enough yet, but I couldn't just fake attraction until I made it, or force it with someone who wasn't genuinely interesting. And I sure as hell would never date anyone just for the sake of being in a relationship.

"We'll cross that bridge when we get there," Ben finally answered. "Wanna go out with me after this and dance it off?"

I shook my head and offered him a crooked smile. "By the time we're done with these, it'll be getting late. I wanna be up in time for the date tomorrow." Darren and Ben exchanged smug looks, and I rolled my eyes. "Oh, shut up."

Ben snorted. "I've earned *some* teasing rights."

I was glad when the conversation moved back to Darren and Ben flirting outrageously. It gave me a good opportunity to excuse myself. Sure, tonight hadn't turned out anything like I expected, but I had something of a plan now, and some advice to follow.

Kev didn't *not* want me. He just didn't know how to deal with it, I reminded myself as I stared out the Uber window for the drive home. All I had to do was show him that it was going to be okay with me—that I'd keep his heart as safe as I knew how.

But did I really know enough to make that promise?

18

KEV

I nearly flung the covers off as soon as I opened my eyes. I was normally perky in the mornings, but this was the most excited I'd been to wake up since moving day.

It was Saturday, which meant I had to get up, showered, dressed, and over to the bridge park by eleven. My sleep schedule was still not back on normal working-world time, so I hadn't been able to sleep until one. It was going on nine now. I didn't have a moment to waste.

"Shower's mine!" I called when I heard rustling in the kitchen. The shitty wall the landlord had added was never thick enough to keep out the sound of Adam rummaging for all the marshmallows in the Lucky Charms.

I knew damn well that was what he was doing, and the guilty tone of his, "Okay!" only confirmed it.

Whatever. I rolled my eyes. I was going to have something a lot better than stale marshmallows today, if all went well. And I didn't begrudge him them, either. For all he pretended to be a lazy jerk, he actually cared in his own way, and he worked damn hard. No guy kept as many part-time jobs as him without caring about his work somewhat. He deserved a treat here and there. I just had to rib him about it, or he'd get insecure about his manhood.

I raced for the shower and scrubbed myself clean, not even stopping to clean the pipes first. A risky decision, but after having had sex once with Charlie, I figured there was a good chance of getting some again. I wanted all the stamina possible available to me, just in case.

"You going anywhere?" Adam called through the bathroom door.

Good thing I hadn't tried to jerk off. Even after all my practice, I had my limits about what I could do, and keeping it up while my roommate interrogated me was a step too far. "Yeah. A date."

"Oh. *Date?*" He repeated the word as if trying to figure out what that meant.

I shut off the water. "Honest-to-god, legitimate, no money being exchanged, only subtle and unwritten rules that everyone seems to follow about reciprocation." I wasn't even cranky enough to add some sass into the words. "Not like *arranged* dates."

"Okay, okay." His footsteps receded as I toweled dry, and then they came back again. "How long will you be out?"

God. What did he want? I wrapped the towel around my waist and yanked the door open to roll my eyes at him. "That obviously depends how the date goes. We're walking around Brooklyn Bridge Park. Probably Pier 3, but it's not like there's much privacy anywhere there, sooo…"

"Oh yeah." He blushed. "Duh."

"Why?"

"I had someone coming over, is all…"

"Strawberry? Watermelon? Gimme a clue," I said, sprinting to my bedroom to find clean clothes to change into. My clothing rack was full, luckily. I thanked the gods for the wash-and-press. Lower income or not, that would be the last amenity to get sacrificed. I knew money would be tight until the course was over, but I was going to the college on Monday to sign the last of the paperwork. It was pretty much official now. They didn't even seem to care about my lack of a high school diploma.

"I dunno until they come over, man."

I paused and grinned to myself. He'd conspicuously avoided using pronouns most of the time, but the occasional *they* had slipped in over the past few months. I was pretty sure he was experimenting, but he wasn't comfortable enough with himself to tell me. He still called himself straight, so…

Not my place to question that yet.

"Text me as soon as you know, then," I told him.

"You're not bringing him back here, are you?"

I could hear the curiosity in his voice, and I didn't blame him. I'd never done that before. I wasn't about to start now.

"No, but I might not actually stay out all night with him," I muttered. "Shocking, I know. Brooklyn Man Doesn't Fuck On Third Date, news at eleven."

I chose clingy black jeans and a thin t-shirt, a thin but warm merino sweater, and a little silver chain with a star on it. When I reached for a bracelet, I pulled my hand back and reminded myself of that cardinal rule: always take off the last thing you put on.

I looked elegant but casual. This was a pretty standard date outfit for me, and I knew I'd look good on his arm.

God, that worried me more than it should when this was just a date. Nothing more than that. Not at the speed we'd agreed to take this relationship.

I yanked open the curtains and headed to the kitchen for toast, then pocketed my phone and wallet while I tried to find my keys. Wisely, Adam stayed out of my way until I was out the door.

"Have fun. Stay safe," he called out.

"You too!"

I was sprinting down the stairs of our building, taking them two at a time until I burst out onto the street. I had somewhere to be, and I wasn't going to miss this date.

One thing was clear: seeing Charlie was fast becoming the highlight of my week. Way too fast.

***

"Hey! You made it!"

"I did!" I exclaimed as I threw my arms around him.

God, hugging him was wonderful. I buried my nose in his neck and breathed in that scent of comfort and solid, self-assured confidence. "I'm glad," he murmured, and I felt his voice rumble through me. "You okay?"

"I'm fine. Just woke up." I'd barely even had time to style my hair, but he didn't seem to notice or mind. Or at least he was good at pretending.

Suddenly, all my doubts about us had vanished. All it took was holding him for a few moments, and suddenly I was dangerously liable to say yes to whatever the hell he proposed. Even if that meant dating. Who was I becoming, anyway?

"How was your week?" He pulled back and took me by the hand as we walked along the waterfront, our gazes straying to the Manhattan skyline now and then.

"It was all right. Busy setting up school. I'm in, I just have to pay tuition."

He grinned. "Awesome! Did you have to fuck around with transcripts and all that stuff?"

That just reminded me of how little education I had compared to him, and I winced. "No. They didn't seem to mind my, um, situation." We wandered down to the coffee shop to grab a to-go cup each, still talking the whole way like nobody else was around.

Charlie didn't falter, though. He squeezed my hand and beamed at me. "That's great news." Despite never seeming to say much, whenever he did give praise, I knew damn well he meant it. That made me blush all the more at what sounded a lot like *congratulations* in his language.

"Um, thanks."

"You're gonna do great. Are you excited for the new life direction?" Charlie asked, and I didn't even get the sense he was just making conversation. He genuinely wanted to know, which kind of put me on the spot, but only in the best possible way.

"I am," I had to admit. "I'm scared as hell that I chose the wrong place, that I'll do the wrong course, that I'll end up in debt and alone forever, but... millennial problems," I laughed, suddenly self-conscious. I tried to let go of his hand and fiddle with my hair, but he only squeezed tighter.

"There's no such thing as alone forever," he promised. "As long as you reach out."

There was so much more he wasn't saying. He was clearly trying to respect me and not push the issue of dating, and I felt bad for a moment. This was a date, but if I didn't have relationship intentions, was it fair to keep leading him on?

I swallowed and shook my head. "You're a good guy."

"Nah," he chuckled. "Just like you, that's all."

Here we were a few minutes into a date, and somehow already discussing our future again. But I found myself not wanting to let go of his hand. Fuck, I wanted to just wander like this, hand in hand, all through New York City. Not just to show off the hot man on my arm, but because...

When I stepped around a kid on a bike, so did he—in the same direction. When I looked at him and smiled, he smiled back. He wasn't distracted by his phone, or by counting down the minutes he'd paid for. He wasn't trying to string me along by choosing what he responded to and what he didn't.

He was just genuine, and there for me in every conversation we had, even this early. That was so damn rare I wasn't sure he *knew* how rare it was. A guy like him, off the market for so long, probably didn't.

"I sometimes feel like I'm just... generating chemistry with you," I murmured with a frown and looked down. While we were being honest, now was the chance to say it. "Like I've done it so much that it's all I can do. I like you a lot, but I don't trust myself."

Charlie squeezed my hand gently and walked for a minute, seemingly thinking about that before he came up with an answer. "That makes sense. Do you think you're more used to letting people come and go in your life?"

Though he spoke carefully, I could hear the fear there. It was obvious to anyone who was paying attention. *Will you just let me go?* "No," I said, and I tugged him over to an empty bench so we could sit and talk. "I was thinking more about our last, um… about what we said about *us*. I still feel like my life is too crazy to commit to anything. But it doesn't mean I'm not into you." My cheeks burned, and even that was unfamiliar. I was used to being totally confident as I negotiated, or even spelled out kinks I would or wouldn't do.

I wasn't used to holding my breath to see how the other guy would answer, but Charlie wasn't just any other guy.

"What are you looking for? Eventually, if not now?" Charlie asked.

"I've always wanted a boyfriend." I smiled as I looked away. It was all too easy to remember the childhood daydreams, and the journals where I'd written *I wonder when I'll get a girlfriend* in case my parents found the journals, but I knew damn well that I'd meant *boyfriend*. Ever since I was little, I'd known. And I'd known that I wouldn't get that as long as I stayed in Tennessee.

Out here, dreams became real.

"I just don't know how all of it works," I told him. "Like you feel about dating after time away… I'm used to dating with, you know, clear guidelines. I don't have many examples of a functional relationship. And… when you find a great guy who seems to be what you're looking for, but so early on?" I bit my lip, not sure how to express this without leading him on. "I thought it'd take longer."

Charlie nodded. "You want to play the field. I'm past that stage, but I went through it, too." He tossed his empty cup in the trash and I followed suit.

"No," I frowned. Was that true, though? I'd always envisioned myself going out and dancing with lots of pretty boys, and not choosing one to settle down with. "Don't you? I mean, just *me*? How can that be enough?"

But I wanted that, too. I'd had more than enough time dating men, even if it wasn't quite the same thing. I knew how hard it was to find a gem like Charlie, and I knew I didn't want someone else instead. It wasn't like there was a single perfect guy out there who could be my entire life. Everyone needed friends and work or hobbies or volunteering just to get out. No one guy could meet my every need and fulfill me forever and ever, amen.

Right?

"I know my heart," Charlie told me, and his smile was confident. "Sure, it might not work out. But if you stop yourself from committing to anyone because you're not quite sure, you'll never commit at all. You're not supposed to be certain all the time. You just have to want to make it work."

I took his hand and squeezed, warmth tightening my chest. "Very mature. Not what I'm used to," I admitted and grinned. "My roommate… well, bless his heart."

"Ouch," Charlie laughed, correctly interpreting the expression. "You planning to get out of there soon?"

"No. Nah, he's okay, for all I complain," I admitted. "The place is crappy, but we can afford it."

"Will I get to see it?" Charlie winked. "Especially if I'm just a friend."

I burst out laughing. Cheeky bastard. "Fuck off," I told him, elbowing him, and he joined in the laugh. "Don't use my logic against me."

"All's fair," Charlie murmured.

In love and war? What about both at once? I met his eyes and, though they glinted with humor, it was easy to tell he was serious, too.

We let the conversation move on from there so we could talk about our weeks, what the hell the street magicians were up to and why the tourists got sucked in by them every time, and which parks were our favorites. Since it was already after lunchtime, rather than one meal, we made do with snacks from the hot dog carts and coffee shops. Restaurants here by the river were way overpriced, anyway.

There was no getting away from the fact that this was a date, though.

Pier 3 was as quiet as usual, thanks to its lack of playground space. The rougher spot around the book cart was my favorite place, because there were boulders and trees and little private nooks. Like I'd said, not private enough for anything serious, but at least we could cuddle.

I settled on a patch of grass and beckoned him to join me.

Charlie didn't hesitate to sit cross-legged beside me, but he soon relaxed and joined me in lying on my back. "This is a nice little spot."

"I come here alone sometimes to daydream," I told him. "Or walk along the waterfront and remind myself that I'm really here."

"I bet," he chuckled quietly. "New York City has always been such a big part of my life that I forget what it must be like to move to. Huge and overwhelming."

"It's big," I agreed. "I dunno about overwhelming. Once I figured out how to take the subway and how not to get mugged... I haven't found it bad. But it is lonely sometimes."

Charlie rolled his head to look at me, and I met his gaze.

On some unspoken signal, we leaned in to kiss. It was like we couldn't resist the attraction that had been pulling us together all day, and damn it, I didn't want to resist any longer.

His lips were soft and warm, and the way his hand rested on my shoulder reminded me of being pinned to the bed and fucked, but also of being cuddled all night.

I instinctively snuggled closer to him as I kissed him back, forgetting our surroundings and my worries. Nothing else mattered when I was here with Charlie, alone together. The traffic was quietest here, and it was easy to forget that anyone else was even nearby.

At least, until my pants started to feel tight. Fuck, it was hard to keep myself in check around him. Just one kiss reminded me of all the deliciously dirty things I wanted to do to him.

"You know," Charlie murmured, his voice low and rough, "we could head back to my place. Whether or not we do anything—"

"Yeah." I didn't even let him finish the sentence. I wanted to be alone with him. As nice as it was to kill a few hours exploring together, we had so much more exploration to do that wasn't public-friendly. *Kind of like the honeymoon phase.*

"I've been wanting to blow you for days," Charlie murmured. "It's kind of addictive."

Okay, with that incentive, we were up and off to the train in moments, making small talk to try to cool off until we got back to Charlie's home.

"Hey, are you on Facebook?" I asked as we strolled for the train platform.

"Hm? Yeah, I guess."

I took a deep breath. I hadn't done this with any client before, or even any friends I'd made since moving here. And I'd cleaned out my profile years ago to cut out anyone who might spy on me and report back to my parents. I didn't let work and play mix. But this was far from work now. "You wanna add me?"

"Oh, I don't go on there much." He swiped his card and headed through the barrier, leaving me standing there for a few moments.

Okay, fine. I guess not. I swiped my card, too, and headed through the turnstile. Just because Charlie didn't want to add me didn't mean anything. He didn't have secrets, did he? I could still enjoy a perfectly good day with him without worrying about what this meant, right?

Blowjobs, I reminded myself. Much bigger priorities right now. I sent Adam a quick *watermelon* text. He'd be happy to hear that. At least he could get some on his own date, and everyone would be happy. He'd be less grumpy tomorrow.

"Train!"

I hastily jogged after Charlie to make this train, putting it in the "deal with later" box that was getting pretty damn crammed full.

19

CHARLIE

Thank God one part of my life was going right, because I was starting to feel like they wouldn't all be in balance at once.

Monday was much less fun than the weekend, which was an opinion I hadn't held in years. Worse yet, because I wasn't spending every spare minute in the office, I had to work a lot harder when I was in. Not necessarily long hours, but absolute focus. I couldn't afford distractions like chatting about my coworker's new kittens.

Was that how I'd kept up with networking *and* my job—by working essentially double-time? No wonder I'd shot to the top of the employee list here. And now I was paying for it dearly.

"I'll leave you two to chat about it," Valerie said with a pointed look at me. She closed the office door on her way out. We were alone in the office now, having had to wait until late at night before our meeting partner was available—and he was up early, at six AM or something stupid.

I knew what that look she'd shot me said. *Close the deal tonight.*

And since our Dubai-based potential client didn't seem interested in working with anyone else, I had to either figure out a way to get them interested in someone else here or get over myself and find a way to work with them.

Fuck.

"Great to meet you, Charlie." To give him credit, Alex did seem like a solid guy. He came across as immediately likable, unlike many a snobby developer I'd met. "I'm excited to work with you, or so I hope." He offered a smile. "Which brings us to this meeting, I guess."

"Nice to meet you at last, too," I agreed, waving slightly and settling back in my chair. The laptop sat in the middle of the polished wood surface, which was bare of any other distractions except a notepad. I grabbed it and balanced it on my lap in case I wanted to keep talking points close at hand. "You wanted to talk about the, um, resort tower."

It was a pretty typical project for the area, with all the challenges of trying to find water in the desert, but the potential reward of boosting my name and the firm's in another developing market.

There were also challenges that most people around me didn't even seem to want to talk about, if they knew about them. Like, even if only in theory, the death penalty for my enjoyable Saturday night.

"Yes. We love your portfolio. The whole firm's, but your vision just fits with what we want. That use of space and the eye for natural environments, the vision for modern, sophisticated, yet green-looking buildings. You take sustainability beyond earthships," Alex enthused.

I knew I was good at what I did, but it was hard not to let the flattery get to me. "Yeah? Thanks."

"You love a good challenge."

A bold statement, but clearly Alex had been doing his homework. For all I complained about other people not knowing they were asking the impossible, I relished the chance to make it come true. "Yes. I've never built in a desert, though. We have other guys here who—"

"Oh, I know," Alex said with a rueful smile. "Valerie's been trying to sell me on them. But the end client only wants you."

Aha. Now we were getting somewhere. There was an end client, which explained why he seemed so reluctant to budge. "Are you being hired by an oil billionaire?"

"Something like that," he nodded. "He wants to maintain his privacy, but you're pretty close."

Right. An ego project, then. If I was never going to get to meet him, that meant relaying suggestions through a third party—not always a bad thing, but added complications when time was of the essence.

"Look, I have some big reservations, apart from labor conditions. I know it's hard to guarantee everyone will be a legal immigrant treated fairly. Especially on this scale of project. Costs go through the roof, or principles get sacrificed." I wanted to make it clear I knew damn well that modern-day slavery was common in the area. Construction and housekeeping were two of the biggest abusive industries, and if I took the job, I might unknowingly be contributing to one.

Not like the West was much better in places. Some subcontractors liked to shortcut safety in the name of cost-cutting. But at least the guys on our sites didn't have their passports taken away as soon as they got there.

"Right." Alex grimaced. "We've done our best to guarantee fair and safe working conditions, which is… a hell of a task in the desert."

"I respect that," I told him, honestly. But there was no point in bullshitting around the real problem. "But I prefer to supervise on-site. If not for the whole project, I have to be there at a few critical phases."

"Right. Singapore and Seoul haven't been a problem."

"And their laws are friendlier to people like me." It was impossible to meet anyone's eyes through the screen, but I did my best to look as close to the camera as I could while still watching his face. "Not *that* much better, in the case of Singapore, but I'm at least willing to risk it."

Plus, there were a hell of a lot of things I wasn't going to get into —like if I'd been HIV-positive, I wouldn't even be allowed into the country on a work visa. They did blood testing for all new arrivals, I knew that much, and they deported HIV-positive people. Which ought to have been a scandal, but then, they weren't the only country to have done that in recent memory. I didn't feel it was fair to the poz guys out there that I got to take advantage of opportunities that were closed to them.

Alex hesitated, scanning my expression, and then folded his arms as he leaned back. "Yeah. I get your reservations. I thought the same before I moved here. But the scene for my friends is a lot safer than I thought it would be. They say there's police raids, but worst-case scenario, foreigners get deported. And there's a lot of underground clubs."

"I didn't establish a life in New York City, of all places, to hide from police raids," I said, shaking my head. Hadn't he even heard of Stonewall? He had an American accent, so surely to God he had.

"If we kept the visits as short as possible, would that be okay?" Alex pressed. I didn't blame him—he had a client to satisfy. "And we could introduce you to locals who can give you a better idea of what to expect."

"I know what to expect," I told him. "When I go to Singapore, I keep it to a week at most. I'm careful not to act too gay in public. I don't want to make it harder for locals. They're stuck afterward, explaining that it's not just an imported idea from the West," I told him.

I hadn't yet said no, though. We were both aware of it. It was a complicated negotiation, and it shouldn't have been. Why was this even a conversation?

"How about I refer you to some of the guys here who are already working in Dubai?"

Alex shook his head. "Valerie gave me their portfolios already. I went through them with my client. They only want you."

Was I being stupid? If I wasn't gonna get the deal closed by passing it on to another architect, it was down to me.

It was one little project in one country. I had others on my plate— the local redevelopment, the Singapore project. I could add one more to my rotation, surely.

"We can schedule most of the meetings through Skype and keep on-site visits to a minimum."

"I need site visits," I told him. "At least every couple months when there's construction going on. Leaving projects in the hands of that team doesn't go well."

Alex nodded. "That's why your portfolio has such a strong vision. A lot of the people we were looking at have great concepts and the real-life execution is... well, missing something."

It was like Charlie-bait: a challenge.

"I need time to think about it," I told him. It wasn't that I was afraid to say no. I was a New Yorker. I was used to saying no on every commute, let alone at my job. But there was more going on here and I genuinely had to figure out what I was willing to do.

Alex lit up. "We can give you a week."

"I might be going to Singapore in a week or two." I ran a hand through my hair, scribbling on my notepad with the other. Singapore raised its own set of problems. "Depends how that timeline unfolds this week."

-Tell K about S'pore.

-Answer Alex by...

My pen hovered over the page as I looked up at the screen. "When do you need an answer?"

"How about next Sunday?"

"That works." I finished writing the note and stuffed it in my pocket. "I don't want to lead you on, but..."

"No," Alex interrupted, waving a hand. "I really appreciate you thinking about it despite your apprehensions. It makes me feel bad I can't guarantee more, but I can pass along all the experiences I've heard about and hopefully you'll reach a decision that everyone's comfortable with."

Hopefully, yeah. Unlikely, from the sounds of things. I smiled and put the notepad aside again. "Yeah."

"Let me know if you want to talk to anyone who has a more... inside perspective."

"Will do." I was tired out, it was late, and I'd probably missed texts from Kev. What would he think of me agreeing to go to Dubai? I found myself genuinely wanting his opinion before I decided. He was smart—and careful, but bold. And he wasn't afraid of saying what he really thought. Exactly the kind of opinion I wanted.

Plus, if I was going to fuck off to a place like that for longer than a few days as I sometimes did when a new project started, he deserved to know there was no chance he could visit me in that time. I could put myself at risk, but not him. Never him.

"Catch you later, Alex. I'll let you know when I have a decision either way," I promised. I raised my hand to wave and trade good-byes before I hung up.

Before I left the office, I shut the laptop and then braced my elbows on the desk, burying my face in my hands. I was under pressure and not thinking clearly, that much was obvious.

I didn't want to support the regime in power any more than any anti-gay country. I didn't want my name on a building in a country that had a terrible human rights record. But then, plenty of countries I'd worked and even lived in had huge human rights problems they weren't addressing.

I sighed and pushed myself to my feet, determined not to think about it anymore tonight.

As soon as I left my office, Valerie cornered me. "Well?"

"I'm thinking about it," I told her, my tone clipped. I wasn't going to give her false hope, either. "He's one hundred percent not inter-ested in anyone else—I tried that already."

Valerie nodded. "I dunno why he's so fixated on you, but it has to be you." She took my arm. "I get it. God, I don't want to go to Dubai, either, as a woman."

I shivered and nodded. Sometimes our country sucked, but I felt relatively safe to be me here.

Why the hell had my work life gotten to the point where this was part of my thought process? Fuck this whole mess.

"But you need to look at the on-the-ground situation before you shoot yourself in the foot," Valerie said. "There will be other projects for us."

That wasn't a threat, was it? No. She wouldn't fire me over something like this. But it was a statement of fact, and I knew she was right. The up-and-coming architectural wonders weren't being built in London or Tokyo these days. They were in countries like Singapore and Dubai. The next hotspots would no doubt have colonial-era laws, too. This wasn't going to be a one-time problem.

"Like I said: I'll think about it. God, it's gotta be nearly midnight. I'm going home," I told her.

"Good plan. Me too." She was clearly disappointed not to have a result, but I was grateful she wasn't pushing that pressure onto me, at least.

I waved and called an Uber before I packed up my laptop. I'd work from home in the morning and recover from the late night. Now that I was starting to get full nights of sleep, I'd found myself counting on them.

I was quiet on the Uber ride home, staring out the window. The gay glass ceiling weighed heavily on my mind. I knew damn well that most of this was the pressure I was putting on myself, and had since Hugh died. I wanted to keep rising within the firm, and then another firm if I outgrew this one. Someday, my own firm.

But someone had specifically requested *me* for this project. It was the first time anyone had been so insistent that it had to be me. Not only was it good for the ego, but it was great for my portfolio. If I really wanted to pursue this career with the vigor I'd put into it for the last five-plus years, it was stupid to ignore this chance.

Plus... I was going to Singapore, for God's sake. Sure, the police presence wasn't so actively hostile, but the laws were against same-sex relationships there, too. I couldn't hold a double standard and argue that one was okay.

I thanked the driver when I blinked and found the car turning the corner towards my home. I climbed out on the corner and stopped by the bodega for a few groceries. I had a full-sized fridge, but rarely kept it stocked with fresh foods. The whole time, my brain was several thousand miles away.

I sleep-walked through my door and straight to the kitchen, dumped everything in the fridge, and then headed straight upstairs to bed without even a glass of wine.

One thing had consumed my thoughts: *what happens if I say no?*

Valerie wouldn't fire me, but there wouldn't be much room for advancement if I started applying silly things like principles to my career and stopped taking jobs in half the countries we operated in. Plus, I was good at Singapore and their building codes. Every country had their own practices and codes to consider, and I liked Singapore.

I was careful not to use social media much so I didn't have to avoid my social media being used against me. I didn't express much of my life, although I was technically registered on a few sites. And I'd always known that was unfair, but who cared? Fairness wasn't the way the world worked. I knew that well enough by now.

"God, it just sucks," I mumbled when I was finally in bed. I buried my face in the pillows and breathed in the faint scent of Kev that still clung to the pillowcases from a few days ago.

Goddammit, I wanted him here by my side. I rolled over again to actually check my phone and smiled at the string of texts from him. I sent one back, but I was so tired I could barely even process the words.

Long day today. Chat in the morning, I'm working from home. Sleep tight.

I got a response right away.

Good night!

It made me smile, at least. This was one tiny bright spot, even if it wasn't like coming home and snuggling up in Kev's arms. I could still remember what that felt like and I conjured that memory up as I pulled the covers over my head.

The fact didn't escape me that if I pursued this with Kev, it was only going to make that very line I was considering right now even harder to walk. A single, HIV-negative gay guy who could kind of pass as straight and didn't especially like to party going to Dubai for a week? Sure, I could avoid any trouble. But as soon as I got a boyfriend, there was that dance of avoiding talking about myself and my life.

I fucking hated that game with a burning passion. I generally avoided talking about myself because it was nobody's business. But not being able to drop in a casual *when my boyfriend and I did this* had already been a frustration, even now that I had five years of solo living to talk about since I'd lost him.

It was a whole minefield of life changes that I wasn't sure I was ready to walk into, but I couldn't ignore the fact that I was still pressing the pillow that smelled like Kev's hair into my face as I drifted to sleep.

Love didn't care about inconvenience, and it never had. The only question was what to do about it—and whether to acknowledge it at all. Not that that was much of a choice.

Why the hell build a life at all if it was going to be half a life?

20

KEV

Exactly how often was I supposed to text a guy who was totally not my boyfriend, but whom I took on dates and had great sex with?

Ugh. Any rules I could think of—the three-day rule, or whatever—were weird and artificial. Nothing made sense except treating him like a friend, and if that meant texting him several times a day… more than I texted Adam…

I lay in bed, holding my phone. It was almost pressed against my nose as I drifted off into a light doze, waiting for Charlie to wake up and answer my good morning text.

Buzz! The vibrating phone in my hand scared the crap out of me, which at least forced me to wake up for the day.

But the text was totally worth it.

Good morning, gorgeous <3

In the privacy of my own room, where I didn't have to defend my weakness to anyone, I smiled. Maybe it made me vulnerable in ways I didn't like, but goddammit, I liked the thought of someone waking up on the other side of Brooklyn and thinking of me first.

I rolled onto my front and called him.

When Charlie answered, his voice was sleepy. "Hi, babe."

"Hey."

"What's up?" He yawned.

I wasn't honestly sure how to answer that with anything that wasn't *I missed the sound of your voice*, which just sounded… well, pathetic. "I just wanted to talk."

"That's all right with me." Charlie yawned again, and I was pretty sure I could hear him stretching and sitting up in bed. "Long night at work last night. Sorry I didn't answer your texts sooner."

"Hey, it's okay." I'd worried a bit about him, but he'd been coping with stupidly long work days for years now. The occasional day wouldn't hurt him too much. "Got sucked into work?"

"We've been invited—begged—to do a project. No bidding and hoping for the best, so the boss really wants it. Had to stay up late to Skype with the guy."

I smiled. "Wow. That sounds prestigious." It was the kind of comment I'd make to a guy talking about his field when I didn't really understand it but wanted his ego to feel good.

The reaction confused me. "I guess," Charlie grunted. "Could be. So, how 'bout you? Any plans?"

"Ugh, I guess not," I said with a sigh. "Thinking about trying to find a job that works around my school hours. I can't really survive without working for a couple years. But that's all boring stuff."

"No way." He was firm. "I want to hear about your journey, too. Oh, speaking of journeys… so, I'm going to Singapore for a week."

I smiled and pressed a hand against my hot cheek. Fuck, he was sweet. Here he was, an up-and-coming famous architect flying to Singapore and Skyping with people God-knows-where, but he was interested in my little vocational school plans? I couldn't keep up with that anymore. Maybe in my old job—I'd gone on a couple of vacations with single older guys who wanted arm candy on their gay trips—but not on my current non-income.

"Have fun there."

"I'll just be working," he said. I was almost getting used to his abruptness. I missed Southern manners, but I couldn't blame him for it. "Anyway, I better get up. Site visit today on this nonprofit's building."

"Oh, enjoy. Hopefully they don't give you many headaches."

At least that got a chuckle. "Hope so too. Good luck with the job search."

"Thanks. Talk to you later?"

"Later, babe." He hung up and I stared at my phone for a second. The pet names were just slipping into his conversation now, like he didn't even notice them—but he was a man of few words. I wanted to believe that every word was carefully chosen.

It felt good to hear those words. Pet names had always felt kind of greasy to me, like guys were trying too hard to turn me on. They knew I was just doing my job, and they always wanted to fulfill their fantasy of seducing the sex worker. Like that would make the sex better or more valuable somehow.

Charlie just dropped them in like I was a person who was important to him, not like he was trying to get something from me.

And here I was, wrapping myself into a blanket burrito and grinning at the ceiling like a total goof while I daydreamed about Charlie. God, I needed to get up and about my day, not lie about mooning over this guy.

Not that I had anything to *do* today. Waiting for school to start, but not really able to start a new job before then, was a sucky place to be in. I wasn't going to try fast food or retail again—I clearly didn't have the ability to put up with abuse in the name of a paycheck that they would require.

Which meant I had to get my ass in gear and do some other kind of work where I'd be respected. My old job was out—and now that I wasn't sure how much my boundaries had been screwed up, it seemed smartest to take a giant step back from it all. Self-doubt had crept in.

Tennessee was an hour earlier, but Josh would be awake on the ranch.

I needed advice, and I needed it from someone who wouldn't judge me.

I dialed Josh's number and bit my thumbnail while I waited for an answer. It was a bad habit I'd kicked years ago, but every now and then when anxiety got the best of me, I found myself doing it again. I rolled onto my front and shoved my other hand under my pillow.

"Hey, Kev! Your phone does work!" was Josh's cheerful greeting.

I grinned. It was kind of like having parents who gave a shit. He meant a lot to me, having taken me in and given me a place to live and a job for a few months. I'd meant to call him before, honestly, but it kept slipping my mind. "Hi, man. How's it going?"

"Great. Business is picking up for the summer."

"How's Evan?" I was glad the two of them had worked through whatever their issues were to find each other. They worked well together—to the point they were finishing each other's sentences by the time I left.

"He's doing good, too. Adam?"

"His usual self," I answered, rolling my eyes. I was keeping my voice down since whatever I said would be pretty clearly heard anywhere else in the house.

"So, if it's not Adam being a massive dick, why're you calling?"

I laughed. Josh saw right through me. "Advice, I guess."

"Shoot."

"Since we got here, Adam's been piecing together odd jobs—you know him. I've been hustling."

"Uh huh." Josh had never judged me for doing what I wanted or needed to do, but the very first time we'd met, he'd offered me a job so I wouldn't *have* to do survival sex work—so I had a free choice. I appreciated that more than I could say.

"But all the crackdowns online… it's making it pretty tough to get work now. Anywhere else like Grindr, they delete your profile. The sites made just for us are all shut down."

"Yep." Josh sighed. "That's a pain in the ass."

"It sure is."

Josh's breath caught. "You're not working street corners, are you? I'll fly out there and kick your ass myself if you are."

"Not quite," I promised with a laugh. "I've been making do with existing clients." I hadn't checked my work phone in a week. Fuck, I'd probably missed so many texts. There was a more graceful way to get out of the business, I was pretty sure, but I never did things the graceful way. "And aiming a little higher-end, so each job keeps me going longer. But I'm sick of it."

"I can get that," Josh murmured. "So, where we talked about other jobs…?"

I grimaced. It was all well and good to learn to keep the books when we were talking one dude ranch in rural Tennessee. But just walking into a hotel or resort or, hell, any kind of small business here with no experience? No way. "I need more training. I'm actually going back to school next week."

"Oh, shit! That's great." Josh sounded genuinely pleased for me, and for the first time, I let myself relax a little bit and celebrate. "What are you studying?"

It *was* good. I was figuring out what I wanted and going for it, instead of just falling back into my routine. "Massage. I guess it's great, yeah."

"What's missing, then?"

"Huh?" I frowned at my phone, not even understanding the question.

"You're still calling for advice, and you don't sound happy about school." Josh was blunt for a Southerner, but I appreciated it. Maybe that was why I could understand Charlie—it came off as peevish, but they were both just the no-bullshit kind of guys.

"No. I'm mostly doing it," I lowered my voice to almost a mumble, "'cause I got fired from a cashier job on day one."

Instead of being pissed at me, Josh burst out laughing. "Day one! Jesus, man. What did you do?"

"I got pissed off when a customer yelled at another employee," I sighed.

"Oh, Kev." Josh sounded fond. "Man, I didn't want you to head off to Brooklyn 'cause of this."

"What? Really?" He'd never let that slip. "Why?"

"You're an idealist. I never understood how, after everything you've been through, but you are. It's not a bad thing, but it's gonna make everything harder for you."

I rolled onto my back and stared at my ceiling. "Yeah? I… I guess I am. I just think if something isn't right, I'm not gonna shut up and put up with it."

"Are you sure massage is where your career calling is?"

"No," I snorted. "But I know where I can get work—start by doing stuff without happy endings, and then maybe transition to something more official, like an actual massage therapy course."

"Or you could take the leap now," Josh said. "What would that be?"

The leap to what? I frowned and rubbed my forehead. "I don't know. Something where I can make a difference. I feel like all bodywork does, but… on a one-to-one basis. There's only so much I can do with that."

Josh hummed. "Well, you're taking a step in the right direction. While you're at college, you might just find something else you wanna do. A lot of kids do."

"I can't afford to screw around in school for years," I told him. "Especially in an advanced degree. I need something that gets me in and out in a couple years."

"Yeah, I feel you there." Josh was one of the few people who understood how much tuition cost these days, having gone off to school himself before his old man kicked the bucket and left him the place. He was also one of the few who understood what it was like to have a shitty parent who treated you like crap. For how little we seemed alike, we had a lot in common.

"Anyway, you think it's a good thing?"

"I don't want you getting arrested, man," Josh told me frankly. "So I don't like the idea of you doing anything that puts you in danger of that. As soon as you've got a record—and you know they'll try to make it a sex offense if at all possible—good luck finding other jobs."

I sighed. He was too right. "I know. I've been playing with fire. The unfairness of it all just fucking pisses me off. Life's unfair, but why treat each other like crap?"

"Wish I knew that, man," Josh told me. "Anything else on your mind?"

I hesitated for a few long moments before I sighed. "Nah. I've gotta build myself a website or something, I think. Figure out what going rates are. If I can't get a menial job…"

"Make your own," Josh filled in the blank. "Good going. Call me up if you need anything. Evan will help."

I smiled. Evan had been big in advertising, so maybe hitting him up wasn't a bad idea after all. "Yeah, I will. Thanks a lot for listening."

Once we'd said our goodbyes, it occurred to me that I didn't really know anyone in the city who I could vent to, apart from Adam—and he was a crappy listener. Maybe *that* was what I was missing—connections.

And with my totally-not-boyfriend disappearing to Singapore and elsewhere for days at a time, that situation wasn't going to get much better unless I actually came up with a plan.

No wonder I was afraid to date him—not only was it a huge

vulnerability to let someone in, but if that was my one friend and I lost him? Fuck, I couldn't let something like that hold me back from what could be a great thing.

There was a plan: find work, find friends, and maybe—just maybe—say yes to Charlie. If he stuck around that long.

Only time would tell.

21

CHARLIE

"Have you had a chance to think about it, or do you want to consider it while you're in Singapore?"

Just what I'd expected to be confronted with over the coffee machine first thing in the morning. Valerie was clearly trying to be casual about it, but the stress lines on her face were obvious. And no wonder—if we got this contract, it wouldn't just be me getting involved. A whole team mobilized at once. Maybe it was small, but the firm was, too.

Why had I fought so hard to get to the top only to waver now?

As coffee finished dripping into my mug, I finally turned away from the machine to meet her gaze. "I'll decide today. I gotta leave early to pack for the Singapore flight. Can you forward me the flight details and pickup time?"

"No problem. Harry will get right on that." She gave me a thumbs-up and strode out of the break room, leaving me smiling to myself in her wake.

She'd taken a chance on me, and she'd given me tremendous

freedom to work on things that interested or challenged me. A lot of firms weren't like that. I shouldn't be too quick to turn my back on her now.

I glanced around on the way to my desk. None of my coworkers would have thought twice about this. And hell, it wasn't like Singapore was that bad when I visited. I didn't really know how locals experienced it, but I'd never run into homophobia myself. Maybe Dubai was like that, really, for most expats.

I could well be making a mountain out of a molehill, but to what end? I wasn't lazy, that was obvious to everyone around me. It sure as hell wasn't a feeling that I couldn't do it. In-situ challenges like lack of groundwater were the most fun to work around and through.

If I said no, I'd be letting my past self down. I'd sacrificed too much in the last five years to stop just short of the… well, not the finish line, but the qualifying race.

I sighed and picked up my phone as soon as I got to my desk and set down my coffee mug. I dialed my boss's extension. As soon as Valerie picked up, I said, "Tell him yes."

She gasped. "Charlie! Final answer, before I call Alex?"

"I want to do my job," I told her. "And I'm not going to let other people's opinions of me change that."

"I could kiss you. Especially if it'll help you blend in over there."

The humor was light and playful—Valerie wasn't one of those workplace creepers. Somehow, though, in the moment, after my days of worrying? That one joke seemed much funnier than it should have. I sank into my desk chair with a laugh. "Thanks, but no thanks."

"Good man. I'll call him right now. We'll set things up. You might be heading straight there after Singapore, though."

"I'm getting back on Friday, right? I think I leave Singapore on Wednesday or something. I want to stay at home for the weekend. I told Alex already, I'm not spending a moment longer there than I have to."

It was nothing out of the ordinary, but for some reason, negotiating this made me uneasy. Like I was shirking responsibility somehow, trying to get away with the bare minimum.

"Fine, we can arrange that. I appreciate how long you'll be away."

Valerie's appreciation manifested in donuts before lunch, and letting me go home right after lunch so I could pack. By the time the Uber pulled up at my door, I'd pulled up my usual Singapore packing list, made a copy, and adjusted it for the current season. Compared to other tropical countries, the weather was pretty steady all year round, luckily.

As soon as I'd thrown everything into my travel case, I bit my lip and texted Kev.

Turns out I'm going to Singapore tonight for a week! Are you free for a goodbye kiss?

Just before I hit send, though, I winced. Fuck. It was Kev's first day of classes.

I backspaced over the last sentence and changed my message.

Turns out I'm going to Singapore tonight for a week! Wish I could see you first, but I hope today's going great :)

"Stupid life," I grumbled. Why couldn't we just be together all the time? If we lived together, there wouldn't be any of that trying to make time to meet up. I'd liked that the most about living with

Hugh. No comparing schedules and finding spare hours, especially in the depths of my busiest weeks with school.

Not what I needed to be thinking about right now.

"Okay, finish packing," I told myself as I headed off to find my laptop bag. It was going to be a nineteen-hour flight, after all. I was going to go out of my mind without something to distract me.

And since that something wasn't the taste of Kev's lips, it would have to be something boring like work.

Somehow, every time I woke up on a plane, I regretted my life choices more than at any other time. Even flying in business class, plane sleeping was a uniquely awful experience.

The windows were half-shaded, and it was way too light in the cabin. Breakfast was coming around, and I was still in pajamas.

It had to be close to nine in the morning destination time—they always waited until ridiculous hours before they dimmed the cabin for sleep. If I had my way, as soon as I set foot on a plane I'd be working on the destination's timetable. But no, they had to serve dinner and wine and let people watch movies instead.

I knew exactly why I was grumpy. I was getting used to waking up and immediately rolling over to text Kev good morning—and I'd been hoping to spend my weekend hugging him good morning, not en route to Singapore. Hopefully we had the weekend before Dubai together.

The plane had wi-fi, at least. I'd used it all evening while trying to ignore the annoying businessman on the other side of the aisle who had chosen to bring the loudest keyboard in all of creation. *Clack-clack-clack* all night long.

Planes were universally the worst part of travel, and I just thanked heaven I had a firm paying for me to travel business class. If I were in economy, I might be testing the door seal by now.

Yeah, it was stupidly late. If I'd been up two hours ago, I could have at least gotten to a normal routine in one fell swoop.

Still, despite my mood, I smiled briefly and nodded at the flight attendant who dropped off my breakfast. It wasn't their fault that planes sucked. Besides, the little plate of scrambled eggs, bacon, and toast made me smile.

It was nothing like brunch with Kev at Bubbles. Sharing a plate of toast with him, drizzling syrup over our stacks of pancakes, giggling over milkshakes like teens.

God, I wanted every morning to be like that one morning, and now I wasn't going to get a chance to experience that for a couple weeks. This was insecurity, wasn't it? That knot of worry in my chest that told me I might never get the chance again?

Calm down, worrywart, I told myself and snapped a photo of breakfast to send Kev before I dug in.

It was early morning, apparently, because I got a sleepy selfie in return. I smiled so wide my cheeks just about hurt, and everything that had been stirring up inside my chest settled again. Just seeing Kev was enough to make me relax and stop thinking the worst.

Was this separation anxiety?

Fuck, I'd hoped I was over this, but it felt a lot like the panic that had settled in my chest every time Ben or one of my parents left the country, in those first few years after Hugh's death.

"Everyone's fine," I whispered under my breath, the plane noise easily covering my thoughts so I didn't sound like a total lunatic to the guy in the next seat. It was a phrase I'd said to myself many times in the middle of the night when I woke up in a cold sweat, terrified that someone else had died suddenly. Checking their Facebook accounts and sending texts just to make sure. God, no wonder I had no friends now.

I'd lost my appetite for breakfast, so I pushed it away from me and sent Kev a followup text. *Looking cute! This plane ride will never be over.*

He sent me a picture of his Lucky Charms. *Notice the missing marshmallows?? This friendship is over.*

I had to struggle not to laugh out loud. I kind of wanted to meet Adam sometime, for all I'd heard about him. He sounded like the typical obnoxious roommate, but then the way Kev talked about him, he didn't hate him. They'd moved here together from Tennessee, after all. There had to be some redeeming quality to him.

I suggest booby-trapping the cereal.

Omg, you genius. But he'll escalate too fast, lol.

I grinned. It was kind of fun to remember what it was like to live with someone. It fit right into what I'd already been considering. *How long are you stuck together?*

Longer than two horny pigs in a blizzard.

That wasn't a mental image I wanted, but I tried not to spray orange juice across the tray table as I laughed anyway. He had a way of getting straight to the point sometimes. When I finally composed myself, I answered, *???!*

Lol. I don't know tbh. We're sticking together as long as that's what I can afford. :)

The optimism that shone through made me smile. He had the spirit of a brand-new New Yorker, and it invigorated me a little bit, too. Brooklyn had grown comfortable around me, and I'd stopped recognizing what city I really lived in. But yeah, it was a pretty fucking awesome place, even if there were so many quirks and compromises. No in-unit laundry? No Walmart? No problem.

Still, I couldn't help testing the waters.

If you guys both start making more money, though? Or someone else takes over the other room? I always had legal agreements drawn up after my freshman year experience. "Assholes," I muttered automatically under my breath. I'd been glad to move in with Hugh after that.

God, you'll have to tell me that story sometime. But yeah, we're flexible on what happens as long as we don't leave each other in the lurch. Why? Planning our future already? ;)

I blushed and fidgeted with my phone. I just kind of wanted to know it wasn't a dead end, that was all. If he was happy where he was…

It's smart to make plans.

As long as I get to help plan the wedding ;)

Now I was blushing hard.

Fuck off, I told him.

All I got was a series of laughing emoji.

I grinned as I added, *We'll be landing in a few hours. Going to school?*

Yeah, getting ready now. First day was great! Sorry I couldn't see you off though. :(

Me too. A week will feel like a long time.

His answer made me smile. *Fly back soon xox.* Then I winced. I had to admit what else was going to take me away from him, didn't I?

Um... on that note... more trip news, lol.

Haha, where to after Singapore?

Dubai. I held my breath as I sent the message and watched it get delivered.

The answer took longer than any of the messages in our conversation had. Finally, I had my reply, and it didn't do anything to soothe my nerves. *Oh I see. Why?*

I winced. *A client asked for my design lead. I'm not thrilled about the idea but I'm flying out for an initial meeting and site tour.*

Hope it goes well for you. :)

It wasn't hard to detect that Kev wasn't happy about it, but goddammit, neither was I. Normally when I made a decision there was no more anxiety or worrying about whether I'd done the right thing. But every time I thought about this project, trepidation crawled into my bones and made itself at home in the pit of my stomach.

What do you think about Dubai?

I would never go, but if you're putting your career first, it makes sense to take the chance. As long as you stay safe. I know other guys who worked and lived there no problem, but I'll worry anyway.

I smiled to myself, even if my heart twisted with guilt. I didn't want to worry him, but it felt weirdly good to have someone care enough about me that my travel choices might affect them. My parents and Hugh's parents had long since stopped paying attention to my trips, and... well, I'd gotten used to the lonely kind of globe-trotting that came with business.

When do you fly back to NYC? His subject change didn't escape me, but this was probably a better subject to talk about in person than through texts anyway.

In a week, arriving next Friday.

Wanna send me your flight details so I can keep a tab on you? :)

God, he was sweet. I immediately messaged back with my flight number.

Fab <3 Are you free between trips at least?

Yeah! I'd love to spend some of that time with you if you're free, I told him.

For you, I'm free ;)

I grinned, not sure if he'd meant that as a joke. It was true in any case. *Boy, am I glad. xox*

The flight attendants were clearing away dishes, and I nodded in thanks despite my barely-touched meal. I'd wait and have something for dinner before I crashed tonight.

Soon enough, I'd be up and at 'em, ready for these next few weeks. Like it or not, I'd made my bed, and now I had to lie in it. This was probably my last site visit on this project, at least. I could worry about the other project after I wrapped up my obligations here.

Just setting down one of my many balls in the air sounded appealing to me. It gave me something to focus on that wasn't the rapidly accumulating distance between Kev and me.

One problem at a time: just the way I liked it.

KEV

Fuck, I really needed a drink.

The first week of classes—half a week, really, since it started on Thursday for some reason—had been pretty damn shitty. I'd gotten lost on campus, and when I finally arrived late for my first class…

Well, my teacher was a hardass who wanted us to memorize a shitload of anatomy before we even touched another person. We weren't going to practice hands-on techniques until the next semester. Worst of all, I had no idea if that was normal for this degree. I'd found other weekend courses, but I was about to pay a lot in tuition to this school. The tuition deadline was next week.

I wasn't even going to learn anything I could put into immediate use, and it was so hard to slow down and remember that this was a long-term game. Not when I didn't have income coming in *now*.

And then there was the fact that something about this plan wasn't sitting right with me—but I had no other choices, besides trying to swallow my pride and take a shitty job and accept whatever the hell conditions came with it. But fuck, I'd run across half the country to escape being treated like shit. If the answer was to suck it up and accept being treated like shit in a different place, what the hell was the point of it all?

On top of that, Adam had been surly all week, probably because his steady yardwork job had wrapped up. The winter maintenance was over, and his clients had hired a real landscaping company to maintain their property during the summer. I'd suggested applying to that company or others, and he'd just grunted and stormed off.

All that, and I wouldn't even see Charlie until Friday. Before he flew to fucking Dubai, of all places. I hadn't thought he'd be the type, but most rich gay guys were like that. They thought they were immune from local laws just because they were important.

I didn't go to any place that scared the shit out of me, and I didn't want him there, but I had no claim whatsoever over his life and I knew it. All I could do was be supportive—and I did genuinely understand why he was going, when I was trying to be objective.

But I couldn't stop putting together scenarios in my head: the border guards checking his phone on entry and finding our sexy texts and throwing him in jail until deported, or him going to a gay club and getting busted in a police raid, or even more outrageous scenarios like his client finding out he was gay and threatening to turn him in to police unless he stayed and designed more buildings for them.

It was ridiculous and I knew it, but I was just afraid. I was losing control everywhere in my life at once, and all of a sudden, everything that had seemed clearcut now seemed like a bad idea—but it was too late to stop.

All of which added up to me needing a good, stiff drink and a little dancing to loosen up. Maybe in the morning, I'd be able to think clearer and stop blaming Charlie for making what was probably a good, sensible business decision. Man, I was not cut out for a traditional job.

Before I could fall down the rabbit hole of "I'm never going to find a real job that doesn't make me feel dirty" and end up in the wonderland of creative horrible endings that suggested for me, I grabbed my keys and phone. "Going out!" I called.

Adam grunted back at me, and I rolled my eyes and strode out.

Friction was only a ten-minute walk from our place, which was one of the best things about our location. We had laundromats—not that we used them, when Adam wasn't being a dick—and small supermarkets, cafes, a bookshop… it felt like a real neighborhood. It wasn't even a whitewashed hipster central like a lot of areas seemed.

I was invisible in the crowd. As well as I knew the neighborhood, thousands of others lived or worked or played around here. It was impossible to know the neighborhood faces, and I still wasn't quite used to that.

For the first time, I started to wonder if moving here had been the right thing to do.

New York City was a metropolis like none other. I missed the open skies and fields, the sunshine and fresh air on my face. What the hell was a kid like me doing in a place like this?

Sure, there were good things about the city—and Brooklyn in particular. But I'd traded the feeling of grass between my toes for the electric sunshine of the city. The 24/7 lights always managed to sneak through the gaps of my blinds. It was like I could never quite escape the reality of where I was.

"Okay, I *really* need a drink," I addressed the bouncer, who grinned and waved me in. Two shots of Jack later, I at least had something to distract me—the burning liquid that slid down my throat.

It took me a few more minutes before I really started to unwind and notice my surroundings, like time had passed in a few heartbeats instead of half an hour.

The place was maybe a third full, which was pretty good for this early in the evening. Once, I would have felt a thrill of excitement at the possibilities. I could be a little more overt when the club was busy, but when it was quiet, I didn't want the bartenders' attention drawn to me by a harsh rejection or a tattletale.

Now, all I wanted was a quiet evening—the kind where you could strike up a conversation with whoever was next to you. Someone who might understand a little of my life, who I didn't have to explain shit to first. Since finding that was hard, I resigned myself to dancing instead of chatting. Different medicine, same effect— forgetting my problems.

The dance floor was already starting to fill in, and I had no qualms being one of the first on it. I didn't have to push through a crowd yet to find a place to dance to the beat. Every song made my mood improve, even with just a couple of drinks in me. By the time I was working up a sweat, I was smiling.

There was liberation in collective movement, and a kind of joy that I didn't have to say a word to share. We all knew the soundtrack, from Britney to yet another It's Raining Men remix, and the DJ tonight was on top of his game.

"Oh, hey," I called out with a wave and grin when a familiar face passed by.

Darren stopped for a moment and looked around. As soon as he spotted me, he shook his head and kept walking. "No, hon."

I opened and closed my mouth for a moment as he headed to the other side of the dance floor. I hadn't even been coming on to him, which made his reaction even more of a slap in the face. I'd never slept with him—we'd gotten close a few times, but he'd never been willing to pay and I'd never been willing to call it a freebie.

Like that, my mood crashed again.

"Fucking fine."

My cheeks burned with humiliation. This hurt worse than it would if I'd been hitting on him, actually. A simple "not tonight" or "not my type" was easy to write off, and I'd gotten very used to rejection at work. But just wanting to say hi to someone I'd seen around, even chatted with, for months, and having that shut down so coldly?

It wasn't the last time, either. Every time I spotted a familiar face and smiled, he turned away or pretended not to see me. The only exception was one of my clients, who pushed through the crowd to get to me.

"Working tonight, baby?" Jack smirked at me. "You haven't been answering your phone." He wasn't bad-looking—another one of those guys in suits who couldn't make time for a real boyfriend, but wanted the experience or illusion sometimes. I'd gone out with him a few times, slept with him every time, and I didn't regret it.

Now, though, I couldn't even muster a smile back at him. I had nothing against him, but my own gut was still twisted too tight from the string of rejections. "Sorry. I'm getting out of the business." I had to speak louder than I'd like over the music in order to avoid leaning in close to him and presenting an opportunity to grope me.

A surprised expression crossed Jack's face. "Got a boyfriend?"

Shit. I hesitated. My first instinct was to defend myself and say no, it wasn't like that. But maybe it *was* like that, just a little bit.

"Hah. Lucky guy. Let me know if he doesn't appreciate you enough," Jack told me, and then headed for the bar.

I stared after him for a moment and then shook my head. The mood was all wrong tonight. It was one of those nights that, if I stayed out, I'd just regret more and more. So instead, I pushed through the crowd that had gathered on the dance floor and headed outside.

All I wanted tonight was community—to be around people like me, and talk to them, and feel like I was at home. Instead, they didn't have time for me. Because of what I'd done, presumably. It was like a scarlet brand I couldn't take off, and knowing that I didn't have another career I actually *wanted* to do lined up…

That was the other realization I was trying to avoid: massage was not where my heart lay. I'd only thought of it because it was the easy, obvious option to transition out of my old life. But now, my old life was starting to feel more like shackles than the freedom I'd thought it was buying me.

Who the hell was I, anyway? It felt like I was a dozen different people, and none of them could agree on what was next. I just knew what I *didn't* want to do: compromise my integrity, or end up broke and homeless, or end up in a situation where I had to make that choice—again.

Rather than drown my sorrows in whiskey, I headed next door to Bubbles. At least there was always a place here for me.

As I walked in, I stifled my groan.

The place was always friendly unless I had the same waitress I'd run into several times, who had never been nice to me. Of course she was working tonight. But I didn't want to head back home and deal with a grumpy Adam swearing at the TV.

The hangover special would kill some time, at least. I swallowed my eye roll when the waitress greeted me without a smile and moved me from the booth of my choice in the window to one at the back, far away from the windows. Like she was worried I was advertising my wares in the window.

"Saving that for someone special?" I half-joked, trying to convey my annoyance without getting confrontational.

"Ya got a problem with that?" She was the picture of a stereotype, popping her bubblegum as she propped a hand on her hip, but then again this whole damn place was. All the bright red seats, counter accents, and menus, and the Americana on the walls, mixed with vintage gay kitsch.

Swallowing the insult to my already battered pride, I raised my hands. "Didn't realize it's not a seat-yourself place anymore, that's all."

"Mmhmm." She kept an eyebrow raised. "It's sit here or get out."

It was the closest table to the kitchen, and no doubt the noisiest, but I gave in. I felt like I was doing a lot of that lately. I didn't want to lose what precious spaces I had, and tonight of all nights, I needed them. "Sure, fine." I slid into the booth. "Hangover special with black coffee."

"Sure." She headed to the kitchen, and I tried not to listen in. Instead, I pulled out my phone and fiddled with it, but there was nothing very interesting there to occupy my attention.

Hours ahead of me in Singapore, Charlie was in the middle of his work day. Was I just being needy, wanting to talk to him now when he was busy with things that were undoubtedly more important than me?

God, I was being a whiny, self-centered asshole. He deserved a good career, even if that career took him to places I worried about, and took him away from me when I was having a bad day. I hadn't survived this many years on my own only to become dependent on someone else.

Vulnerable at their loss, more specifically.

I nodded at the waitress when she dropped off coffee. I liked my food spit-free, after all, even if she seemed to hate me for some reason I couldn't work out. And having just been on the other end of that shit, I couldn't bring myself to yell at an employee, even if they were treating me like crap.

A shadow fell across my table and I looked up. At least my mood was already at rock bottom, so Darren's appearance couldn't ruin my day for the second time. "Yeah?"

"Hey. Can I join you?" I shrugged noncommittally, and Darren slid in with his cup of coffee. "You're looking pretty down. Why you hiding at the back? You're always up front!"

"Apparently that's where they put the whores." I couldn't bring myself to lower my voice in case she heard me. "I tried to sit at the front and she moved me."

Darren blinked and then leaned back to see into the kitchen. "Hey, Enrique? You guys taking reservations?"

A peal of laughter and then a hearty, "Fuck off," was his answer.

Darren shrugged and turned back to me. "Talk to Jared when he's in."

"I don't wanna get in trouble. Uh, get *her* in trouble." The slip made me cringe. Maybe that was closer to the truth than I'd meant. "Or start anything. I'm not ashamed of what I did."

Darren frowned. "Did?"

"I'm quitting hustling. Dunno what I'm doing next." I sipped my coffee, not bothering to hide the moody scowl. "Now I just need a face transplant so people will give me the time of day."

"I'm sorry," Darren sighed. "I shouldn't have been a dick earlier. I assumed you were..." he trailed off with a guilty expression. "Looking for business," he finished when I didn't interrupt.

I didn't have the energy to console him or pretend it had been okay. I shrugged. "Well, I wasn't. Just wanted to say hi."

"Yeah." Darren looked at me closely and then leaned in. "What's wrong? Nothing bad happened, did it?"

I hadn't expected him to care. I gave him a slight smile and shook my head. "Just trying to make a legal life for myself. Do something more interesting now that I've got the option. It was good for me while it lasted, but..." I shifted uncomfortably. "If not good for me, whatever. It got me through."

"Fuck," Darren murmured. "I had no idea you were having a rough time."

I wanted to defend my old career, but my ability to bullshit was at an all-time low. It felt like life was slowly sliding a rug out from under me, and whatever I grabbed just gave way. "And I'm into this guy who's too good for me. I'm just a nobody trying to make ends meet. I was screwed up way before I started screwing for money. And now I'm... just generally screwed all over." I choked up and folded my arms tightly, trying to get myself under control as I stared at the table.

Fuck. I was not having a meltdown about this—especially not in front of an acquaintance I barely knew.

"Hey," Darren said gently. Then, he did something I really hadn't expected—he got up and moved to my side of the booth, and he put an arm around me.

Even more surprising was my reaction to being held. For all I'd told Charlie he was skin-hungry, so was I. Once I got used to the touch, my muscles unknotted and I slumped into the hug, resting my forehead on his shoulder. He was even rubbing my back gently.

The waitress cleared her throat loudly and set plates down in front of us so hard I half-expected them to crack.

I tried to pull away, but Darren held me tightly. "What's your problem?" he snapped.

"You know what."

"No," he said, his voice still razor-sharp. "I don't. Tell me."

"The only business on these premises is Bubbles, all right? Take it to a hotel or back alley or *wherever*," she said. I didn't have to look up to hear the sneer in her voice.

I was perfectly capable of ripping into her, but before I could gather my strength, Darren let go and stood up. I wiped my eyes as I gripped the back of the booth to keep myself both calm and upright now that my support had abruptly vanished.

She stared at him. "We got a problem, mister? I gonna have to call the cops?" she taunted. Behind her, Enrique poked his head out of the kitchen and stared. The diner was quiet now, so everyone heard when she added, "Bet *he* wouldn't like that."

"Yeah, I've got a problem," Darren told her icily. "You can't treat him like shit."

"Jared told me what he is."

"It's none of your fucking business, is what he is," Darren snapped. "If you have a problem with a couple gays hugging, you're working at the wrong place. He's more than whatever you think he is, and I bet Jared wouldn't want you treating him like crap."

My heart was in my throat. I'd never dealt well with raised voices, and I was starting to shake.

All I could think of was being screamed at. *You're dead to us, Kev. Get out. Forever.*

I touched his arm. "It's okay," I mumbled.

"No, hon. It isn't." Darren shook his head, and I gave in. The emotion choking my throat was gratitude. I was grateful for the support, and that she was facing off with someone else and not just me, terrified of losing my safe place in this community…

Honestly, if he wanted to absolve his guilt by standing up for me, I wasn't going to stop him. It wasn't even about *this* in particular—it had just been a long time since anyone had stood up for me in any way at all.

"Sounds like you're causing a disturbance," she murmured with a smug grin.

"If you call the cops, I'll call Jared," Darren retorted.

Enrique's head was snapping back and forth between them like a tennis match. When she turned to him and gestured toward the phone, he didn't move.

"Call the police, bitch," she snapped at Enrique.

Enrique's brows climbed. He was only about her age, but his confidence came across even in the way he stood. He folded his arms. "The fuck did you call me?"

"Numbnuts, I'll beat your ass later. These assholes are a bigger problem."

Enrique laughed out loud. "I'd like to see you try."

"The way I see it," Darren interjected, "one person here's causing all the problems." He moved past her for the door.

"Good. Get out!" she called after him and then turned her gaze to me. It was hard. She'd dug her heels in now, past the point of reasoning. "You too. Go get your money off him, you *whore*."

Before I could do anything, though, Enrique snorted. "Stay where you are," he told me. "Darren isn't leaving."

"Yeah, he is, fuckface." She gestured to the door, and I had to agree with her, even if I wouldn't say as much. Then she paused, an expression of horror crossing her face.

"Uh huh." Enrique smirked and looked around the place. "Lots of regulars in here tonight. Hope you're ready to stand by your words, 'cause I ain't putting my neck on the line for you, *fuckface*."

Before they could get into an actual catfight, the door opened and Darren came in again, with Jared—the owner of Bubbles—in sweatpants and a t-shirt, hot on his heels, and looking pissed.

How the hell he'd found Jared so fast, I didn't know, but the gasps were audible as he came in. Most patrons had abandoned any pretense of ignoring the unfolding drama.

"What the fuck is this shit?" Jared addressed us, a scowl on his face. His hair was pushed up at weird angles, and he looked like he'd just been in bed.

"These two," the waitress gestured between Darren and me, "were getting it on."

"Really?" Jared looked at me, raising an eyebrow. Enrique laughed in the background, and Jared pointed at him. "Were they?"

"I wish. Would've made a better show," Enrique said with a shrug.

I shook my head, my cheeks burning. "I was just… he sat next to me and hugged me. I'd never…" It was hard to hold back the mix of emotions now. I was still shaking, staring at Jared in a silent plea not to throw me out.

"You know what he is," the waitress snapped.

"Tara, shut up," Jared told her. He looked around and pointed at a guy sitting at a table—someone I didn't even recognize—and pointed at him. "Billy?" He was a total queen rocking silvery platinum hair and a gorgeous red floral wrap.

"That guy," Billy pointed at me, "was pretty upset. Darren hugged him and then that—" he pointed at the waitress and glared before continuing, "*gorgeous* individual told them to break it up. Told him to take his business to a back alley."

The thundercloud gathering in Jared's expression was frightening to watch for someone like me, who didn't deal well with conflict. I found Darren standing next to me, and I grabbed his hand to keep myself from running out the door.

"It's okay," Darren whispered and pushed me gently to sit in the booth again and scooted in next to me, keeping himself between everyone else and me. I could have cried, I was so grateful for the physical shelter.

All I wanted was Charlie there, shielding me from everyone's stares, joking to cheer me up, holding my hand.

Fuck. This was not the moment to think about all that.

"Tara, with me. Now." Jared stomped toward the kitchen and pointed for her to keep going past us. He stopped and turned to us, his body language softening. "Sorry you guys had to go through that. I can't apologize enough."

I gaped. I hadn't expected that answer. Half of me still felt like I was kind of sneaking around here, somewhere I shouldn't be, and I'd been about to get caught out.

Darren squeezed my shoulders. "It's fine," he murmured again. "Jared's solid."

I could hardly tell up from down to know who to trust, but my gut instinct said Darren—and thus Jared—was safe. I just nodded slightly and managed a smile. "It's… thank you, sir."

"No, thank you. You come here a lot." Jared reached out to offer a hand. "You belong here."

Fuck. My cheeks were hot and wet, and I found myself staring at his hand instead of making eye contact as I took his hand. He had no way of knowing how much I'd needed to hear that. "Thanks," I whispered as my voice cracked, and I shook firmly.

Then Jared nodded and headed into the kitchen while Enrique snickered and crept in after them.

When I finally wiped my eyes and looked around, everyone was pretending not to look at us again. Conversations were resuming, and the silence was no longer squeezing in around me like a ring of spikes. Darren hugged me hard around the shoulders again and gestured. "Eat up."

The idea of eating seemed laughable, but my stomach grumbled and reminded me that those hash browns *did* look really good. I picked at first, but as we listened to the rumble of voices and clattering pans in the kitchen, my appetite slowly returned.

Finally, Darren mumbled, "So. This is a night to remember."

I laughed weakly and washed down my late-night meal with a swig of coffee. "You're telling me. But… um… why'd you even come talk to me?"

Darren shrugged. "You looked like you needed a listening ear. I wish someone had done that for me, so I try to do it when I'm not being a massive dick."

I laughed again, this one coming to me a little stronger. "You made up for it."

"Nah. One right doesn't make one wrong... right..." Darren waved his fork. "Whatever. You get the idea. So, spill the beans. Anything else I can help with while I'm kicking ass and taking names?"

I dabbed my lips with flimsy napkins and shook my head. "I've just been having one of those come to Jesus moments about my relationship. Not quite relationship. Fling. I don't know."

"He doesn't wanna be serious?"

"I'm more of the problem," I admitted. I trusted him enough now to talk about it, even if I wasn't going to admit to who I was talking about. If Darren only knew it was the guy he'd introduced to me. How weird life was. "I thought it was 'cause I don't trust that love exists, but... I don't know. Maybe I'm just afraid he can hurt me."

In this mood I was still emotionally raw, if not actually shaking. I was talking without filtering my words first, and I was surprising even myself.

"Maybe," Darren agreed. "That's always the risk. But you don't need the answers right away. You've had a hell of a night." He clapped my shoulder. "Give yourself a break."

Before I could thank him for listening, Jared reappeared, looking distinctly disgruntled. "Tara's no longer with us, effective immediately. I'm taking over her tables. Also, I seem to have lost your check," he told me. "Don't wait around to pay. You either, Darren."

It took me a second to understand before I blushed. "Oh. Um. Thanks." He really didn't have to, but it spoke well of him that he was putting my meal on the house.

Jared shrugged it off. "I got too much other shit to do to worry about a couple breakfasts. Go away so I can turn over your table," he waved a hand at us. I had to try not to smile. There was that grumpy New Yorker kindness again—an enigma I was slowly growing to understand.

"I'm going home to get some sleep," Darren said and patted my shoulder. "You?"

I nodded. After all that, I was ready for bed, whether or not Adam was going all Eeyore back at home. "And me."

"Come on. Let's head out."

I had to admit that having him by my side made it easier to escape through the whole length of the diner without worrying about whether people were looking at me. I wasn't normally self-conscious, but having my business broadcast was nothing I ever wanted.

When we were on the sidewalk, the chill of late April just touching my exposed arms, Darren wrapped me up in one more hug. "You okay tonight?"

"I'll be fine," I assured him but relaxed into the hug, hugging him back tightly. Something about the simple contact bolstered me in a way I hadn't known I was missing. I was going to have to make an effort to keep getting this kind of touch.

"Don't stop believing in you," Darren murmured into my ear. "Or this city will break you."

I pulled back slowly and nodded, finally able to meet his gaze. "I won't," I promised. I'd been pretty damn close, but he was right. I didn't move here to give up at the first sign of trouble. I was just the average twenty-three-year-old kid, trying to figure out who I was and what to do about it.

With friends on my side, maybe things could shake out okay. As long as I got on the same page with Charlie as soon as possible, whether or not it put my heart in danger.

"And for God's sake, don't break both your hearts when you like each other already," Darren murmured, avoiding my gaze. He looked up as if searching for stars. Fat chance of that, in Brooklyn. "Even if that's all you're used to doing... screwing up is a self-fulfilling prophecy." For the first time, I wanted to ask if he was okay, but Darren was already turning away. "Have a good night," he added.

"Y-You too. Thanks again. For everything."

He just raised a hand and beat a swift retreat, leaving me standing there for a moment and watching the bouncer search girls' handbags on the way into Friction.

The confrontation had seemed like the biggest deal in the world just ten or twenty minutes ago, but life carried on just outside the door like nothing had ever happened. Maybe Darren was right, and I could reinvent myself. Brooklyn was big enough, and I was young enough.

All I had to do was believe it was possible.

23

CHARLIE

"This has been a long road."

Nobody knew that better than Vince. I'd cursed the project manager in my thoughts many times, but ultimately he'd managed to pull the team together to execute my vision and the client's specifications. A little piece of the Singapore skyline had changed forever because of him.

I held up my glass. "It sure has. To all of us," I toasted them. The local beer was good—and this was the first time I'd indulged since flying over here. I didn't tend to drink much anyway, but I hadn't wanted to make the jet lag any worse or interfere with my ability to think clearly.

The biggest perk and drawback of being part of a small firm like mine was that we were involved in every step of the process. If I left for a bigger firm—of whom there were plenty in New York City—that wouldn't happen. I'd just be designing all day long, and never seeing how my designs got bastardized further down the line.

After years of drafting on computers, the chance to actually get involved in the hands-on was so damn welcome. The internship period was the most painful for an architect, unless you were the kind of weirdo who liked drawing tiny details over and over all day long. We didn't do headline-grabbing skyscrapers, but what we did, we did well. This hotel was going to be a pleasant *and* beautiful place to stay.

I'd been avoiding thinking about the next project to begin all week. I was never gonna make principal before fifty if I turned down projects. That was just the way it had to be.

This was a time to celebrate construction drawing to a close. From here on out, it was just finishing details, and everything had been successfully sourced. Vince was in charge of making sure all the subcontractors came together to deliver and install everything correctly, but there was no more design work to do.

"Cheers!" someone called out, and everyone drank. We'd taken turns toasting ourselves all evening. Good thing we were at my hotel bar. They'd been accommodating of me, since I'd tried to insist I couldn't go out partying. Instead, they'd brought the party to me.

"I'm happy to forget about this week," said Vince with a laugh, clapping my shoulder. "You've been on fire, though. We couldn't have pulled through without you."

"Thanks," I said with a grin and toasted him for another sip.

"But you look a million miles away. Looking forward to getting home?"

I nodded. It was more than that—so much more. The week had indeed passed in a blur of site meetings, last-minute drafting until late at night, and then redrafting in the morning when the fucking construction crew fucked up. I drew a breath and let go of my resentment over that. It was over now.

But I'd spent the week thinking of Kev in all those few spare moments. Even my favorite Singaporean foods couldn't pull me out of my funk. Nothing tasted like kissing Kev, and no comfy hotel duvet was like snuggling into him at night.

I had to face the fact that I'd fallen hard and fast. Way harder than was smart, and way faster than was believable. I'd taken my time to get to know Hugh—our love had been the kind that slowly grew over months.

What I had with Kev? It felt like I'd known him my whole damn life and just picked up where we left off when we first met.

"Are you coming back when we hand over the keys?"

"You've got to!" called someone else, leaning over Vince and giving me a thumbs-up.

I normally tried to be there for that meeting, when we celebrated what we'd accomplished and I could see what everything looked like totally finished, dusted, and polished.

"Bringing anyone? A new wife?" Vince added with a sly smile. When I stared, he shrugged. "You have that look like you miss someone."

"Yeah, I do," I said slowly, then shook my head. It was that usual conversation where guys bragged about their wives and those traveling tried not to say that they missed them, in a manly way.

This was the personal phase of a work relationship, when I couldn't change the subject back to the project at hand. I had nothing to hide behind.

"I'm sort of single," I told him with a shake of my head. "So I'd be surprised if I got married before this place is ready. I'd better not!" I added, laughing.

He hastily rapped the bar top, even if it wasn't wooden. "From your lips to God's ear. But, dude. *Sort of* single?"

I didn't want them thinking I was playing a few people at once, whether they were thinking of girls or guys. "We're going on dates, but not really dating."

Vince hummed and nodded. "Congrats, man. Good luck with it. What's she like?"

It took all I had not to brag about Kev. I knew the chances were slim I'd ever get in trouble for promoting a homosexual lifestyle. I wasn't exactly hiding myself in the office, either. But on a construction site? "One of the kindest, most optimistic, and most driven people I've met," was all I said.

"Cheers to that."

More toasting, more drinking, and my mind was wandering far too much for my own good. I was feeling guilty about my non-answer, and about shrugging out of answering.

If I was shooting to make partner someday, or even own my own firm... well, what would happen if it became public knowledge? I wasn't living in the closet, but with my sexuality on display on Wikipedia or somewhere, what the hell would happen to projects like this? And the next one?

It was a thorny mess of issues I'd just avoided addressing in the last five or more years. Plus, nobody cared about the sexuality of the junior architect stuck behind a computer day in and day out. It was only out here, in the field, where I'd fought so hard to get to, that it mattered.

Telling people was ripping a Band-Aid off, and I wasn't ready for that. I couldn't very well stick it back on again afterward.

I made my excuses after another hour or so, shaking hands over and over again before I finally managed to peel myself away from the whole group.

I paced the elevator as I waited to arrive at my floor. I hadn't even had more than two beers despite my pretenses of drinking to socialize, so it wasn't even the urge to move around that so often came with being drunk. I was just restless after being cooped up in offices or hunched over my laptop for most of the week, troubleshooting this critical last structural construction phase.

I wasn't exactly feeling social, but I needed to do something. "Fuck this," I muttered by the time I got to my room. I felt like going for a run, but at this hour? No chance. On the other hand, the hotel had a gym… and a pool.

Now that I was thinking of swimming, I remembered throwing my swimsuit into my suitcase at the last moment. Nobody else was likely to be around at this hour. Though I hadn't deliberately held back from drinking, I was now glad I hadn't, so I could safely go in by myself without risking a stupid drowning incident.

Most visitors to this hotel were here for business, so the bar was busy right now and I was willing to bet the pool was quiet.

Or, I could entertain myself some other way. I caught myself glancing at the clock and doing math to figure out what time it was in New York City. I was going to see Kev soon enough. Why the hell did I need to call him now? He was busy with new classes, no doubt. Setting up a whole new life for himself.

And I was proud of him for it. Seeing him go for what he wanted inspired me to do the same, however uncomfortable it might be in the short-term.

Swimming was a much better idea.

I changed into my swimsuit, wrapped up in the hotel bathrobe, and shoved the one-size-fits-all hotel slippers on before grabbing my towel. At the last moment, I remembered my room key. Just as well—it would be pretty embarrassing to parade in front of my coworkers, bare legs and all, to get another key from the front desk.

The chlorine-thick air greeted me before I was even in the pool hall. By the time I chose a locker for my stuff and padded across the spotless, dry tiles toward the pool, my lungs were protesting.

Still, a vigorous swim would get my heart working and maybe take the edge off my anger and guilt. As I set off swimming laps, I indulged in some of the anger that had stewed since that casual chat about my "wife" an hour or two ago. I hated pretending I was straight, or even just lying by omission. Plus, it made me feel like I was hiding Kev. And I was, if I let myself think about it.

Two strokes quicker than my usual speed, I reached the end of the pool, turned, and set off again in a backstroke.

I don't have to tell anyone a thing, I reminded myself as my breathing settled into a quick, deep rhythm. I didn't owe the world an explanation of my sexuality or romantic life. I sure as hell hadn't dragged my problems into the office with me when I'd been lucky enough to score and keep the internship despite all the other hell going on in my life at the time. There was no reason to make a big deal of it now.

Except there was, and I had the feeling that reason wouldn't take kindly to being told I couldn't talk about him. Quite rightly, too. I'd be pissed off if he were still in his old job and tried to hide my existence. I'd want people to know he was mine, and vice versa.

Wait, no. That was not a parallel, and now I was jealous about some hypothetical man... jealous over a man I had no right to claim as my own.

I groaned as I smacked the back of my hand on the concrete side of the pool. "Motherfucker!" At least I was alone, so I didn't have to apologize for my French to any small children.

I clung to the edge of the pool at first, and then trod water awkwardly as I rubbed my hand. I really should pay more attention to where I was going.

Oddly appropriate. That was how I'd found myself in this situation with Kev. I hadn't really paid attention to my destination until I'd passed the place I'd thought we were going. And now we couldn't get off this ride—and I didn't want to.

I was lonely, though. That was the truth behind the gnawing ache, more so than either guilt or anger. I just wanted Kev here, by my side. Whether or not I was supposed to want that was irrelevant.

My career had never been stacked against my love life before, and I'd never considered that I couldn't just add love to my existing life without making changes. That fact seemed so obvious now, and if I'd known it beforehand, I sure as hell wouldn't have started this.

But then I wouldn't have met Kev, and I'd choose to do it again knowing that.

I had a foot each in two worlds which seemed incompatible. Now they were slipping apart from each other. Which foot would I pick up?

I kicked off from the end wall of the pool again, and I swam.

24

KEV

This was either the smartest or stupidest thing I'd ever done. No wonder people said love made us all go crazy. It had only taken a week away from Charlie—totally unable to see him, only hearing from him once or twice a day—to realize that I wanted to show him what he meant to me.

And, if he'd still have me, I wanted to give this a shot between us.

I clutched the flowers against my chest tighter, ignoring the smiles and jealous expressions of onlookers as I jostled my way into the JFK arrivals area.

His plane had landed a few minutes late, and then he'd have to make it through customs and pick up his bag. He was probably stuck in that annoying phase of travel.

Now that I saw people waiting with placards, I kind of wished I'd thought to do that myself. I could have done some cheesy *Will you date me?* sign. We'd probably wind up in some Humans of New York photo post that way.

Then again, the chance of hearing a *no* was worrying. Better do it this way after all.

I fidgeted, my eye automatically drawn to each and every person who walked past. Some were scanning the crowd, looking for someone to reunite with. Many, though, were just heading straight out. That was the saddest thing to me—knowing nobody was waiting for you.

Maybe someone was waiting at home, but still…

There he was!

Charlie was tired, with strangely wrinkle-free trousers, but rumpled t-shirt. His gaze was on the exit, and I knew I only had a few seconds to get his attention or I'd have to run awkwardly after him.

"Charlie!" Well, that had been a little louder than I'd meant. Several heads turned to me, and one cab driver standing nearby jumped. I was too distracted by Charlie turning to me to apologize to anyone else, though.

"What…" Charlie trailed off, stopping dead in the middle of the zone and staring at me. A few travelers tutted and strode around him with wheeling suitcases. And then he smiled, and his face lit up, and my heart melted.

"Over here." I waved my flowers at him.

He was grinning as he hurried across to me, cutting off several other people as he leaned over the barrier to hug me. I barely got the flowers out of the way in time to avoid crushing them. "Oh, my God. Kev!"

I'd had a whole thing planned to say—*I missed you and I wanted to say welcome home. By the way, do you want to date me?* "Surprise," was all I could come up with.

It was enough.

"Hi. I *am* surprised." Charlie laughed, the sound hoarse but light-hearted.

He finally pulled back and I offered the flowers before realizing his hands were full with his briefcase and rolling suitcase. "Oh, I can help carry them, though. I didn't think about that."

Charlie balanced the bags on top of one another and took the flowers. His expression was just glowing with an expression I hadn't quite seen before. "You planned this all week? You sneaky man."

I beamed, proud of myself. "Yep." When I'd asked for his flight details, I'd had a vague idea of doing it, but it had only become a pressing must-do when I'd realized...

Well, when I realized how I felt.

"Come on. Let's go home," I told him, nodding toward the subway.

He grinned and shook his head. "I've got a car booked. I'm sure they won't mind two. Let's go."

Separating from him for even enough time to walk around the crowds on each side of the barrier was the hardest thing I'd done all week. When we met again, he'd looped the briefcase handles around the rolling suitcase so he had a hand free. Instead of taking the flowers, though, he took my free hand.

I beamed up at him. "Welcome home, by the way."

"Thank you. I'm the luckiest man here." He looked down at the flowers and then back at me. "I... I don't even know what to say." It was rare that he gushed, and I was walking on top of the world with pleasure that I'd managed to pull it off. He deserved to feel like someone was waiting for him.

"No, I am. I missed you like hell," I admitted. "It's been quite a week."

As we found his driver, explained that we were both coming in the car, and climbed into the back seat together, I gave him bits and pieces of the story: I'd stopped college classes before the tuition deadline and I was in the process of exploring other majors.

"Maybe psychology?" I offered. "Counseling?"

Charlie, bless him, didn't bat an eye at hearing that I'd dropped the whole idea of massage and I was veering wildly down another path. "You'd be great at that."

"You're not even fazed." I wasn't sure if I was more surprised or amused. "Not even a bit."

He grinned sheepishly. "I wondered if massage was really what you wanted to do, to be honest. But I didn't want to discourage you."

I squeezed his hand across the gulf of the backseat between us. "I feel the same way about... well." About *his* job. But the last thing he probably wanted to discuss was that.

He'd caught it, though. His lips crooked into a little smile. "May as well tell me. You're pissed about Dubai, aren't you?"

I blushed. It wasn't really my place to tell him off for a career decision. "I'm just... worried about your safety. And I don't like the idea of supporting human rights violations."

"Me neither." He surprised me at how much he lit up, his expression suddenly intense and passionate. "The developer says he's working to guarantee all labor is freely chosen—and that things aren't as bad as the exposés say—but I don't know. I couldn't live with myself if people were being treated like shit just for *my* step up the career ladder."

Oh, fuck. I might actually have loved him a little more now. That was why he wasn't at all disappointed in me for quitting the grocery store after a day, then. He got what I meant. I'd never met someone so practical, yet apparently, idealistic, too.

"Yes," I breathed out. I was safe to say how I really felt with him. "Exactly. So why do it at all?"

He recoiled and pressed his lips together, staring out the car window for a few moments before he looked back at me. "I've been waiting for this big break for too long to fuck it up now."

"Unless something better is around the corner." I wasn't going to give up yet.

He shook his head. "I doubt it. I've been through my internship and my junior years. Five years," he reminded me. "Five years of shitty menial jobs. The drafting nobody wants to do. I learned a lot, don't get me wrong. But this is much more interesting... fulfilling, too. I get to see it all take shape. And this is the first time someone's asked specifically for *me*."

I frowned at him. I expected better of him than to take a job because of his ego, but I could understand his career progression worries. "Should we talk about this when we get back to my place? Or, um, yours?"

He'd lit up, though. "To yours?" he echoed. "Your house?"

I squirmed, my grip tightening on his hand. "Well, I've been thinking about stuff... and we can't really date if I'm, you know, hiding part of me from you."

Thank God I'd already quit school, or I couldn't have cleaned the place from top to bottom first. Adam's mess was contained to his room, and he was out all day anyway. Not working, but he wouldn't say what he was up to—he was still being moody. The rest of the place looked as presentable as it could.

"Yes," was all he said. "I'd love to."

There was a kind of unspoken understanding between us, like our energies had naturally synced up again the moment we'd touched after a week apart.

I leaned forward and gave the driver my address, and then we sat back and held hands, watching the world pass by. The sheer size of the city was easy to forget until it took this damn long to get from the airport to my home. He was quiet, too, seemingly lost in thought.

But we didn't need to talk every single moment. Just being alone together was okay with me. Another piece slowly sliding into place in my life, until I couldn't imagine how I'd lived without it— without him.

"Fuck!" I was too choked to say anything else, and not in the way I'd been anticipating for the whole car ride home.

We'd barely made it into the front hallway before I spotted patterned shards across the carpet, distinctively radiating from the kitchen. The only way a cup could have broken and flown into pieces so far was...

"Kev!" Charlie tried to grab my hand and hold me back, but with my shoes on, I didn't hesitate to sprint across the hallway carpet into the kitchen.

It was a disaster. Like a crime scene, shards sprayed out in a blast radius from the wall that had once held my precious shelf of cups.

One of the brackets had crashed to the floor. Even the wooden shelf had cracked with the force of the impact.

A few of the cups had clearly hit just right so they just chipped or cracked cleanly, but most of them…

Most of them were write-offs.

It was a stupid thing to cry about. Altogether, I'd probably spent twenty bucks on the collection. But I'd painstakingly gathered them from thrift stores across Brooklyn in the last four months. I associated each with a particular memory. Some more than others, because anything cracked or chipped, I'd carefully fixed with gold glue, like the Japanese art of kintsugi.

The philosophy was beautiful to me: an object that had been put back together was seen as more beautiful than something shiny and new. I'd always hoped someone would see me the same way.

Those cracked pieces I'd painstakingly restored to useful glory were in too many shards across the floor to process.

Gradually, I became aware of a pricking pain in my foot. I cursed and hopped off that foot, leaning on the kitchen counter as I wiped at my stupid eyes.

"Oh, no." Charlie frowned as he picked his way around the stream of shards that had hit the carpet. He tried to scoot inside, but there were too many pieces lying everywhere to do so without stepping on them. "Shit."

Grief was very rapidly dwindling, and my chest was tight. "Adam!"

No sign of him.

"Adam, if you're in your fucking room, I swear to God, I will kill you."

Still no answer, and Charlie gently cleared his throat and glanced down the hall to the bedroom. Adam's room was visible from the doorway, but not the kitchen where I stood. "There's a bedroom there with nobody in it."

"Good, or I'd fucking—I swear, this has to be him."

I'd just about had it with Adam and his clumsiness. Breaking cheap mugs was one thing, but *my* shit? And then skedaddling out of the place? Like he could just skip accountability, yet again, for everything he fucked up in life?

Oh, I was going to wring his neck.

"*Mea cupa?*" Charlie offered. He was smiling as he reached out to touch my arm.

I jerked away from him and flipped him off. "It's not funny." Fuck, now I was crying again. It was only a few stupid cups, and I was hurting myself—and him—over them.

But, like a spring-loaded Jack-in-the-box, my feelings didn't seem to want to go back in the box now that I was admitting to them. And I was pissed.

"Sorry. It's just Latin," Charlie said, frowning again.

"I know what fucking *mea culpa* fucking means," I swore, supporting myself on the counter as I took one more look around the carnage. Once again, I was gonna be the person sweeping all of this up. "I'm not some redneck trailer trash who just landed in the city."

Charlie's jaw dropped. "Kev. No, I—"

"No, forget it," I moaned, pressing my hands to my face. The poor guy was standing there with his rolling suitcase and flowers and I was yelling at him because my roommate was a giant dick who couldn't keep his feet straight. "I'm sorry. *Fuck.* I thought my week of bad luck was over."

"Dunno how much bad luck a bunch of cups is," Charlie said, but he'd opened the broom cupboard and pulled the broom out. "I'll help. You stay still. You're in the middle of it now."

My foot still stung and I tried not to let my lip quiver like a big baby. "Yeah."

He swept his way to me, making a path through the wreckage. As soon as he could, he leaned the broom against the counter next to me and hugged me. "I really am sorry."

I buried my nose in his shoulder and hugged him tightly. "It just feels like I can't hold onto anything nice."

"You've got me," Charlie murmured. "Arguably not at all nice, but I'm a good lay?"

Finally, I managed a little laugh. It bubbled up from inside me, and then I couldn't control it. "You're… I don't… fuck off," I said, but I was laughing.

And I couldn't stop thinking about those words. *You've got me.*

"I never promised to be nice," Charlie murmured, and then he squeezed my backside. "In fact, I think naughty is what you're after."

I ran my hands down his back. "Before we fuck, can I clean up my foot?"

Charlie's gasp was sharp as he pulled back and held me by the elbows. "Did you step on something? It went through your shoe? Here, lean on me and take your shoe off. Oh, my God."

The concern was sweet as anything. God knew I'd had worse, but it was kind of nice to just let him take care of me for a few minutes. I limped to the bathroom with his help and pointed out the first aid supplies, and then dried my eyes and splashed water over my face.

"And by the way," Charlie murmured as he knelt on the floor in front of the toilet while I sat on the lid, "I don't care about where you're from. I sure as hell don't think you're whatever you called yourself—redneck trailer trash. You're sophisticated, but that's not why I care about you, Kev."

"I don't *feel* sophisticated right now," I muttered. Here I was in my nice Diesel jeans and Tom Ford shirt, and he was in rumpled practical clothes taking care of me. It was a sudden shift in my priorities when I realized that I didn't have to dress up for him— or anyone.

I'd never given a shit about brand names for their own sake, but I'd felt like… like I needed to prove myself.

And here he was, taking care of me when I'd just been horrible to him. If Darren had felt like a jerk last weekend, I sure did now. "I'm sorry," I mumbled again, trying not to flinch away from the antiseptic.

"No, I'm sorry I joked about it," Charlie assured me as he put a Band-Aid on my foot and kissed the top of my foot teasingly.

That, at least, made me smile. I grabbed him by the arms to pull him to his feet and then leaned on him as I stood, too. Good. My foot still ached, but without the shard in it, I could stand on it a lot better. "I never told you I collect that stuff."

"No, you didn't." Charlie offered me his arm like he was taking me to the ball. "Let's leave that mess for Adam to clean up if he made it. Show me your room."

I breathed a sigh of agreement and leaned on him to hobble down the hall. He was polite enough not to show his surprise at the shabby little setup, either. He just pushed his way into my room, settled me on the bed, and sat next to me.

"Thank you," I murmured. I was suddenly aware of how close we were again—and how many days I'd been yearning for this. "I missed you."

He lay down beside me, propping his chin on his fist as he ran his hand up my side gently. "Yeah. So did I. The guys were asking if I had someone I was looking forward to getting back to."

My heart skipped a beat. "And?"

Charlie gave me a fond look like I was being dumb. "I'm here, aren't I?"

I smiled and snuggled into him, running my hands up his shirt. "And thank God for that." His body was hard and warm and everything I needed right now.

All my armor had fallen away. Partly because I'd willed it to, and partly because I was kind of a mess in every aspect of my life. But no matter what, Charlie didn't seem to care about that. He was just here for me, as he had been since we'd talked about not-dating.

"I kinda said I was dating someone, too," I admitted in a murmur. "When I was talking to people last weekend. And it was nice."

Charlie's breath caught. He pressed his lips against my cheek. "And?"

I wasn't letting him away without a proper kiss. I cupped his cheeks and pulled him in for a long, slow kiss. The kind that would make my knees wobble if I were still standing. As it was, it made my cock harden in my jeans, and I felt him reacting to it too.

I moaned against his lips and rolled my head back, and he nipped my throat before swinging a leg over me. He was straddling me now, his hands settling on my shoulders as he leaned down to capture my lips.

He wasn't kissing me—he was claiming me. The way he kissed now was fiercely and unapologetically sexual. The raw energy coursing through him was burning under my skin, too, and I lost my patience.

I got his t-shirt off as fast as I could without ripping it, and then he fought my clothes off and out of the way. Our hands slid over one another's torsos, fingers teasing nipples and tracing lines along our ribs. I couldn't be parted from him for a single second right now.

"I need you," I whispered. "Would you fuck me?"

"I'd love to," he whispered. Either that or *I love you*. I couldn't hear which, and it took me a few seconds before I even realized I wasn't sure.

By then, he was busy peeling the rest of our clothes off.

"Babe, I… got tested while you were away." I'd always been careful to use protection at work, and to track the window periods. "I'm going to stay on PrEP until we get tested together. I'm happy to stay using condoms if you want, but…"

"I'd love to bareback my boyfriend." Charlie offered me a teasing smile.

Was that him asking me? I squirmed under him, naked and hard and full of more feelings than I could contain. They were bursting out of me now in stupid words. "Are you—are we—can that be me?"

Charlie laughed gently and pressed a few more kisses against my lips. "That's what I wanted to ask you, baby. I'd love to bareback. And… since I got tested a couple years ago…"

"Yeah," I breathed out with a smile. "Just me."

"Nothing *just* about you," Charlie murmured as he ran his thumb along my jaw. I blushed and looked down, but he kissed me again and wouldn't let me shy away from the attention. "I'm serious."

"I... thanks?" I offered weakly, not really sure what to say. "Wanna fuck me and seal the deal?"

Charlie laughed and looked around. "More than anything, but lube would be a good idea."

"I *guess*." I grinned as I grabbed the bottle from under the bed and wriggled to get enough space. "Stand back, I'm going in."

He laughed and knelt between my legs, casting an admiring gaze up and down my body. Being the object of his gaze made me hot all over. I couldn't fucking wait to have him inside me again. All I wanted was to stay like this forever and forget about all the rest of the world's bullshit.

The thought of his cock inside me made my fingers feel all too thin. I bit my lip and slid them out. He took the bottle to add a little more lube to his cock, and my eye was drawn to the sight of glistening liquid spreading across flushed pink.

He was so fucking hot, and he was all mine. The thought made me smile.

Charlie spotted the expression, as always. "What's on your mind?" I shook my head, but he slowed his strokes and gazed at me. "I wanna know."

"I'm happy," was all I could say. There weren't any better words for it besides that. And how long had it been since I was able to say that without qualification?

Sure, life was shitty in some ways, and I was scared I wouldn't cut it in the big city, and I was afraid about what our careers would do to us, but…

We were here, together and officially dating, and that was all I could ask for.

"I have a *boyfriend*," I added, my voice squeaking slightly.

He grinned broadly. "So do I. And I'm about to make love to him. Or would you prefer a good fuck?"

"Make the headboard hit the wall. Not too hard, though. Those walls are crappy."

Charlie's laugh was beautiful. His fingers caressed my hip before he guided himself to my opening and inside. He was thick inside me, stretching me open slowly with every inch of himself. I breathed deeply and tasted the scent of sex, of his particular musk, of the flowers I'd seen him briefly press his face into while we were in the car.

I didn't know where I was going, but I knew what I wanted, and that was him.

He slowly thrust, and my nails dug into his hips as I hissed. "Slow." I hadn't even been playing with toys as much as usual lately. And more than that… it was taking my brain some time to wrap around the fact that he was *here*, and inside me.

Charlie did indeed take it slow, like the sweetheart he was under that gruff exterior. Our gasps and moans were the soundtrack to a movie I'd been on edge and eager to experience for the last week —longer, really. And it was everything I could have hoped for.

His pace gradually sped up, and I couldn't stop myself from touching him. Whether I was curling my hands around his biceps, running my fingers up his spine, or gripping his ass as the muscles flexed under my hands, the emotion suffusing me was unmistakable. I hadn't thought I could get any happier, but apparently I'd been wrong.

"This is perfect," I whispered, and he pressed his lips against mine.

"I know."

I smiled. "You're perfect."

Seeing Charlie get embarrassed was the best thing. I giggled under my breath as he scoffed and kissed my cheek. "Your gorgeous little ass is the perfect one here."

"Romantic," I said with a laugh, but I hugged him close. The way he held me made me forget about anything outside of him. I could face it all with him by my side.

I was burning up from the arousal crackling along my skin. Every inch of me needed him pressed down against me, and buried so deep inside me that it felt like we'd never be separated. I couldn't control my gasps of pleasure now, and my hands finally fell to the bed, where I twisted them in the sheets.

It was unbearably good for me—*he* was unbearably good to me. His grunts and moans of appreciation made me feel on top of the world, too.

And before long, I was clinging to the edge, resisting the ecstasy that I so badly wanted. My muscles were so tight it was hard to breathe, and making it even harder was the way he pressed his lips against mine after every few thrusts. Some kisses were gentle, and some were hard and rough, but his pace never faltered.

"I'm so goddamn close." I was clenching involuntarily around him, but I knew I wasn't quite gonna get there without a hand. My cock was so sensitive that I could feel the breeze in the room, let alone the touch that came next. A firm hand wrapped around the shaft, fingers sliding down to the base. "Fuck!" I whimpered, and I held back with all I had to keep from coming on the spot.

"You're beautiful," Charlie whispered. "I wanna feel you getting there, baby."

"I'm about two pumps of vanilla away from making you a frothy latte."

He tipped back his head and laughed richly, and I gazed up at him, just grateful he wasn't seeing the way I looked at him. If it was anything like I felt, my emotions had to be written on my face right now.

"I love your mind," Charlie murmured when he'd caught his breath. He slowed his pace but pushed himself in deeper, not looking away from me. Finally, he stroked at the same slow pace, and I lost my mind to the tightly wound pleasure bursting free at once, an overloaded spring.

I made a hell of a mess, but I didn't care. "Yes!" I whimpered as my every breath caught in my throat, my body pushing up and into his. My nails were nearly ripping into my sheets, my teeth bared as I struggled to contain the seismic power that shook me apart.

"I'm almost there, hon."

"Fuck me," I growled. "Now." Before I was too sensitive, I wanted to feel him come, too.

Charlie didn't argue. He pressed my knees into my chest and pounded me hard, his hands tightening around my thighs. "Yes! Kev, I'm... gonna..."

"Inside," I demanded, grabbing his back when he made like he was going to pull out. "Make me yours."

That did it for Charlie. He clutched at my skin, his thrusts erratic and deep now as he gasped for breath. "Yes!"

I loved watching him come just as much as he did me, it seemed. It was all I could think about, but to be fair, my mind was still kind of blown from my own climax. Apparently, a little less sex made every orgasm that much better. It was a persuasive argument for self-control and shorter showers.

"That was… fucking amazing." Charlie had barely pulled out before he wrapped me in his arms and pulled me in tightly. "You're amazing."

I'd just caught my breath, and I grinned as I pushed my hair out of my face. "You're telling me."

"For real. I can't even believe…" Charlie trailed off, smiling.

"What?"

"That you're mine."

I poked him in the chest with a finger. "Creampies don't lie."

"Oh, God. I'll get you a tissue!" He lunged for the box as I laughed my head off.

I didn't give a fuck if we were disturbing the neighbors, or Adam, or anyone at all. This joy was ours, and I was going to keep it safe against the world, whatever it took.

I wanted to keep *us* safe.

This first visit to my house had gone pretty damn well considering how it had started. Vulnerability wasn't the worst thing ever, apparently. It made it all the easier to cuddle into his chest, pressing my cheek against his ribcage as it thudded gently and evenly under me. Charlie must have been tired from the plane, because his breathing quickly evened, too. I could tell without even looking that he was asleep, which was precious.

It felt all too much like the tighter I held on, the more likely I was going to have this precious, fragile thing we'd built smashed to pieces.

Well, fuck if I was gonna let that happen. I'd fight to keep Charlie if I had to. How the hell I'd ever thought I could ignore the pull toward him, I didn't know. I was done trying to second-guess my heart. With him, I was contented in a way I hadn't been for days. Everything else felt bearable now.

Charlie had the right idea. One little nap couldn't hurt before I let the outside world fuck with me again.

25

CHARLIE

A door slamming startled me awake, and it took me long seconds to figure out which country I was in. My only clue was a man tucked against my chest, my arms around him and my nose buried in his hair. It felt like a long time since I'd last woken up like this, and I glowed with satisfaction.

Kev.

I smiled, the haze of last night lifting. I remembered arriving on the flight, Kev greeting me at the airport...

Oh, right. The broken china that had bothered Kev so much. If I went to make coffee, it would take me a few minutes to get there safely. I could always try, anyway. One less heartache for Kev if he didn't have to see his prized collection in pieces again.

Kev hadn't budged when the door slammed—the walls were so thin here that it sounded like a neighbor's front door—and the apartment rattled. When I tried to peel myself away from him, he made an unhappy noise and gripped my forearm. Apparently, I was going nowhere.

I laughed gently and settled down again as Kev gradually stirred and rolled over to face me. "Morning, you."

"Morning," I greeted, brushing his hair out of his eyes and pecking his lips. "Sleep okay?"

"Like a log, apparently. Don't remember much of it," Kev admitted. Then he smiled, sleepy but definitely awake. "Except the bit where we're boyfriends."

"That's a good bit to remember. Good morning, boyfriend." Man, I was gonna have to call Ben today and tell him the news. He'd want to meet Kev immediately. Maybe I could put it off for a week or two. I didn't want *all* my embarrassing college stories out there yet.

Kev giggled quietly. "Good morning." He looked precious wrapped in the duvet, his hair splayed across the pillow.

I just wanted to capture this memory for those mornings I had to wake up alone. I cuddled him for a minute, not saying anything to break the silence.

Kev was the first to do so. "When do you leave for Dubai?"

There it was: the sinking feeling in my stomach, much worse than leaving for Singapore had been—or any other country I'd visited for work, for that matter. "Um… Monday," I muttered. That was one way to pop my bubble.

He hummed quietly and didn't say anything, rolling onto his back and stretching his arms above his head.

"What?" I knew that look—he was biting his tongue about something, and it bothered me.

"Just planning when I can sext my new boyfriend."

I sighed and pulled him into me, rubbing my hand along his

stomach and up to his chest to try to soothe him. "Anytime you want. It's not all that bad."

"Unless by some freak chance it is. Like, the police search your phone for whatever reason." He shrugged. "You can't guarantee it won't happen."

It was maddening that he was right. "Lots of people travel there."

As much as I could fool myself into using that excuse, he wasn't buying it. "Sure they do. And there are headlines about a few of them every year."

"The US isn't always safe either."

Kev hummed and rubbed sleep out of his eyes as he pushed the covers off. "You can go to Friction without sneaking in the back door."

I smirked, about to make a *back door* joke, but the look he gave me silenced me. Instead I sighed, sitting up and watching him gather clothes for the day. "I know."

"I'm not saying not to go," Kev added slowly, laying underwear and socks on the bed. He chose jeans and a shirt from the rack. "Just that it's scary how much I miss you even when you're going somewhere pretty safe. And it scares me how much it scares me to think of… well, that."

I rubbed my hand down my face and nodded. "I know. I'm sorry. I've been having second thoughts, but I can't back out now."

"Can't you?" He frowned before he picked up a towel. "But then, I can't even hold down a job. Don't listen to me," he chuckled.

"I'll get us coffee," I told him. I didn't want him getting down on himself if I could help it.

"Nah. The kitchen stays like that until Adam cleans up his fucking mess. Bet he's not even home." Still grumbling, Kev disappeared down the hallway.

I smiled fondly after him. Even when he was in one of these rare grumpy moods, he was adorable. I just wished I could help him find the direction he seemed to so badly crave in his life right now.

Leaving on Monday suddenly felt that much closer, even if we had the weekend ahead of us. It meant I was going to miss a meeting with the charity building, but that was pro bono anyway. They understood if I couldn't keep a close eye on it.

Oh, that was right. I'd meant to ask about volunteering at the LGBT hotline. Not exactly something I could manage if I was about to add more international travel to my schedule, though. But I'd found my own way of making friends. Linda would be happy.

It hit me out of the blue: last time I'd been in the office, I'd seen a draft of an ad for telephone operators. Counseling skills required, and the pay wasn't great, but...

Could that be something up Kev's alley? He was passionate and clearly justice-oriented. He was eloquent and good at listening, when he wanted to be. And that made him understanding, but his sense of justice was so strong that I knew he'd never forgive me— not for violating his moral code, but for letting myself violate my own.

Fuck.

I weighed my phone in my hand for long moments, but the decision had already made itself.

I dialed Valerie and crossed my fingers she would answer. Lucky for me, she did.

"Hey, Charlie. What's up?"

I grimaced. "I'm sorry to do this to you, but we need to talk about Dubai."

"What is there to talk about?" She didn't sound surprised, though.

That was a good point. Either I was in or out. Sitting around being indecisive didn't benefit anyone.

"I can't do the project. I was lying to myself, thinking that I can." I drew a breath. "I know I'm screwing up planning, but... I'll happily talk to Alex about it."

"No need," she told me. "I'll call him myself." I wasn't imagining the annoyance in her tone.

"Sorry," I added. "I can't betray myself to get ahead in my career. I understand if this makes me a bad fit for the firm."

"We'll talk more on Monday," Valerie told me, which didn't at all leave me with an ominous foreboding. "See you at eight."

"I'll be there."

When I hung up, I pocketed my phone and sighed. Sitting here stressing about being let go was only gonna drive me nuts. May as well put myself to good use.

But just as I reached the kitchen, the bathroom door opened behind me. "Nuh-uh," Kev warned me. "We're going out for coffee and leaving that mess for him to clean up."

Far be it from me to get in the middle of this. Like sibling rivalry, roommate arguments were best stayed out of. "Can I treat you to Bubbles?"

Kev's smile warmed me inside. "I'll let you," he decided. "Did you want to stop by your place?"

"I'll need to bring my luggage home first. Then we can get coffee, lunch, a sneaky makeout, and then I'll go crash?" I suggested. I didn't plan to stay out long and I really didn't want Adam losing his temper and wrecking my stuff.

"Sure." Kev almost skipped to his bedroom and I chuckled as I followed. "Gimme ten minutes."

Watching him get dressed, I could kill more time than that. "Take all the time you need." I stretched out on his bed, hands behind my head. When he dropped his towel, I tilted my head and made it obvious I was watching him walk around his room naked.

He giggled and threw his towel at me, and then wiggled his way into his clothes. Seeing this goofy, rougher, less meticulously self-conscious side of him was its own reward.

Oh, yeah. I'd missed him.

<hr>

The stop at my house was just long enough to drop off my luggage. I wanted it out of the way for the fun day I had planned. We were out of my house in five minutes flat, and very quickly found ourselves at Bubbles.

"Breakfast?" I suggested with a grin.

I hadn't expected him to wince as he looked at the door and then me. "Sure," Kev finally concluded and turned to lead the way into the diner.

I'd have to ask him about that later. For now, I followed him to his usual booth in the window.

"Need a menu?" I asked.

"Hangover special," he said with a shake of his head. "I never get anything else. Well, just toast when I… I don't feel like eating."

There was so much he didn't say, for all his openness and communication. I respected that, though. He could talk at his own pace and I'd never try to force anything out of him.

"Morning, Kev," Jared—the owner—greeted. "The usual?"

"Yessir." Kev looked at me.

"I'll have what he's having."

"I bet you will." Jared winked and flipped his book shut as he headed off.

Kev's cheeks were red. When Jared came back with the pot, he cleared his throat. "It's not like that."

I was in the dark here. I'd thought he was teasing us about showing up together, but now… why was Kev denying anything was going on?

Jared just smiled. "I know."

"How?"

"I've got ears everywhere," Jared told him and finished filling my cup. "Enjoy."

When he left, I just stared at Kev, brows knitted. He tried to touch my hand, but I pulled it back. "Not like what?"

"Don't rub it in." Kev shook his head. "I'll tell you later, when it doesn't make me spitting mad."

"Oh." I had no idea what to think, so it was just as well that Kev changed the subject with less subtlety than he'd ever shown.

"So, you gonna see me before Dubai?" He was keeping his expression carefully neutral, I could tell. The self-control it took was obvious.

"About that…"

He held up a hand before I could explain. "I'm not going to criticize you or make you defend yourself. You sure as hell have the right to make up your own mind. I courted danger for years, after all. I ain't no hypocrite."

"It's not that dangerous," I said, shaking my head. "That's what they tell me."

"Can I visit?"

"No." I wasn't sure how to tell him I'd changed my mind on the whole damn thing. "No need."

He raised his eyebrow and didn't say anything.

"I never wanted to put you in danger," I said, sighing.

Kev raised his other eyebrow now. At least they matched. "So you don't think you're worth taking safety precautions? The worst-case scenario wouldn't bother you?"

I blinked a few times. From a guy who'd just denied we were together, this was giving me whiplash. That made it click. "You're not pulling back because of my trip, are you?"

Kev looked just as confused. "Pulling back? I'm here with you."

"But not *with* me."

Breakfast arrived, so he couldn't answer until Jared had left us alone again. When he had, Kev looked right back at me. "Are you changing your mind?"

The whiplash intensified. "Am I?"

"I don't know!" Kev exclaimed, but at least he was laughing. "Make up your damn mind!"

"About what?" This was why I preferred spreadsheets and diagrams to people. None of this vague assumption-based bullshit.

"Dating me."

"No," I scoffed, my jaw dropping. "Why would you think—are *you* changing your mind?"

"Hell, no." He looked just as confused.

"Why did you tell Jared we're not together then?" I tried not to let that sound as wounded as I felt.

"I didn't!" Kev cradled his mug of coffee by his chest like a shield. "I—" He looked around and lowered his voice as he leaned in. "I almost got thrown out last week by a waitress."

"What?" All of a sudden I didn't want to eat. I pushed my plate back. "Why?"

"She had a problem with what I do—did. Jared fired her."

My appetite returned and I grabbed a crispy strip of bacon to nibble on while we talked. "Right. So you weren't saying we aren't boyfriends." The opposite, in fact.

"Yes. I mean, no. You're right." Kev breathed a sigh of relief and I nudged his foot with my own.

"I'm sorry," I offered up. "I just feel like…" No, that was a waste of time.

"Like?" Kev stubbornly prompted. I waved at him to forget it and eat, but he wasn't giving in.

"Used up. Like I had my chance the first time around, and now

I'm... not the twenty-something model you could have instead. You know you could."

He quirked a smile, refusing to indulge my rare moment of self-pity. "Babe, you're thirty-two, not three hundred."

"You don't need to say that so loud," I muttered. "Besides, you said before that *you're* old for Grindr."

Kev's smile disappeared. He picked at his food before he finally looked up. "I do feel old, because I never expected to make it this long." He said it without emotion, like he was afraid of what would happen if he gave me another crack in his armor.

Oh. That was a punch to my gut, distracting me completely from what we'd been saying. "Fuck. I'm sorry."

"It is what it is." Kev's smile gradually returned, like a lightbulb being dialed up. "Whole new Kev is on the way."

"Not whole new, I hope," I told him with a soft smile. This time, when he touched my hand, I turned it palm-up to take his. "I like a lot of this Kev."

Kev's blush was so worth it. "Maybe not all-new, then. Just refurbished."

I laughed, but it was a good word. He'd done that for me without even knowing it. With Kev in my life, I had more to look forward to than I had in years. "And I'm not going to Dubai."

Kev's grip tightened and almost crushed my hand. "You're not?" The relief was so evident that he gripped his chest for a moment.

"No," I said, and finally, everything felt a little more right. "I have too much keeping me here."

"But..."

"Damn the opportunity. I'll make my own," I told him. "Eat up and get ready to go shopping."

"For what?" Kev looked startled.

"You'll see." I nudged his foot again. "Before it gets cold."

"I… okay." Kev gave in and smiled. This time, he dug into his hash browns with an appetite.

And so did I.

2 6

KEV

"Where are we going?" I bit my lip, just hoping he wasn't going to dress me up like a doll. Now that I was backing off buying new clothes, my closet looked more manageable.

And I wasn't wasting time worrying about keeping myself looking like a magazine centerfold, which meant I could sit around parks, lean on bus stops, and spend less time hyperconscious of my body. That could only be good.

But instead, Charlie smiled. "You tell me. Where do you go thrifting?"

I stared at him. I hadn't expected him to do more than look down his nose at my place and the things I loved. He wanted to get new teacups with me? "We don't have to replace them right away."

"No, but if they have something you like, you can get a start on rebuilding your collection," he told me.

I had to blink quickly and look down so I didn't cry. Damn his sweet heart. "Okay. Treasure Aisle is around the corner from the bookstore."

He led me there, hand in hand. "I noticed a lot of those things had gold glue. Did you get them that way?"

I shook my head. "I like the single ones that aren't all pretty and matching in a set, or the ones everyone else would give up on. I like making them new and pairing them with a complementary saucer."

"Like me." Charlie smiled. "You're the saucer. I'm more of a coffee guy, but I like the metaphor."

I scoffed. "Like you're old. I like things with history, that's all."

"Not convincing me. Again, like me," Charlie said with a laugh. "It's not beauty like a catalog, but at least I have experience."

I shook my head. "Everyone's definition of beauty is different."

"What's yours?" We waited at a red light, and Charlie squeezed my hand as he looked at me.

I hadn't thought to put it in words before, so I thought about it as I spoke slowly. "Beauty isn't in anything so new it gleams. That's just possibility. Beauty is in the broken, chipped, worn pieces. The well-used heart is a well-used cup. The more it's been filled, the more it's held—the more precious it is."

I wasn't sure how to bring it up, but I wanted him to know that I didn't resent his past with Hugh. It had made Charlie who he was, and I'd always have Hugh to thank, even if a part of me was afraid I couldn't measure up.

"I saw you as possibility at first," Charlie admitted, but he was looking away. He raised his other arm to swipe across his face. "I think a lot of people do, with the image you always held. But you're a lot more than that."

"And I see the possibilities with you," I murmured.

Charlie cleared his throat, his voice thick. "Around the corner, you said?"

"We're nearly there," I promised.

And how true that was. Piece by piece, we'd slowly been finding the ways we fit together. All we needed was a little glue.

"I liked the cheesy blazer I kept showing you." I smirked. "You should have gotten it. And it would match the yellow teacup we decided belonged to Aunt Maddy."

"The lemon cake expert?"

I grinned. "That's the one. Three blue ribbons at the county fair. She probably has matching walls, too. Her nephews— the gay couple, of course—"

"—of course—"

"—have finally talked her into remodeling and ditching the yellow walls, but she secretly wants neon purple countertops. That teacup—and especially the blazer—would clash so horribly." I nudged him again. "Shame you'll never be able to scar her fabulous gay nephews. Especially with the shoulder pads."

Charlie looked horrified. "Wait a second. Are you calling me skinny?"

I laughed and bumped him with my hip, careful not to get the bag with its breakables caught between us. "No, silly. I'm scrawnier than you, anyway." I snaked my arm around his waist to keep him close before he could pull away.

"I don't understand retro fashion," Charlie declared. "We've moved on. Why pretend we're still in the era of big hair and... muscle cars and lemon cake?"

It made sense for an architect to be looking at the future, but it still made me chuckle. "Some trends should come back, though. Crop tops for guys."

Charlie stared at me. "Why? That doesn't seem like your thing at all."

I raised an eyebrow. "More abs on display is never a bad thing. And even guys without abs—soft tummies are adorable."

That made Charlie crack up as he poked his own. "Phew."

"Shut up. I've felt those abs." I smirked. "Carefully, one by one."

He was blushing now, glancing around to see if anyone was overhearing. Silly, for a New Yorker—he should know that nobody else cared what anyone else was saying. Everyone was too busy with their own business.

"I've missed those abs," I purred, leaning in. We were only a few blocks away from home, but I wanted to wind him up. "And your cum-gutters."

I didn't even see it coming: Charlie yanked me by the arm into the next alley we passed. My heart rate doubled in moments as he backed me up against the wall, and I tried not to think about how many windows looked onto this alley or how many guys had pissed in here after a late night at Friction. It had rained this morning. Phew. That took care of one concern, at least. It still smelled awful in here, but with Charlie smelling like travel shampoo, I could ignore that.

"When you say things like that, you make me remember how long I was celibate," Charlie breathed out. The plastic bag of paper-wrapped cups hung from his forearm next to my head as he pressed a hand to either side of me.

I grinned at him and ran my hands slowly down his sides to his hips. "What does that make you wanna do?"

"Everything." Charlie's body rippled forward as he ground against me and pressed me up against the wall. He laced his fingers with mine and dragged my hands above my head.

I shivered. "In what particular order?" If we got a free bonus round of sex in before he went home today, so much the better. I found myself kind of hoping Adam was out, despite spending the afternoon hoping he had a miserable time cleaning up his own mess.

"I thought we could see about that," Charlie breathed out.

A sharp voice cut through the air. "Hey! Asshole!"

By the time Charlie let me go and I turned to see who it was, he was up in our faces. "Whoa—" I tried to stop Adam, but it was too late.

He took a wild swing at Charlie, his muscles barely restraining the coiled fury that was so clear on his face. "Get off him! You don't get to do whatever the fuck you want!"

Charlie was backing away, his hands up slightly, but he seemed reluctant to leave me by myself. "Don't hurt Kev, okay? We can talk this out." The bag dropped to the ground with a clunking noise that made me wince. We didn't seem to have good luck with china right now.

"*You* don't hurt Kev! Did you hit him in the kitchen, huh? I saw the state of that place!" Adam's cheeks were red, and his eyes red-ringed. Had he been... crying?

Before I could process that, Charlie was brushing Adam's hands away from him, circling him like a boxer. "I never touched him. Well, not in ways he didn't want."

"Adam, whoa. We're dating," I gasped.

"So? I asked about the watermelon situation and you never answered any of my texts," Adam hissed at me. Now he was sheltering me from Charlie in some bizarre turn of events.

I couldn't help myself—I started laughing. "Wait, you're—oh, my God. You *read* my check-ins?"

Charlie looked confused as hell, his hands hovering halfway between his sides and his face, like he wasn't sure if the fight was over yet or not. "The what?"

"You didn't even answer your work phone. Fuck. Is this—wait, is this *really* your boyfriend?"

"Duh!" I exclaimed, throwing my hands up and pushing Adam away from me. "I'm not Princess Peach, dude." Thank God he hadn't interrupted anything more personal. If he'd walked in last night... "And where the hell were you, if it wasn't you that broke the shelf?"

"Of course I didn't break the shelf!" Adam exclaimed, his cheeks flushing a deep scarlet as he folded his arms. "Are you kidding? You'd fucking kill me."

"I was about ready to, and that's before you interrupted hot wall sex."

"Ah, roommate bliss." Charlie picked up the bag and peeked inside.

"Shit. Don't tell me," I groaned. We'd spent a great afternoon lovingly picking up the first teacups in my new collection and imagining histories for them. It had felt like such a defining moment in our developing relationship.

Adam looked even more grouchy now as he swiped at his face and stared at the ground.

"They're intact!" Charlie announced, and I half-hugged him.

"Thank God." That left me with one thing to deal with—a pretty big one. "So, uh, if it wasn't you and it wasn't us…"

Adam grumbled, "That fucking shelf. I bet it wasn't properly anchored into the drywall."

Knowing how run-down our apartment was, that wouldn't surprise me. "Ugh. And here I've spent a day being mad at you."

"While I spent hours thinking you'd gotten the shit beaten out of you."

"What?"

"Broken dishes everywhere? Blood in the hallway? They said they saw you with a guy this morning at Bubbles, and you two looked wound up about something. And then you didn't send any safety texts. *And* you didn't answer mine."

It was my turn to blush, but my mood was soaring, too. Holy fuck. For all he acted like he didn't care, Adam had actually worried about my safety that much? It gave me pause, and it made it a lot harder to hate him for all his annoying quirks. "Fuck. I didn't think about it that way. Sorry."

"It's lucky I stumbled on you here." Adam huffed, shoving his hands in his pockets. "I might have put an APB out on you." I grabbed him around the shoulders for a tight hug, and he made a startled sound. "All right, all right. Whatever. You're *not* dead." Still, I hugged him insistently until he returned the hug.

It was hard not to notice those subtle signs of distress—like his red-rimmed eyes. And he'd been so out of his mind with anger on my behalf that I had to wonder if this had hit Adam's hot buttons.

He'd never talked much about why he hated his parents. He'd always said they pressured him into working or joining the military so he'd be a better man, but he'd carefully danced around his sexuality. As far as I knew, even Josh and Evan and the other guys had never found out much. Josh had met his parents once and said they seemed like the average couple—nice on the outside, but God knew what had happened behind closed doors.

At last, Adam relaxed into the hug and squeezed me back, properly. "It smells like trash here. You were gonna fuck? God, you're a horny hobag."

"Fuck off!" I laughed, slapping his chest as I pushed him away. "God, you're a dick."

At least it felt like a little normalcy had returned here. I took Charlie's hand again and waved between them. "Charlie, Adam. Adam, Charlie. Let's get out of this gross dumpster-land."

Charlie nodded and shook hands with Adam as they traded a few grudging words of respect on our way out of the alley. Before I could suggest coffee to warm things up between us all, Charlie handed me the bag. "I better take off."

"Yeah?" I'd been hoping for more time with him, but even if he wasn't going to Dubai, he had to have things to sort out after his trip. "Okay, sure. See you soon?"

"Later," Charlie promised and leaned in to peck my lips before he strode away.

That had all felt so abrupt that I found myself staring after him. I felt none of the warmth he'd shown me one-on-one. Was that just because of Adam's presence? Was he jealous?

"Okaaay." Adam clapped my shoulder. "Should we go clean up that crap, then? Sounds like we have a lot to catch up on."

I found myself grateful for his presence, for the first time in a while. "Yeah. We sure do."

I couldn't spend all my time wondering what was wrong with other people and how I could help. I had my own life to clean up and get back on track, and Adam's words were a welcome reminder of that. Which reminded me of one of those things I had to tell him.

"So, I quit school."

Adam's response was to laugh loudly. "Did you swear at the teacher?"

"Oh, fuck off!"

Still, as we took potshots back and forth, I found myself grinning as I walked alongside Adam back to our cozy little place. Annoying little shit though he was, I was lucky to have someone like him around. I only wished I could read him better.

God... men. "Let's grab wine and pizza on the way back. I have the feeling we'll need it."

Adam pumped his fist. "Bring it on."

27

CHARLIE

Another exhausting night: not exactly what I needed right before the most important Monday morning in my career for the past five years.

I gave up on sleep at five and tossed the covers aside like a tarp at a breaking-ground ceremony. A shower improved my mood slightly, but not much. It was hard to ignore the knot of fear that had gathered in the pit of my stomach and was now occupying every spare moment of my thoughts.

I'd spent Sunday occupying myself with work, so I couldn't justify any more time on my laptop. Instead, the next couple hours were spent cleaning my place from top to bottom. As I descaled the sink and polished the shower taps, I kept half an eye on the time. I poured all my fragmented attention into the tasks, trying to exhaust my brain out of overthinking everything.

As long as I got my ass to work on time, I could probably take off early if I really needed to. The Singapore project wrapping up had to give me a little leeway, right? I was totally lying to myself, but whatever got me through the hours until eight.

A cup or three of coffee later, I managed to nibble toast while I called an Uber to get to work. If I was upset, I didn't want to be driving in Manhattan traffic. A distant part of my brain noticed that I was already making contingency plans in case I got fired. Always the efficient machine.

Couldn't hold down a relationship, but at least I could keep my career together, right?

God, I wished my brain would shut up and let me relax. When I had a good thing going, I was bound to screw it up. I knew I must have fucked up on Saturday because I hadn't gotten a good night or good morning text from Kev since. I'd meant to send one myself, but I'd fallen into a restless sleep almost right away. And texting at three in the morning to apologize was so not an attractive look.

I made myself send a text after I had another quick shower.

Morning :) Big day today. I hope yours is relaxing and the landlord fixes the shelf soon.

It was about all I could think to say without worrying him. I didn't need to stress out even more people over my worries about things like getting fired. And I certainly didn't want him feeling guilty for pressuring me not to accept the Dubai job.

Plus, there was the weird conversation I felt like I'd missed half of, between him and Adam.

The Uber arrival notification took me by surprise and I sprinted for the door, grabbing my coat. Damn thing must have reversed down my street or something to get here early. At least the ice had melted within the last few months. Sprinting down the sidewalk to the curb wasn't the risky choice it was in January.

"Morning," I greeted as I climbed into the backseat. I prayed I didn't get a chatty driver, and luckily for me, he didn't say much aside from returning my greeting.

That allowed me to settle back and stare out the window at the familiar passing scenery. My phone went off and my heart leapt into my throat.

God, I'd half-expected it to be Val saying not to come into work today, or ever again. I was really on-edge—much more than I'd even admitted to myself.

What's going on? Fallout from the Dubai cancellation? xox

Yeah. She wants to talk about my future I think, I answered, chewing my lip as I stared at my phone screen.

The answer came quickly. *OMG, you didn't say. Hugs xoxoxo*

At least that made me smile. Kev had a lot to learn about me and how I hid my stress, but he was trying to be supportive, and that meant a lot.

Hugs xox, I responded, trying not to feel like I was a kid writing letters to my grandma in Maine. It was much more Kev's language than mine, but it earned me several kissing emoji in response.

I pocketed my phone and ran my hands through my hair. All I could do was wait for eight o'clock. The Uber got to the office a few minutes early, probably by violating traffic laws. He could have pressed a flying button on the console and I wouldn't have even noticed, I was so wrapped up in my thoughts.

"Thanks," I mumbled once I got there and loped into the elevator.

I was early enough that I missed the main rush of coworkers arriving one or two minutes before eight, at least. I'd probably have time for another cup of coffee—no, tea was a better idea at this stage of the morning. Caffeine jitters wouldn't help anyone.

I managed to occupy enough of my attention with the hot water tap that Valerie had to call my name twice from the break room doorway.

"Oh. Oh, shoot, sorry." I nearly spilled the cup as I snapped the lid on and followed her to the office.

"Still on Singapore time?" she said, not unsympathetic.

I half-smiled. "Oh, I've gotten used to that spacey feeling."

She stopped in her doorway, and I had to stop sharply on my toes so I didn't spill hot tea down her back. That was not the way to keep my job. "Do you want to do this another day?"

"No," I said strongly. "No way." The suspense would kill me. I'd rather get this over with, even if I didn't speak perfectly or take in all of it, than wait days for the outcome.

"Close the door," she told me unnecessarily before heading for the desk. Once it clicked shut, I joined her and sat opposite, and she folded her hands. "How did the trip go?"

"Great. The ceremony was good," I said automatically. I never took much pleasure in grandstanding and ceremonies like that, but at least we'd gotten some photos for the firm's website and press releases. The final opening ceremony would be a few more months while the finishings were done, but as far as I was concerned, my job was over.

"Glad to hear it. So, I've called Alex and canceled everything." Valerie's displeasure was easy to read on her face as her lips turned down. "We were all pretty disappointed."

"So am I," I told her. If I'd learned anything from Kev, it was how damn important it was not to tiptoe over something that really mattered to me. Like Kev wouldn't accept being treated like shit, I wasn't going to, either. "It's a shame they're building in a country that wants me dead."

Valerie paused for a few moments, looking at me. "Yeah," she finally agreed. "But our firm is expanding operations throughout southeast Asia and the Middle East as economies grow there. I'm going to need all hands on deck when we win bids. You know, through the normal process."

I winced, not needing any more reminders of how rarely a job was handed to us on a silver platter. I'd really screwed things up for them. "I'm sorry I caused problems," was all I said. "But I have a hard line. I tried to get over it, but I can't. I won't go there in the future. If that's a problem..."

"I don't know if it will be," Valerie told me. "Most of our senior architects—gay or straight—have been flexible about where they're willing to work."

"I get that. That's their choice, and this is mine," I told her, my confidence growing. Looking for a new job sucked, but at least I was alive to do it.

This had once been my dream job—I'd been thrilled to be accepted as an intern, even as the rest of my life crashed and burned around me. They'd gotten the benefit of my desperation to drown myself in work, and I'd gotten... well, the start of a career.

But it was starting to feel a hell of a lot like a relationship that I'd outgrown. Which I hadn't noticed before now, perhaps because I'd never had that chance. My few high school boyfriends had been childish, full of easy dumping and getting together. Then came Hugh, and... well, I'd never had the chance to outgrow that relationship.

"I'm getting the impression I'm not the best fit for this position," I said calmly. It was a perfectly reasonable conclusion to draw from the available evidence.

Valerie's look of relief was obvious, too. "Well…" she hedged.

"As long as I'll get a good reference, I'm happy to move to a different firm. Somewhere I'll either be responsible for projects here in the States, or stick to behind-the-scenes work."

"That might be best for everyone," Valerie agreed without hesitation.

Sounded like I'd just saved myself from being shunted out the door. I drew a breath of relief. "Right. I appreciate all that I've learned here." And I'd miss my coworkers, sort of. They hadn't been the worst. I didn't really know many of them outside work…

Hell, who was I kidding? I'd just been coasting here, doing my time and gaining experience. As much as the position had outgrown me, I'd outgrown it in a different direction. And the culture had never quite been right for me.

"I'll talk to the charity project today at my site meeting about who they want to take over my role," I said, automatically working through my mental checklist. I'd miss walking away from the pro bono work. "Do you think Angus would be happy to take over?"

"He's probably open to it," Valerie said. "You can always ask."

"Will do." I stood up. "I'm not sure how long it'll take me to find another position."

"With our reference and your skills, I'm sure you won't have trouble finding something you're comfortable with," Valerie told me, reaching out to shake hands.

I shook on it. "Thanks."

As I headed out of her office for my desk, I added *look for a new job* to my mental checklist. At least I'd saved myself from a dubiously legal firing experience. Leaving on my own terms left everyone happier and saved face all around.

Just another happy Monday in the office.

Thankfully, I had a break mid-afternoon for the site meeting, and that passed in a flash. Toward the end, I brought up the uncomfortable conversation—asking if they'd be okay working with Angus to complete their vision.

"Oh, that's a shame for us—but are you leaving for greener pastures?"

I hadn't expected the reaction. "Uh… I hope so, yes."

"Then congratulations are in order." The guy shook my hand and grinned, and God, for a moment I envied Neil. He had a hell of a task in leading an organization trying to cut down on LGBT suicides nationwide. It had been my pleasure to take away as many headaches as possible with this process, at least.

But he was making a difference in a very concrete way. He could point at call logs. All I had to point to was vague statistics about my preferred architectural techniques and the psychological theories behind them.

"One thing," I said, suddenly unable to help myself. "Look up kintsugi floor tiles. I was planning on using them, and I think Angus would appreciate that style."

"What are they?"

I smiled to myself, thinking of those tea cups. "Tiles that have been cracked and are repaired, and they're all the more perfect for it. Say, do you still have that job open?"

Neil blinked at me a few times. "Well, if you happen to have a counseling background as well as that architectural degree…"

I laughed abruptly. "No, not for me. Not even for someone who fits it yet. But I think it could be a dream job for someone." When he raised an eyebrow, I added, "My boyfriend is looking for... a new direction in life."

"Oh!" Neil lit up and beamed at me. "I had no idea—you never mentioned..."

"That I'm gay?" I quirked a smile. "Yeah. It never seemed relevant." Even as I said it, I chuckled. I'd had several conversations about mental health and sexuality with him, and the ideal ways to support his staff's mental health in this design. Still, I'd always felt like it was *too much* to mention what or who I was.

No more of that. I was going to make damn sure that I was present in every way from now on.

"Here you go," Neil said, rummaging in a drawer of the desk to pull out the job ad. I snapped a quick photo to text Kev, though I didn't have time to add a caption without being rude to Neil.

"Great. Thanks," I told him and shook hands. "It's been great working with you. I might just look at volunteering here if I find myself with more spare time in my next role."

"For our sake, I hope so. We'd be delighted to have you," Neil told me and smiled. "And your boyfriend, in whatever capacity."

I finally let myself relax and enjoy the small talk just a little. It was the closest to a connection I was likely to find in this city, in this job. Just a little slice of community I'd found, but it was enough to make me feel that much less alone. Hugh's mom had been totally right. I did need more.

I had Ben and Darren to talk to, though. And I hadn't updated either of them on the status of this relationship in a while. Maybe I should do that. It felt like I was relearning how to be a good friend, but I sent a quick text in the Uber on the way back to work.

Tonight, I'd try to be a decent friend. I could relearn this if I just put my mind to it.

Maybe after that, I could be ready to be a decent boyfriend, too.

KEV

Okay, that was it. I was sick of reading between the lines. All I'd gotten from Charlie since he'd gotten off work was a cryptic message about his meeting turning out the best for everyone. Then, he'd texted an *xox* like he thought that was all I needed to know.

I was sick of playing therapist to everyone around me, interpreting their moods and trying to help them before they even noticed they needed it. And now Charlie was sending *me* therapy links? Like I was the one who had the issues here?

If Charlie expected me to be his hunk, his sweetheart, and his emotional interpreter, he was wrong about that. From leaving abruptly on Saturday to his short texts, something was clearly wrong. If that was work, that was fair—but he couldn't just leave me hanging on here, guessing at what was wrong.

Finally, I gave in and called him, retreating to my room for some vague air of privacy.

"Hey," Charlie answered after a minute. "Kev? What's up?"

"Can we meet up?" I asked. "I'd like to talk." I wasn't going to hash all this out on the phone. Especially not the, *So, you think I'm crazy?* bit. I'd only barely glanced at the photo, but a LGBT mental health counseling hotline sounded a lot like *you're crazy*, and I'd heard that enough for one lifetime.

Charlie hummed. "I'm going out this evening with a couple friends, and then seeing my—well, my… Hugh's parents."

Oh, boy. There was a reminder I didn't need that he probably didn't want me around when talking to his last, late boyfriend's parents. "Right. I can drop by for a couple minutes," I offered. "I just need to talk about things as soon as possible."

"Is it a today thing?"

"Yeah," I said, biting my lip. Was he trying to stall me?

"I don't believe in going to bed with a grudge," Charlie said. "Come on over. Want me to call you an Uber?"

"I've got it," I promised. I'd figure out the money for it later. Right now, I just wanted to see Charlie. While our relationship was so new and fragile, letting resentments go until we were "less busy" was a bad idea.

"Okay, babe. See you in a few."

"Bye," I wished him, already grabbing a sweater and my keys. By the time the Uber arrived, I'd been shifting impatiently from foot to foot on the sidewalk for several minutes.

I couldn't get to his house quick enough. Now that I'd apparently decided I needed to be around him more often, even an entire day without him had been painful. All the more so when he wasn't giving me anything solid about how he was doing. After that kind of day, who knew what to expect?

Charlie greeted me at the door with a hug and a kiss, which was a relief. I smiled up at him as I stepped inside.

"How was your Monday?"

"Oh," Charlie shrugged and gave me a roll of his eyes. "You know. Monday."

I sighed and grabbed him by the hand to tow him to the couch. "Okay, boyfriend rules. Number one: none of this vague *I could be better* shit. I'm not going to play emotional oracle to guess what happened."

Charlie blinked a few times and let me push him down to sit on the couch. "Oh."

"I'm sick of trying to interpret what everyone's thinking all the time," I told him.

When I crashed next to him, he wrapped an arm around me and pulled me in. "Yeah? I didn't mean to do that. I just didn't want to worry you."

I kissed his cheek and shook my head. *Men.* "I've been imagining you getting fired, or getting blacklisted from any new projects, or something… for my sake."

"No," Charlie said quickly, but he didn't quite meet my gaze. When I nudged him, he sighed. "Okay, so… I'm moving to another company."

Fuck. I sat up straight. "You *did* get fired?"

"Not quite." Charlie took my hand. "I didn't want you thinking it was your fault or anything. It's the best move for me, and I would have done it regardless." Then he smiled to himself. "Sort of."

"More," I told him, poking him in the ribs until he laughed.

"Sorry. I'm used to thinking through everything myself," he told me, his lips quirking into a little smile. "Not used to having someone around who wants to help."

I rubbed his back gently. "I know. But if all I get is silence from you, or if you shut down on me… I just start guessing, and that doesn't end well."

Charlie nodded. "Noted. I'm sorry I rushed off the other day." He rested his head on my shoulder, and I held him close. It was an admission of vulnerability, especially with the way his voice had just softened. He seemed like he'd given in and he was talking now. "What did he mean about watermelon texts?"

I half-smiled. "When I worked, I'd send safety check-ins to him. Addresses, photos, that kind of thing. I didn't realize he thought I was working…"

"Oh. That's… smart of you."

"I get by," I shrugged. "But what else is going on?" I felt like *I didn't know what was going on between you* wasn't enough reason to rush off like that. "Something else was, wasn't it?"

Charlie nodded. "I was stressed about the meeting today. I don't like the idea of giving up what I've worked so hard for. But you've reminded me that I *do* have principles, and if I break them for money… well… what does that make me?"

I kissed the top of his head. "Plenty of good people do things they don't love just to get by." I sure as hell wouldn't judge him for that.

"Yeah," Charlie murmured, "but I can also walk away. When you have another option, or you can make your own… go for it. You taught me that."

I blinked as he turned to look at me. I hadn't expected him to look so sincere, and even… grateful. "Me?" I almost squeaked. I'd somehow expected that he was more… well, more put-together than me. He'd had another nine years to practice, after all.

"Yeah, you." Charlie looked fond. "I don't know what I would have done if I hadn't met you."

I bit my lip. "So, when you sent the counseling thing… you're saying I've got issues?"

It took Charlie a few seconds before he gasped. "What? No. It's a job."

"But I can't do that, so—" I suddenly broke off. "Oh, shit." Here I was, spending the afternoon thinking he was telling me I needed to stop being so… whatever he thought. And I'd just fallen right into the trap of putting words in his mouth. "Shit. I didn't even look at the photo for more than, like, two seconds." I was blushing so much I could barely look at him.

Charlie just rubbed my shoulder gently. "It's just a suggestion, anyway. There's a lot of stuff you could be good at."

But he had my attention, now that I'd stopped leaping to conclusions like a dumbass. "No, I… I'm good at listening. Normally. Not with my boyfriend, apparently, because I'm a dumbass…"

I was too damn used to having to read the mood of the room around me to stay alive. I could afford to take a step back and *ask* now.

Charlie laughed and kissed my cheek. "Now *that* I don't believe. You're smart. Everyone has those moments. And I've been stressing you out today. I really should have said something when I sent it to you."

I breathed out a little sigh and shook my head. Thank God I'd insisted on coming over. At least I knew that much about how to have a relationship. "Thank you for agreeing to talk to me, like, right away."

"I think that's a smart move," Charlie murmured and rubbed my back. "Glass of water? Anything stronger?"

"Yes, please. Just water."

Charlie grabbed two glasses and brought them back. By that time, I'd at least pushed my embarrassment to the side so I could talk with him properly. "Thanks," I told him and sipped. "So, if you give me a little more to interpret, I'll try not to interpret *for* you," I said. "Deal?"

"Deal," Charlie said with a smile. "Did you want to meet my friends and my second parents?"

I stared at him. "You... you want me to?"

"If we're doing this," Charlie told me, "we're doing it right." He touched my knee. "Unless you're not ready. But I don't want you to think I'm hiding you."

I let out a breath of relief as stress I hadn't even been aware of melted away. Yeah, I was used to being hidden. But this was different. "Thanks. I'd love to." As long as they didn't judge me for not having an answer when the inevitable, *So what do you do?* question came up.

"And for my part..." Charlie trailed off, setting aside his glass and lacing his fingers with mine, "I've just been adjusting to the idea of being in a relationship again. I've thought of myself as single—or widowed, kind of—for so long that... I'm almost afraid of being happy."

"Because you might lose me?" I asked, as gently as I could.

Charlie flinched and looked down, and I gave him some silence and space to figure out how he felt. "Partly that," he finally said, leaning into my shoulder again. "And partly, I guess… if I'm happy with you, what does that mean about me and Hugh?"

I bit my lip and forced myself to acknowledge the moment of emotion in my chest. It wasn't jealousy—I knew that much. I was just afraid of being the inferior option. In my job, I'd been the backup boyfriend—the emergency last resort for guys who were desperate. I didn't want to be that in a relationship, too.

"How so?" I asked, trying not to get defensive.

"Like, if we were… you know, soulmates… but then I'm with you, and I feel like we click just as much as I did with Hugh in those early days…" Charlie's brows knitted together.

I grimaced. Soulmates—there was no worse word, in my opinion, but Charlie clearly valued something about the idea. "Yeah?"

"I guess I'm just challenging what I believe love is." Charlie's voice was quiet, but he looked at me steadily now.

My heart nearly skipped a beat. "Was that a—do you mean…"

"I love you," Charlie said softly. "It's early days yet, I can tell. But it's going to grow, if we're careful. And I think it could be a long-term thing. I'm invested in you in a way that… kind of scares me."

I took both his hands and squeezed them. Poor Charlie had only been trying to test the waters, and he'd tripped and fallen into… well, me. That would throw anyone off. "For what it's worth, I think I love you, too. I haven't really felt like this about someone else." I struggled to put it into words for his sake. "Like I want to be there to see them grow and become the person they were meant to be. Like I… I just want to be around them all the time. I couldn't even be away from you for a day," I laughed, resisting the urge to cover my face with embarrassment.

"Someone wants the D," Charlie teased.

That broke the mood and made me laugh. "You jerk," I scolded, smacking his knee. "I was trying to be serious."

"Sorry." Charlie's lips twitched as he clearly hid his grin.

I snorted. "The moment's over now!" I declared, but I threw myself into him and let him catch me with a quiet, *Oof!* "Take me to your friends."

"Aye aye, sir." Charlie kissed my cheek. "I'd be delighted to."

29

CHARLIE

"My roommate drinks all the milk at night." Darren folded his arms and pouted. "Imagine no cereal in the morning, ever."

Kev high-fived him. "Mine eats all the Lucky Charms marshmallows. God, it's annoying."

I laughed at the way Kev and Darren had immediately bonded over crappy roommates. Even so, I sensed Kev didn't hate Adam. Especially not after he'd tried to come to his rescue, awkward as it had been for him. It was just a series of little annoyances, and it was good for him to finally have an outlet.

Darren held up a finger. "No, I can still one-up you here. He always told me he was lactose-intolerant."

Kev and I gasped at the same moment before I shook my head. "Shit. That's dedication."

"How the hell did you end up with a roomie that bad?" Ben wanted to know. He looked confused and alarmed at all these stories. "And why haven't you moved out?"

"Oh, money." Darren waved a hand. "I need to split the bills with *someone*. Better the devil you know."

"Even the ex you know?" I asked, quirking a brow. I wasn't sure about it, but I'd gotten the impression from the way he talked that his roommate was his ex.

Kev gasped again. "No."

"Yeah," Darren said with a sigh and a roll of his eyes. "Fine, I admit it: we're exes."

"You're living with your *ex*?" Ben exclaimed. "Dude."

I winced. "I think Darren wins the pity drink of the night." I flagged down the waitress to ask for one more round, on me. I didn't want to get too drunk before bringing Kev to meet Hugh's parents, but a couple drinks would sure steady the nerves.

"It sucks, but whatever. The regret-fueled sex is hot." Darren smiled, but none of us missed the hint of bitterness. "Anyway, you two are *too cute* together. Restoring all of our faith in true love, etc."

"Seconded." Ben toasted that. "I have a good excuse for my next foam party. I might just meet The One in Friction, too."

I laughed. "Well, we didn't exactly…" I traded looks with Kev before shrugging. "Yeah, I guess we did."

"I know damn well you met in front of me," Darren said, smirking. "I knew you two would get along."

"Yeah, right!" I laughed. "You shooed him away!"

"Before I could even give him my name," Kev added, punching Darren's arm lightly. "Asshole."

"We always want a taste of the forbidden," Darren said sagely.

Ben snorted. "You're so full of shit," he told Darren, who just flipped him off and laughed. The two of them were getting along just fine, too.

It made me smile. I'd suddenly formed a little friendship group. Not many strong, but so far, so good. Maybe I wasn't as bad at this friendship thing as I'd thought.

All that talk got my mind turning, though. As much as Kev seemed secretly fond of Adam, would it make his life easier if he didn't have to share a place with him? My house was a hell of a lot nicer. I just wasn't sure when normal people would ask each other to move in. Hugh and I had waited a couple years, after all.

But was it too soon? God, I wished I had a relationship guide—other than the ones sitting in front of me, with Kev right there listening in. My instinct told me that every relationship was different, and judging this one by my last successful relationship wasn't a good idea.

I had to follow my heart, as hard as it was for me.

When we were finished our drinks and several rounds of goodbye hugs, I finally escaped the place, leaving Ben and Darren to keep flirting outrageously.

"So, that's Ben."

"You didn't tell me *Darren* was gonna be there." Kev grinned at me. "Did you know each other from before, at the bar?"

I chuckled. "Nope. That was the first time we'd met, too."

"Weird how life works out." Kev took my hand as we waited for the Uber. "You can go out night after night and then find yourself with a new friend and a boyfriend all at once."

I noticed his faintly possessive tone when he took my hand.

"Mmm." I squeezed his hand and smiled. "Now for the tricky part."

"At least you don't have to meet mine," Kev murmured, but he was gazing down the street. I could tell it was a bittersweet victory, having cut them out of his life.

"And I've got two sets. That's more than enough to go around," I murmured. Kev swayed into me and I snuggled up against his back, wrapping my arms around his waist.

"Charlie?"

"Hm?"

Kev's voice was soft as he covered my hands with his own, resting his arms along mine. "Thank you."

"No," I murmured. "Thank you for being you. I'm the luckiest guy in all of Brooklyn. And Manhattan, too. All five of the boroughs."

Kev laughed and rubbed his thumb along mine. "Whoa."

"I believe it," I insisted. "And one of these days, so will you."

"I hope so. At least, I hope Hugh's parents believe it."

"You'll be fine," I assured him and kissed behind his ear as we spotted the Uber heading toward us. "They'll love you." I just hoped like hell it was as true as I made it sound.

"Welcome! Come on in."

As always, Linda greeted me with a hug, and Chris said hello with a handshake. This time, they extended the same courtesy to my new boyfriend.

God, this was a weird moment, but if anyone else felt awkward, they didn't show it.

"Pleased to meet you," Kev told them. That charming megawatt smile was turned all the way up, but it didn't feel fake.

He listened with interest as Chris whisked him off to describe the barbecued meal he was preparing, and Linda took me to the kitchen to serve drinks.

"I'm so glad you brought him to meet us," Linda whispered and passed over the fancy drinking glasses. "We've been waiting for so long."

I sighed and shrugged. "So have I. But if I hadn't been, I wouldn't have met him at the right time, so…" I picked up the tray of glasses and brought them to the table. I eyed her as I set them by each place.

"Oh, I'll save the interrogation until Chris gets in," she assured me with a wink.

Just then, they both came in, carrying plates of home-barbecued food. Kev was laughing, and I managed to knock two of the glasses over. Thankfully, neither broke. Linda winked at me, which only flustered me more, but mercifully, didn't say anything.

Even the dreaded careers conversation went fairly easily. "What do you do?" Chris asked after dessert, and before I could interrupt, Kev had his answer ready.

"I'm about to go back to school. I want to study psychology and political science."

I blinked at him. "Poli sci?"

"You aren't two-faced enough to be a politician," Linda teased with a smile. "Our Charlie wouldn't have you around otherwise."

Both of us blushed—I knew from my own warm cheeks and the way Linda and Chris laughed at us. "Well, uh. Thanks," Kev answered with another of those charming smiles. "But I don't know. I think in local government there's room for someone who really wants to make change. That's more of a long-term goal, anyway. Politics doesn't really pay until you get to a career track."

"Too true," Chris agreed. "And psychology?"

"Well, counseling. My college has a fast-track program. I was going to take another trade, but I've been thinking about my options. I may as well go for something I really want." This must have been a recent decision. He looked at me with trepidation as he said it. "I made my mind up pretty quickly when I finally gave myself permission to go for what I want."

Oh. He was drawing a parallel here, wasn't he? I wasn't going to stop blushing any time soon. "Um. That's fantastic," I managed with a smile, and leapt to my feet. "I'll get the dishes."

Everyone laughed at my hasty escape as they kept asking him about how he liked New York City. They were being gentle with him, and I appreciated the hell out of them.

"What about your family? Where do they live?"

I winced. Shit. I was too far away from them to be able to rescue him here, and all I could do was listen as I loaded the dishwasher.

"Tennessee, still, I assume. I unfriended them long ago."

I raced to load the cutlery in the basket, but there was no need to hurry. Linda just gently said, "Oh. We didn't realize—I'm sorry."

"They can't live with me, so I'm not gonna put up with that," Kev said simply. "Not when I have a lot of life to live."

"Good for you." Chris scoffed. "Wish I could tell those kinds of parents what I think of them."

When I came back, the conversation had changed to TV shows. Kev offered me a little smile when I took his hand. No disasters to avert.

So far, it had been so damn easy for Kev to fit into my life.

Honestly, I wasn't sure what I'd expected. An interrogation? A litany of stories about Hugh and how he couldn't compare to him? My friends and family weren't those kinds of people. Even my blood relatives, distant though they sometimes were, loved me. They wouldn't want to make more trouble for me.

And for this, I got to call Kev my boyfriend? All it had taken was the strength to stand up and admit that I wanted this man by my side. That was a price I'd pay any minute of any day.

"Speaking of career changes," I told them, "I'm making one of my own."

"Oh?" This surprised them more. "Are you getting out of architecture and joining the circus?"

Kev laughed along with them, and even I smiled. "No. I'm switching to a bigger firm. I'm starting interviews tomorrow."

"Congratulations on moving up," Chris told me. "What prompted this?"

I had a long list of possible answers, but in the end, it was simple. "I have to follow my heart. That much is easy to decide. I'll let you know how I get on with the rest."

"The two of you are clearly well-matched," Chris finally concluded as he stretched. "Are you staying for wine, or would you rather get home?"

"I think we should get home for tonight," I answered. "We've got a lot of plans ahead of us. Let's take a raincheck on the wine."

"Raincheck written," Chris mimed writing one and handing it to me. "Kev, it's such a pleasure to meet you. It's nice to see Charlie happy with you."

"I—I hope I can keep making him happy." Kev audibly gulped. "I know it must not be easy for you, and you've been so gracious tonight."

Linda and Chris exchanged looks, and Linda was the one to speak. "Honey, don't you feel bad about what happened before you came into the picture. We'll never stop missing Hugh, but that doesn't mean we won't welcome you."

"As far as we're concerned," Chris added, "we had one son, and now we're blessed with three. You don't get a lot luckier than that."

I'd never seen Kev's eyes water before, except in the great cup disaster. He quickly moved in to hug Linda and turn his face away from us. It was hard to watch, but even I was getting a little misty-eyed.

"Thank you," Kev finally murmured.

When we made our escape to the Uber, Kev held onto my hand all the way into the car, and even afterward, he reached across the gap between seats to keep doing so.

"You good?" I asked once we were on our way back to my place.

"Yeah," Kev murmured as we sped through the relatively traffic-free streets, his voice barely audible over the hum of road noise. "I'm really good. You?"

"I don't know what I was worried about," I admitted and smiled. "I guess I've been planning for contingencies, making up obstacles in my head…"

"No need to make it harder than it is," Kev said. I bit back my grin, trying to think of a solemn response, but he joined in my snicker with a laugh of his own. "God, Charlie. Such a dirty mind."

"I blame you completely," I told him.

"Blame I'm happy to accept." He ran his thumb along my palm, and I spent the rest of the ride planning all the sweet ways I could make love to him tonight.

Every building needed a solid foundation, and this night felt like the last cornerstone of ours. That deserved a celebration.

30

KEV

"Remember when I asked if you believed in love?"

Oh, boy. I tapped my water glass and winked at Charlie. "Changed my mind. I'm going to need wine for this conversation."

"My pleasure." Charlie laughed and went to grab the bottle and two glasses.

I followed him to the kitchen. Many of my most important conversations had happened in the kitchen. There was something about it that just seemed to lead to good conversations. "Yeah, I remember. What about it?"

"Well," Charlie hummed, carefully rotating his hand to drive the corkscrew into the cork. "You seemed kind of skeptical of it. I don't know if that's the right word. But I wondered how that's changed, if we're… you know, in love."

I should have expected this. He was whip-smart and had a great memory for everything involving me. I wasn't used to people remembering my feelings—just my appearance, or what I'd done for them sexually. It took me off-guard for a few moments. "Um… right. I did say things about that, probably."

"You were concerned about not being Pretty Woman-ed or something," Charlie reminded me as he handed over a wine glass.

I clinked it against his and sipped before smiling. We shared a taste in wine—simple and sweet, not fancy and dry and awful-tasting stuff you had to pretend to smell for notes of candy apples or some crap like that. "Yeah, that's always been a fear of mine." We headed back to the couch and snuggled in together as I cradled my glass against my chest.

"And is it still?"

"Yeah, a bit," I admitted. Everything had gone fine with his friends and family—a bit too fine. "Especially if you believe in soulmates like you said earlier."

Charlie looked as confused as I'd felt when I realized that having that idea challenged actually upset him. "Why does that worry you?"

"Because…" I breathed out a quick laugh, forcing myself not to joke and cover it up. If I wanted emotional vulnerability from him, I had to give it, too. "Because one guy has control over me somehow. I've fought since I was sixteen—longer, really—to be out of anyone's control."

"Love is vulnerable. That's the beautiful part of it. You both have to bare your hearts to bear each other's burdens."

I swallowed hard around the lump that had risen in my throat. A little wine helped wash it down for now. "Yeah," I managed hoarsely. "The last few weeks talking with you, so much stuff has unwound in my head. I realized you're not trying to change me, you're trying to help me be what I want to be."

"Exactly." Charlie smiled. "Whatever crazy thing you're up to, I want to know about it and help and… you know, support, if you'll let me."

"I didn't know how to take that," I admitted. "I mean, I feel like I've just begun my real life. Like all those years back in Tennessee were just training. And meeting you almost right away… I mean, it's actually a good thing. You're patient and you're experienced. And I like that you have a life history you haven't run across half the States to escape."

Charlie cracked a smile. "It's been close sometimes. But I just figured you're not used to committing to one guy. Especially after your job…"

"Whoa." I held up a hand. I'd learned from Adam—I wasn't going to let comments that made me uncomfortable slide. "There's a difference between work and pleasure. Yeah, I quit my job. But that has nothing to do with commitment. I've just never had the chance."

"Right." Charlie looked sheepish. "But work still got in the way of dating, didn't it? Meaning you didn't have the chance?"

When I picked apart my defensiveness, the statement sounded true, so I slowly nodded. "Somewhat. Mostly the rest of my life did. Like, I didn't have time to date back on the ranch in Tennessee when they were teaching me odd jobs and accounting and hospitality. Or here, when I was settling in. Or before that, when I didn't have a fixed address."

Charlie nodded again, his arm sliding around my shoulders protectively. "I hate the thought of you going through all that. I just wish I could have… helped you earlier."

"Pretty Woman-ed me?" I teased, but I was smiling. It was kind of nice to be rescued, in its own way. Only because I knew he respected me, and he wouldn't dream of telling me what to do with my life.

"If you like," he said with a laugh. "*Would* you like?"

I sipped more wine and tried to give honest thought to the question. "I'd hate to feel like I'm not paying my own way."

"But if you're in school… hell, that's hard enough. You don't need the stress of money, too." There was something nervous in his voice, and I sat up a little straighter to listen. "What I'm saying is… if you want to take therapy courses, or political science… go for it. I'd like to help."

I shook my head. "What I need to do is choose."

Charlie gestured with his glass carefully at me. "There's always another solution. What if you moved in with me, so you only had to worry about tuition?"

I stared at him for a few seconds, trying not to burst out in an embarrassing series of excited noises.

Sure, we'd only known each other for a month, but it already felt like years. I missed him when I woke up without him, and I waited eagerly for his texts after he got home from work.

"You'd do that for me?"

He hummed. "It's a practical solution. It would solve several of our problems at once."

I tried to restrain my giggles but utterly failed. Of course my boyfriend was thinking of the practicality of combining households rather than the romance of it all—sharing a roof, and a bed, and all those little daily things we could do together. That was fine, though. I knew he secretly loved it, too.

I wanted to say yes, but I needed time to make sure he really meant it. After all, I hadn't lived with many people who'd treated me well. It would be a whole new experience.

"What?" Charlie looked miffed for a moment. "What did I say?"

"I love you," I told him. "And I love your problem-solving, and that you're… you're so willing to help me. I'll think about it."

Charlie rubbed my shoulder and kissed me before he held his wine glass for a toast. "Whatever you decide, here's to us. We'll find a way to make it work, Kev."

With this man by my side, no dream felt too big. I loved Charlie's vision. All of a sudden, I could see the kind of work he must do. Nothing was impossible to him—it just needed to be carefully planned and meticulously done.

"Now's the time to be bold," I murmured, setting aside my glass and standing up. I offered him my hand.

Charlie looked between his glass and my hand for a moment, set the glass aside, and took it. "Hm?"

"I want to follow my heart, just like you said," I told him. "And my heart's wanted you all fucking night. Don't make me wait any longer."

Charlie didn't hesitate to lead me by the hand upstairs as soon as I told him what was on my mind. He swept me off my feet when we got to the top landing, as much as I squirmed and giggled and protested that I could walk perfectly fine.

"You could," Charlie agreed, kicking the door closed behind him. "But this way I get to show off all those muscles you've so carefully memorized."

I laughed again as he dumped me on the bed, and I grabbed him by the belt loops to haul him on top of me.

"Whoa!" Charlie hadn't been expecting that, and he crashed on top of me in a flailing tangle of limbs and half-hysterical laughter.

I hooked my leg around the back of his and wrapped my arms around him, then rolled us over in one quick move before he could see that coming, either. "Surprise," I grinned down at him. "My turn."

Charlie's lips parted as he gazed at me. "Yes. To whatever that is."

"Well," I said with a grin, "I was gonna ask how you felt about bottoming."

"Hell yeah." Charlie was already plucking at my t-shirt, trying to get it off. "I'd let my gorgeous boyfriend fuck me into the mattress if he wants to. And then I'd return the favor, all damn night."

I pressed my hand against my chest and mock-gasped. "Taking turns on the top? That's real love."

"If you don't hurry up, I'm gonna finish on the spot from all this dirty talk," he warned me with a wink. "And then it'll be my turn next."

"Oh, no, mister!" I exclaimed. "Keep your shot in the barrel until I tell you otherwise. I'm not missing my chance."

We kept joking around as we stripped and found the lube, but before I slicked my fingers with it, I took one more chance to gaze at him. "You're sure?"

"Sure as I've ever been," Charlie said with a smile. "I never say yes unless I really mean it."

I kissed him as I pushed a finger inside, taking it as slowly and gently as I would for a guy trying it for the first time. God knew how long it had been since anyone had done this. Judging from his quick breathing, just as long as I'd suspected.

Still, within a few minutes, he was starting to relax and push into me for more, so I followed his cues and added another finger. By the time I had both fingers pumping into him in a slow, easy rhythm, his eyes were open again, and he was gazing at me with such affection that it almost hurt to see.

I managed to make eye contact, though, and then I found I couldn't look away.

"I love seeing you in charge," Charlie whispered. "And I love making you feel good, too. And I love just cuddling you. How damn lucky am I?"

"You're about to get real lucky," I teased, bringing my other hand down to cup myself and stroke gently.

Charlie moaned and spread his legs. "Hurry up, then. I can't wait much longer."

I fumbled with the pump to add more lube to my hand, and then stroked myself a few times. Fuck, I was so turned on just from hearing him moan and feeling him squeeze tight around me. I could barely believe I was going to get to feel this in just a few moments.

Sex could be wonderful with someone you didn't know—there was a kind of intimate understanding that formed from learning each other's bodies before your pasts. But this was something new to me, and I couldn't get enough of it. Even though I didn't know all of Charlie's past, I *knew* him—what kind of guy he was, and how much I trusted him.

I wanted this to be perfect for him, and I took it as slow as I could stand. By the time I pressed myself against him, he was bucking into me needily, his fingers digging into my thighs. "Now," Charlie begged. "Please, Kev."

How the hell could I resist that? I leaned down to kiss him as I eased myself inside, slowly filling him with me. Every time he gasped, I stopped for a second or two and rubbed his chest or his hip, murmuring to him how well he was doing—how beautiful he was—how much I loved him.

By the time I was fully inside, Charlie was blushing but smiling. "It feels good," he assured me. "Really good."

"You feel amazing, baby," I praised him. I was smiling just as much as him. My cheeks hurt from it. "I'm… fuck, I don't even know what to say."

"Don't say," he whispered, pulling me down for a long kiss.

I lost myself in that kiss—the warmth of it, and the tenderness, and how unspeakably intimate it was to kiss him while buried to the root inside him. I felt his every shudder and clench around me, and how fucking easy it was to turn him on when I sucked his lip or flicked my tongue along the tip of his.

"Tell me how it is," I whispered when I finally caught my breath and started to move my hips. Thrust after thrust, the motion grew more comfortable for us both. Before long, I caught his hand creeping down to stroke himself.

I didn't mind the view, so I let him get away with it for now. As much as I wanted to tease him to the very edge and push his limits, I could save that for another night. Tonight, he deserved to feel good over and over.

"I hope you weren't planning on a good night's sleep." I kissed his jaw and then his neck, running my fingers up his ribs toward his chest. I played with his nipples idly as he tried to form a response, and all either of us got from him were breathless moans.

"Not fair," he finally gasped. "Trying to… ah, distract me like that."

"Is it working?" I flicked my nail gently along the sensitive nub.

His body arched and he squeezed tight around me. Fuck, that felt good when he clenched around my shaft, fully enveloped inside him, stopping me from moving for a few seconds.

I pressed him down to the bed again, hands on his chest and shoulder, and started to move a little harder and faster. My body was demanding it by now, and he was begging for it with every moan and gasp he gave me.

I earned a light scratch of nails down my back and moaned to encourage him to do it again. To my pleasure, he did—this time, harder. The stings of pain just stirred the embers within me, and I was kissing him hard and fast, open-mouthed now. I kissed him with every dirty intention in my mind.

My thighs ached and my heart was hammering a mile a minute, but I couldn't get enough of him. As our bodies moved together, I felt my orgasm thundering toward me like a charging bull. All I could do was grab it by the horns and cry out Charlie's name, pressing my face into his neck as I came. My whole body shivered, and nothing outside us mattered even for a second.

All I wanted was Charlie right here—with me, under me, around me—forever.

I'd never meant to fall for him, but here I was, whispering that I loved him while he squirmed under me and stroked himself hard and fast. Before I could even pull out and prop myself up on my elbows again, he clenched around me and groaned. "Kev!"

"Yes, baby," I moaned. "Come on."

By now, Charlie couldn't be stopped. He rolled his head back and I kissed his bared throat as he groaned and writhed under me. Our bodies were pressed together, so his sticky mess covered us both in short order.

Did I care about that? Not a bit.

"I love you," he whispered as he came down from his high and wrapped his arms around my back. "I don't care if I'm not supposed to. I don't give a single fuck about anyone who tells me otherwise. If I've got nothing else going for me, I know my heart, and I know what love feels like."

I tried not to choke up as I rolled onto my side and rubbed his chest gently. "I know, baby. I have no idea what it's supposed to feel like, but I know what it is, too."

Charlie pressed me tightly against him, nearly crushing my ribcage in the force of his hug. "Stay right here with me."

"I am, Charlie." I kissed his shoulder gently once he let me breathe, rubbing his chest. "I'm here."

He shook his head slightly. "No. I mean, *stay*."

I caught my breath and pulled back enough to see his face. "You're still serious about that?"

"Very." Charlie might think he was stoic, but I could read his every emotion: apprehensive, hopeful, and above all, totally in love. "I know I said it'd make our lives easier, but I'd also like... *you* around. For your own sake."

I blushed as I noticed the way he watched me, almost forgetting the question. "Um. Huh? Yeah. I mean, yes. Moving in. I... I wouldn't say no."

"It would solve a lot of problems, and..." he trailed off.

I held my breath, just waiting to see if there was more.

Charlie cleared his throat and brushed imaginary dust from my arm. "It would just be... nice."

A grin spread across my face, and I laughed. "Yeah, you goof," I teased. "Nice."

"Leave me alone," Charlie protested with a laugh. "Take it as a credit to your lovemaking abilities."

"I think it'd be *nice* to live with you, too." I smirked as he groaned and pulled a pillow over his face. I had no intention of letting that one go. "And maybe romantic, and fulfilling, and scary, but... nice, too."

"You're such a jerk. Maybe Adam's the nice one, really," Charlie groaned.

I gasped. "You take that back!" Tickling his ribs didn't seem very effective, but then I found a spot under his arms that made him gasp and pull the pillow off his face to smack me with it.

"I won't take anything back." Charlie winked. "I only say what I mean."

"Well, if I'm such a jerk," I pointed out with a grin, threatening to tickle him once more, "I notice you're not retracting the offer."

"Like I said," Charlie murmured, his grin fading to a soft smile, "I only say what I mean."

I let the pillow drop beside us and lay down again, my head on his chest. "I know. And I mean it when I say yes."

"Yes to... moving in?"

I nodded and peeked up at him. "As soon as I find a roommate for Adam. I won't leave him high and dry."

Charlie kissed the top of my head. "I never expected that of you. We can wait as long as you need to get your affairs in order."

I smiled as I tucked my face into the crook of his arm. "Good. I love you."

"I love you too."

We lay still as I contemplated a nap, and then wondered what he was thinking. A moment later, I giggled, unable to help myself.

"Hm?"

"You're nice."

Charlie's groan was nearly drowned out by my laughter, and then my squeal when he grabbed the pillow for another round of pillow wars.

A new and delicate strand was forming between us, like the glue I used to repair chipped pieces to their former glory. It still needed time to strengthen into a lifetime bond, but what we'd found between us was more precious than gold.

I'd never thought I'd find it, or even that I'd deserve it if I could, but now that I had, and I finally felt like I did? It was pretty damn nice.

31

CHARLIE - TWO WEEKS LATER

"Another interview? Should I be expecting a call soon?" Valerie asked, poking her head around the corner of her office.

I nearly jumped out of my seat at the sudden voice. I'd been zoomed in as far as I could go, laying out details in a mind-numbingly boring bit of drywall. "Lord almighty!"

"Sorry," my boss added with a laugh. "I just got your email."

I'd asked her for the afternoon off. She was pretty laid back about it, as long as I pulled my weight in the hours I did work. In return, I'd thrown everything into drafting, since I was pretty useless at any long-range project planning or management while I was waiting to leave. But I could do the grunt work that was usually left to interns, and I could do it damn well.

"It's my third with these guys," I said, nodding. "So yeah, they might need references, if that's okay?"

"Fine by me." I knew she'd already lined up my replacement and was just waiting for me to have a departure date—the sooner, the better. Nothing personal, just business.

To be honest, I was looking forward to the change in pace. These last couple weeks of grunt work had popped a much-needed hole in my ego. Instead of dreaming about skyscrapers, I was back to the nitty-gritty details that nobody liked to deal with, but I found a weird kind of joy in the monotonous work. Every bit of it had to be done perfectly. It wasn't just the ribbon-cutting and last minute conference calls with construction managers that mattered.

"I just wanted to let you know we really appreciate you pitching in to help with this bid," Valerie added, pointing at my screen.

I shrugged. "Of course. It's only fair that I help where I can, if I'm not..." I trailed off. I didn't want to sound bitter that I wasn't needed in the firm's future of wooing developers in places I didn't feel comfortable going now that I had a new boyfriend on my arm.

"Right." Valerie nodded briskly. "Take the afternoon off, no problem. We're ahead of schedule on this project now."

That would earn me a good reference from her when they called, but more importantly, the job would get done well. That was what mattered most, at the end of the day.

"Thanks." I shut down my computer and headed for the door once I'd saved my work in progress, my heart light.

It wasn't until I got to the parking lot that nerves struck. The drive was short—the new firm was located just a twenty-minute walk from here, but it was raining today and I didn't want my interview suit to get soaked.

Third interview had to be a good sign, right?

I could only cross my fingers and hope for the best. Sooner or later, even Valerie would get tired of waiting for me to move on.

"Did you get it?" Kev nearly dove into my car, and I had to fight back the squeak of alarm. He hadn't even warned me by tapping on the window first.

"Jesus, everyone's out to get me today!"

Kev laughed. "Sorry. Did you?" He looked just as eager and nervous as I'd felt walking into the huge corporate building. He was dressed a bit differently now, too—more casual, and the look suited him. Sure, he looked pretty in catalog clothing, but not *him*. This was much better.

I tried to hold back my smile and surprise him, but something must have given me away.

Kev squealed and dove across the console for a hug just as a cab behind me started to beep. "That's amazing!" he congratulated me, kissing me. More honking and he flipped off the guy in the rearview mirror before buckling up.

"You're becoming local!" I laughed. "Used to be you'd roll down the window and apologize."

"You say that like we've been dating for ten years," Kev scoffed.

I smiled fondly. "Feels like it sometimes."

"Hey. Is that a good thing?" Kev eyed me as I pulled away from the curb.

I winked. "Why don't we find out later with celebration sex?"

"Yes, please. When do you start?"

"Sometime after I peel your underwear off, which is not long after I get you through the front door. Maybe up against the closet—"

"The job!" Kev was laughing, and he conspicuously adjusted himself. "Don't turn me on *before* the meeting. That's not fair."

"Oh." I grinned. "Two weeks. It's totally fair, by the way. You knew what you were doing this morning."

Kev, the little minx, had made sure to wrap himself up just right in sheets that barely covered his morning wood when I came in for a goodbye kiss before work.

"Mmm." Kev pretended not to know what I meant.

I kept flirting and teasing to distract him, all the way until we arrived at the hotline's cramped, industrial building.

Kev's nerves kicked in then. "Are you—this is the place? Are you coming with me to the lobby, at least? Where is it?"

"I'll come with you if you want," I promised, shutting off the car and squeezing his hand. Once he was calm enough, I brought him to the building and kept my hand in his as I buzzed to get in.

It was strange being greeted and welcomed in with my boyfriend by my side, and not here for my own sake.

"How's things going?" Neil asked with a warm smile. "With the job move?"

"Just accepted a new position today."

He clapped my shoulder. "Great news! And Angus has been wonderful, by the way. Not the same as you, but he's doing his best," he winked. "You must be Kev?"

"I am." Kev shook hands, too. "Thanks for seeing me."

"No problem at all."

I wasn't sure how nervous Kev felt, so I offered, "I'll wait out here, unless—"

Kev smiled at me and nodded. "Okay. See you in a bit."

His confidence had always seemed high, but it felt more genuine now. Over the last few weeks, he'd seemed to settle into his skin better. Knowing that he had a future ahead of him had stopped him from feeling quite so insecure, and he didn't rush to conclusions as much.

In return, I'd been working on showing him how I really felt—which was hard when it came to everything except how I felt about him.

Darren had been more than eager to move in with Adam and ditch the living situation with the ex, but he needed some time to get his things together and start moving them over, so Kev had started moving out, too.

The most important things were already at my place: that growing collection. Just two cups and saucers for now, but that was all the two of us needed.

Time passed in a flash as I daydreamed about our last few weeks together, and the upcoming moving days. By the time Kev bounced out of the office again, I'd planned the next few days off and how we'd get the rest of his stuff to my place.

"Thank you so much for your time," Kev told Neil, shaking hands enthusiastically.

I'd never seen him all smiles like this, and I gave Neil a huge, grateful smile of my own as we made small talk on the way out.

We'd barely gotten to the car before Kev turned to me. "He thinks I'd be a good fit, personality-wise. I talked a bit about my past, and he didn't—you know, get all judgmental. He said I'd be perfect to understand where people are coming from. He gave me advice on the kinds of courses I should take, and in the meantime, I can volunteer..."

I listened to his rambling with a smile, nodding at appropriate moments, but I barely had a chance to get a word in edgewise.

Volunteering sounded great, though. I'd made sure my new job had consistent enough hours that I could commit to a shift at the hotline and get to know a little bit of other people's realities. Kev's especially, but there were lots of others who needed a community or a friendly listening ear. Even if I wasn't that ear directly, I could support their work. In the background, just how I liked it.

"So, I take it you'd like to head to the college now?"

Kev gasped. "Could I?" He looked at me, and then the clock. "Do you have to get back to work?"

"Nah. They've given me the afternoon off for good behavior."

"In that case, I'd like to visit the college, and then go home and behave *very* badly to reward you for all that hard work you must have done," Kev winked.

It was my turn to shift, adjusting myself under the steering wheel. "Count me in."

Whatever happened with Kev's career, I hoped he'd keep talking to me about it. He'd started opening up more about his past in the last few weeks, and while I expected it would be years before I heard it all—if ever—this was progress.

I, too, had been opening up. Whenever I talked about Hugh, he seemed to listen without envy or trying to shut me down. He even asked smart questions sometimes, about what Hugh had been like.

God, some small part of me wished they could have met, though they couldn't be more different in some ways. But then, I reminded myself again, I never would have gotten to be with Kev.

There was no good or bad about it—it was just life, and it was crazy and unpredictable and utterly intoxicating.

I was done with missing out on living by being some boring office drone. And just like Kev refused to subject himself to abuse in order to work, neither would I. It might make my job a little trick-ier, but my new bosses had completely understood—sympathized, even—when I talked about why I was leaving my old firm.

The future looked rosier than it ever had, and Kev? Well, he held the keys to it all.

If I could be his rudder and help steer him on the course that made him happiest—one which would no doubt change the world in one way or another, or many at once—then that was my pleasure.

So long as I got to be by his side, anything was possible.

"Ugh, Darren doesn't even want to pay for press-and-fold!"

I bit back a grin as Adam lamented to me over the phone about his roommate. The honeymoon phase had passed, and now Adam was undoubtedly making Darren's life harder in some ways while being a sweet asshole in others.

"Uh huh. And how does that make you feel?"

Adam groaned. "Dude, you haven't even started class yet! Don't think I don't see what you're doing."

"Yeah, but I've read the first five chapters."

"Oh, God. I should've known you'd be an eager beaver," Adam said with a sigh. "Now you're gonna be testing all your skills on me."

"Yep! Aren't you glad I didn't end up in massage, then?" I burst out laughing at Adam's noise of horror. "Don't worry, I wouldn't give you a happy ending."

"Good. I don't need one from a guy. Especially you." Adam was still resolutely pretending to be straight, then. Something about him had tripped my gaydar—maybe bidar—for a while. I'd teased him about giving guys a try a hundred times and he'd always pretended to miss the hint.

He was a hell of a character, but I counted myself lucky to have him as a friend. He'd also come with me to help me buy textbooks, something I'd never had to figure out in my life, and taught me how to navigate the new college campus last week.

"Uh huh," I hummed.

"How about you?" Adam finally asked. "How do you feel?"

"Pretty damn nice." I giggled to myself, but that was a joke for just Charlie and I. "I mean, he's great. Two months in and we haven't killed each other. We haven't even broken up."

"I'll start saving the date now."

"Don't even," I laughed, trying to hide the flutter in my chest. It felt nice to have something like an engagement to daydream about, but we'd taken so many steps so fast that we'd agreed to take it all nice and slow for a little while. We both had a lot of life changes recently and coming up, after all.

"Charlie's just getting started on a new project. He's not managing or leading things anymore, which sounds like a demotion, but he's way less stressed. And he doesn't have to travel. He seems happier."

Adam hummed. "That's the main thing. And you?" he grumbled, as if he were almost unwilling to even ask.

I smiled to myself as I wandered to the kitchen and crouched by the oven, making sure the lasagna was keeping warm without burning.

Compared to the years I'd spent scrounging for a solid meal, twenty bucks for a bed, or a guy who'd make me believe in the fantasy I constructed for him?

"Happier than I can believe," I murmured. "I'm so fucking glad we came here."

Adam grunted, but he didn't disagree. "At least you're getting laid. You're a lot more cheerful, even if you psychoanalyze me now."

"Oh, fuck off," I laughed. "Call me and tell me how the new job goes, huh?"

I wasn't the only one who'd gotten a new job. Adam had been promoted to a full-time employee in the landscaping company he'd started working for, and that meant he could ditch all his cobbled-together jobs. I knew the stress relief must be immense for him. Best of all, he could quit that fucking grocery store job and its lousy customers.

"Yeah, yeah," Adam grumbled. "It's no big deal."

"You know it is. We're doing celebration pizza and beer at your place next week, all right?"

"You wanna come back to this dingy little place?"

"Anywhere you are," I told him.

Adam was quiet for a moment—several moments. Finally, he answered me, just when I was thinking he hadn't heard. "Thanks, Kev. For... you know."

I grinned. That was as much as I was getting from him for the whole year, probably. "Of course. Thank you."

Who would've thought a couple small-town kids, butting heads every other day, could wind up here in Brooklyn, happy—or at least on the way, in Adam's case—and right at home?

Life had turned out better than I'd ever expected, or even hoped or dreamed for. And it was all thanks to one man seeing straight through me, and not giving up until I saw the potential in me, too.

With Charlie's love, and a little help from friends, I could get by.

Dear reader,

Thank you for reading *Electric Sunshine*, the first book in the Brooklyn Boys series!

I want to take the chance to thank a few people who brought this book to life. Many huge thank you hugs go to Amelia for that day in Central Park and many more since, Helen for many feels, John and Leslie for making this book so much better than it was, Meg and Kitti for expertly sifting out the errors, Aubrey for all of her love and cheerleading, Lucy for inspiring my leap into a new pool... and gosh, so many more. It's about time I got around to thanking my whole crew—without whom not just this book, but the last few dozen I've written, wouldn't have happened. You know who you are and can redeem your hugs anytime (besides when I'm in the shower, Zach excepted).

And, of course... my thanks always to the boy for being my sunshine.

The next Brooklyn Boys novel is *Live Wire*. Darren's bad luck takes a turn for the better, but Adam quickly finds out that no good deed goes unpunished.

If you'd like to meet Josh and Evan, check out *Tremble* (also where Adam and Kev first met)—and, of course, the rest of the Significant Brothers series! And to find out what happened between Shay and Jared at a speed-dating session back in January, check out the short story "Wind Tunnel" (you can grab it for free by subscribing to my newsletter).

Make sure you follow me on Amazon to hear about Brooklyn Boys and my other new releases, or subscribe to my newsletter to hear about new releases and sales, get sneak peeks at upcoming books, and hear about audiobook releases, event appearances, and other exciting news as it happens!

I also have a reader group on Facebook here if you want to tell me what you loved about this book, see cute bee and flower photos, and keep on top of my upcoming releases with a whole bunch of fun, lovely readers: https://www.facebook.com/groups/edavies

Last but not least: always be you!

~Ed

Freak

Faux

Forever

After series:

Afterburn

Afterglow

Aftermath

Hidden Creek books:

Shelter

Adore

And, of course, stay tuned for more books in the Brooklyn Boys series!